WE FADE
TO GREY

WE FADE TO GREY

edited by
Gary McMahon

featuring
Paul Finch
Stuart Young
Gary McMahon
Mark West
Simon Bestwick

with an introduction by
Mark Morris

Pendragon Press

First Published in 2008 by
Pendragon Press
Po Box 12, Maesteg, Mid Glamorgan
South Wales, CF34 0XG, UK

Typesetting by Christopher Teague

Printed in Wales by Print Evolution

ISBN-13: 978 0 9554452 8 6

CONTENTS

The systems fail,
The lights go out;
We fade to grey:
Frail ghosts of doubt.

- Charles Urban, *'Fader'*

This book is dedicated to all the readers, writers and editors involved in the small press: those who keep the flame burning.

As always, this is also for my wife, Emily, who keeps *my* flame flickering in the darkness.

Acknowledgements

Love and thanks for giving meaning to my life must go to my son, Charlie; indeed, here's some more of that love to my whole family.

There are too many names to remember, so forgive me in advance if I've forgotten you. I just wanted to take this opportunity to thank some people who have in some way provided inspiration, compassion, friendship, and encouragement over the last few years, as well as during this project:

Paul Finch, Simon Bestwick, Stuart Young, Mark West. Chris Teague. Peter Tennant. Ramsey Campbell. Gary Fry (for so fucking much it should have its own list; but most of all for "discovering" me). Simon Strantzas. John Probert (Britain's Best Living Horror Writer!). Adriana Capozzi. All at the RCMB. GCW, for musical accompaniment during the editing stages. David A. Green, Trevor Denyer, Jason Andrew, Charles Black, David Longhorn, Barbara Roden, Ellen Datlow. Conrad Williams, Tim Lebbon, Sarah Pinborough, Joel Lane, Mark Samuels, Tony Richards. Micheal Kelly, T.M. Wright, Mort Castle, Vince Liagnuno, Nanci Kalanta, Joe Kroeger. The Humdrummers: Guy Adams and Ian Alexander Martin. Apologies if I've missed anyone off this by no means exhaustive list: I'm rubbish with names.

INTRODUCTION
Mark Morris

If there's one thing you can say about the new generation of horror writers, it's that they certainly ain't in it for the money.

Back when I was starting out in the late 80s, horror was enjoying something of a boom period. Subsequently my first novel, *Toady*, became a real bells and whistles production. The promotion that the paperback received from Transworld was enough to propel it to number 7 on the national bestseller list on its first week of release. This was a time of dump-bins and big colour posters (one of which I have framed on my study wall), of promotional tours and meaty advances. In the words of Mary Hopkins, 'Those were the days, my friend. We thought they'd never end.'

But oh, how wrong we were.

The bottom fell out of the horror market around the late 90s. All at once horror writers began to find that long-term publishing contracts were not being renewed, and that publishers' horror lines were starting to disappear. For those already working within the genre, it was a simple case of adapt or die. New, unpublished writers, however, those who had grown up reading and loving the work of everyone from Blackwood to Barker, and who themselves had ambitions to become part of the noble tradition, were faced with a yet starker choice: Either abandon the genre you love and try writing something else, or continue doing what you're doing and fuhgeddabout making any kind of living out of this writing lark.

I suppose we'll never know how many decided to take the former option, because such individuals are now lost to us. Of the

1

latter group, only a smattering of UK writers have stuck to their guns and – largely by doggedly establishing a reputation by way of the American independent presses – actually managed to make enough money to chuck in the day job (Tim Lebbon being the name that springs most readily to mind). The others have, by and large, had to bite the bullet and keep on producing good work for the small presses, who – though they do an excellent job with the resources available – can offer their contributors only minimal print runs and scant (often non-existent) financial reward.

My only hope is that the likes of Finch, Fry, Cooper, West, Young, Hughes, Samuels, McMahon, Bestwick, Probert, Lockley, Lewis et al do not, in years to come, become a kind of 'lost generation'. It is not for me to say whether, if circumstances were more favourable, some or all of these fine fellows would be enjoying the benefits of lucrative contracts from mainstream publishers by now (the vagaries of editors are notoriously difficult to predict), but certainly they are all writers whose work has garnered accolades and awards aplenty these past few years, not only from fans and peers, but, perhaps more significantly, from many of the elder – and highly respected – statesmen and women of the field.

As I write these words, less than three weeks into a shiny new year, there are tentative indications that horror as a literary genre may finally be in the ascendancy once more. At least two mainstream publishers are on the verge of launching bona fide horror lists, and others are either actively looking for 'smart, contemporary' horror fiction, or are at least finally prepared to consider the kind of overtly supernatural fiction that has been anathema to them for much of the past decade.

So, who knows? Some of these writers may yet find that they haven't missed the boat, after all. I, for one, certainly hope that this is the case, because judging by the collection of novellas you currently hold in your hand, every one of the writers whose work is contained herein certainly deserves a fair crack of the whip.

The book kicks off with *The Pumping Station* by International Horror Guild and British Fantasy Award-winning author, Paul Finch. What always strikes me about Paul's work is his ability not only to establish an incredibly vivid sense of place, but his evocation of Britain as an ancient, haunted realm. His stories, it seems to me, have a weight and a history to them, and as such the sense that dark magic and forbidden secrets are forever lurking beneath the hard, rugged crust of reality suffuses his work like the mulchy odour of rot on a wet and dreary autumn day.

Such is the case in *The Pumping Station*, a tough and uncompromising tale which takes place almost exclusively in a landscape of squelching mud and driving rain. Reading this reminds me of one of those deliciously grim British horror movies from the early 70s – *The Shuttered Room* or *The Beast in the Cellar*. I mean this as a compliment. To my mind Paul's writing captures the best aspects of the movies produced in this very unique, very fecund era of British film-making – their bleak stoicism; their often banal (and therefore all-the-more shocking) depiction of human evil; their ability to conjure up what is often an almost overwhelming sense of bucolic dread. Paul's small cast of characters in *The Pumping Station* are blunt, flawed, sometimes annoying but nonetheless sympathetic – just like real people, in fact. For the short time that we are in their company, their plight becomes our plight. But be warned, gentle reader – Paul Finch is an ex-policeman and a big feller, and as such he is not the kind of man who pulls his punches.

Fellow British Fantasy Award winner Stuart Young follows Paul's tale with *Bliss*. If these five novellas have anything in common, it is a certain amount of Northern grit and a preoccupation with death. However, in contrast to Paul's rain-lashed and downbeat tale, Stuart offers us a deliriously bonkers story of pensionable psychopaths, murderous MPs, indestructible bodyguards and alien parasites.

Bliss starts soberly enough, with a senselessly shocking death, a grieving family and a funeral. However, it soon escalates into a fast-paced romp that manages to walk a fine line between gruesomely shocking and blackly funny. Stuart's writing is slick and sure, and he handles the action with aplomb, whilst at the same time never losing track of his grounded and likeable protagonists – soldier-boy Lee, back from the war in Iraq for his father's funeral, and his ingenuous younger brother, Adam. What prevents *Bliss* from becoming the joker in the pack, however, and therefore perhaps more throwaway

3

than its grittier bedfellows, is its denouement, which – without giving too much away – effectively takes the form of a coda not only about life and death, but about the very nature of human existence. It provides a sombre, thought-provoking and ultimately horrifying end to a powerful and inventive tale.

If *The Pumping Station* is akin to a grim British horror movie from the 70s, then *Heads* by Gary McMahon strikes me as its TV equivalent. Back in my adolescence and teenage years, I used to adore (and still do – I've got them all on DVD now) the British anthology shows that seemed to cram ITV's late evening slots on Thursdays, Fridays and Saturdays. *Journey to the Unknown*, Brian Clemens' *Thriller*, *Hammer House of Horror* and its evil twin, *Hammer House of Mystery and Suspense* – all of these shows are classics to me. And reading Gary's *Heads*, it struck me that a dramatisation of his novella would slot right in to any of them. The set up is perfect: suburban couple unearth a trio of spooky stone heads in their garden, which they subsequently discover have links to local tales of witchcraft. This leads ultimately to a series of spooky goings-on, culminating in supernatural mayhem.

What this perhaps suggests is that *Heads* is the most traditional of the stories presented here, and in many ways I guess that's true. But again this is certainly no bad thing. Tales of witchcraft and ancient evil have proved one of the enduring bedrocks of the genre, and no doubt will continue to do so for as long as horror stories are written and told. There's nothing wrong with tradition as long as it's presented well, and Gary's novella is certainly a well-constructed and satisfying tale. Furthermore, it is given a very human angle by dint of the fact that Morris and Helen, the young couple at the centre of the story, are desperate for a child after a couple of miscarriages. The fact that the supernatural intervenes to subvert their plans only serves to add poignancy to their modest ambitions and renders their very human tragedy all the more acute.

The Mill by Mark West is a beautiful story. Though it shares a very obvious parallel with Paul Finch's *The Pumping Station* in that an archetypal Bad Place is established as the focal point of the narrative, the real horror in Mark's tale comes from the harrowing and affecting depiction of our protagonist, Michael Anderson's, grief

4

following the premature death from cancer of his beloved wife, Nicola. The journey that Michael takes, from the couple's first discovery of a lump in Nicola's breast, through the different stages of her illness, and eventually to her death and its aftermath, is one of the most moving pieces of writing I have read in a long time. It is wrought with such a precise and excruciating elegance that it manages to convey the complexities of Michael's emotions – his deep love for his wife, his desperation and anguish, his sense of futility and helplessness – without once becoming maudlin or resorting to saccharine cliché. Anybody who has ever lost a loved one will sympathise absolutely with the emptiness and despair that Michael feels after Nicola's death, and his desperate yearning to turn back the clock, to press the restart button and somehow divert the terrible events that have destroyed not only Nicola's life but his own as well.

The supernatural element of this tale is subtle and insidious, and – rather like the illness that has taken Michael's wife away from him – both merciless and indiscriminatory in its choice of 'victim'. Ultimately, Mark's tale is perhaps most effective simply because it reminds us that the malevolent phantoms we can all too easily dismiss as harmless flights of fancy have the ability to adopt more tangible forms, that can be just as deadly but are not so easily dismissed.

The Narrows by Simon Bestwick, which wraps up this quintet of novellas, is a brooding, claustrophobic tale which accesses some of our most primal fears. When the story opens, mankind's worst nightmare has already occurred – the bomb has dropped, the apocalypse is now, and the flimsy construct of civilisation is nothing but radioactive dust.

The entirety of the story takes place in a darkness that is both metaphorical and all too physical. A disparate band of survivors – teachers and pupils from a school on the periphery of the blast – flee from the encroaching radiation via a series of long-disused underground canals linked to a vast network of old mine workings.

If you like your horror fiction to be reassuring, gentle reader, if you want the evil to be overcome and the monsters vanquished by the time you tuck yourself up in bed at night, then *The Narrows* is not for you. It is the bleakest of tales, in which the characters with whom we identify are doomed from the outset. Their world is destroyed; there is nothing on the surface but poisonous ash and dust. They have no plan, nowhere to go, and very little food. Their only instinct is to survive, whatever the cost. They carry on living simply because they are terrified of the alternative. They are crawling through a world without hope, and yet at the same time it is a kind of blind hope which drives them onward.

It is rare, and oddly heartening, to find darkness this impenetrable even in modern horror fiction. One gets the impression, from reading *The Narrows*, that Simon is striving for something *beyond* horror. Even more heartening is the fact that he does this by – literally – keeping his readers in the dark. At no point does he give in to the temptation to resort to the cheap shot, or to offer glib explanations for the plight of the world, or for what the survivors find in the underground caverns. By showing restraint he manages to convince us that there are worse things waiting for us than death – however painful, lonely and terrifying that death might ultimately prove to be.

So there you have it. A show of strength from the new generation. And now, having prepared you for your journey, I'll release your hand and nudge you along the way, and leave you to explore the darkness alone. It will be quite all right. As long as you keep to the path you'll be perfectly safe.

I promise.

THE PUMPING STATION
Paul Finch

Everyone local knew about the windmill standing in the middle of Probert's Field. How in the true sense of the word it wasn't a windmill – it had never been used to grind flour or hoist grain. How in actual fact it was a pumping station – it had once drawn water from an aquifer and despatched it uphill through underground pipes. How even in that capacity it was now derelict and closed up. And how no one would even go near the place if they could help it, because of a curious incident in the year 1919. All the locals knew about this.

The trouble was that Paul, Josh and Maxine were not locals.

The plaque over the pub door said that the licensees were 'Vera Bates and Neil Bates'.

"I wonder which one's the *master* of the house?" Josh said.

Paul sniggered.

Maxine pushed him. "Don't be so crude."

Laughing, they went indoors.

They'd found *The Gauntlet Inn* about five miles off the A59, twelve miles north of Clitheroe in the heart of Lancashire's famous Bowland Forest. The area was completely rural, and the pub very much suited this environment. It was located on a winding B-road hemmed in by fields and patches of woodland, and was built almost entirely of old, yellowed stone. It had Georgian mullioned windows and a black weathercock on its tall, slate roof, which swung from side to side in the gusting March wind. Josh had been most impressed, however, by the pub's name, *The Gauntlet*. He'd thought it very appropriate, though the gauntlet on the pub sign – a clenched, mailed fist – was a different sort of gauntlet entirely from the one he had in mind.

Inside, they were pleased to see that a small room on the left, probably the snug, was dominated by a hearth in which a fire crackled brightly. The décor was traditional: whitewashed walls, polished wood beams, the spaces between them hung with horse-brasses, leatherwork and farm tools recycled from an earlier age. As it wasn't yet noon, the tables and chairs were still neatly arranged, the atmosphere dust and smoke-free. There was a long central bar, and behind it a smiling lady who simply had to be the licensee, Vera Bates. She was short, middle-aged and busty, but very well presented in make-up, jewellery and with her silver-blonde hair done in a large bouffant.

"Morning," she said cheerily. "Cold day, eh?"

The threesome nodded as they approached, opening their cagoules and stripping off their gloves. "I know it's a bit early," Paul said, "but is there any chance of us grabbing some lunch?"

"Sure," she replied, handing them a menu. "Drinks first?"

"Just a lemonade for me," Paul replied.

"And me," Josh added.

That left only Maxine, who, after some consideration, piped up: "A pint of bitter-shandy."

The landlady smiled. "I'll bring them over."

They moved into the snug and sat down beside the fire. From here, one of the windows gave out onto the pub's car park, which was exceptionally large; it completely dwarfed their vehicle, an old Terrano four-track, which at present was the only one there. As they gazed out, the cold winter rain that they'd been subjected to on-and-off throughout the morning, started up again. It made them glad that they'd thought to put a waterproof tarpaulin over the trailer on which their three quad-bikes were secured.

"You guys students, by any chance?" the landlady asked, as she brought their drinks on a tray.

"Used to be," Paul said. "Not any more. We're all taking a year out, to do a bit of travelling and have a few adventures."

"I could tell you weren't from round here, and the tourist

season's a good two months off yet," the woman replied. "Flaming weather's awful, as well."

Paul was from the West Country, Josh from London and Maxine from the South Coast, but it amused the group that the woman had noticed this. Cosmopolitan Britain clearly hadn't reached this part of the Lancashire hills yet.

"We prefer rough weather," Maxine said. "Makes it more exciting."

The landlady looked puzzled. "Makes what more exciting?"

The group exchanged furtive glances. This was always a fun part of the game; seeing how much they could actually reveal to gormless bumpkins who asked too many questions.

"Life generally," Josh finally answered in an airy tone. "We think of ourselves as outdoor types."

"What, camping and that?"

"Some camping, yeah," Josh agreed. "But we like a bit of sport as well. You know, of the extreme variety."

If the landlady suspected that they weren't being completely truthful with her, she didn't show it. A tall young man in jeans and a t-shirt had now appeared in the bar behind her, yawning and scratching his belly. She indicated him. "Neil there goes to watch Accrington Stanley."

"Not quite the same sport," Josh said, trying not to catch Maxine's eye.

"No, but you've got to be an extreme fan to actually go and watch them."

There were polite titters from the group.

"Now," the woman said. "Any decisions on lunch yet?"

Paul ordered steak and ale pie with chips and salad, Josh chose chicken in a basket and Maxine opted for a tuna sandwich. The landlady wrote everything down, then teetered back to the bar on her high heels.

"Thought she was never going to shut up," Maxine said quietly.

Paul dug into the pocket of his cagoule. "She's just being friendly."

Maxine snorted. "Like we asked her to be."

Paul now spread a map on the table in front of them. It was dog-

11

eared and tacky, having passed through various pairs of hands; its margins were filled with scribbled notations. However, being Ordnance Survey in origin, it was a good map, accurately portraying the immediate district surrounding the place where they were now: primarily a crazed patchwork of woods and fields, with streams and minor roads cutting across it here and there. Down the very centre of the map someone had drawn a zig-zag line in red biro. A closer examination would reveal that this red line respected no boundaries. Slowly, Paul slid his thumb along it.

"So here we are," he said. "The Cresta Run of illegal off-road race tracks."

"Doesn't look like much on there, does it," Maxine remarked.

Josh chuckled. "You say that every time we arrive anywhere, and you always finish last."

She glared at him.

Paul intervened: "It may not look like much, but this is as challenging as they come. It's ten miles and it's all downhill. The one on Dartmoor was fifteen miles, but that was mostly flat. The one in the Lakes was a lot steeper than this, but that was only two and a half miles. This one's a shallow descent, but it's a *non-stop* descent – that's ten miles of steady acceleration. Imagine how fast you'll be going when you reach the other end."

"Yeah," Josh said, prodding Maxine's leg with his foot. "That's if you don't hang onto the brakes all the way."

She was about to respond in her usual heated fashion whenever her prowess was questioned, only for the young guy they'd seen earlier – the one called Neil – to come loafing up, smiling sleepily. He laid down some cutlery wrapped in napkins, a salt-shaker and a bottle of vinegar. Paul whipped the map away. He then watched the young guy closely, to see if he'd spotted anything untoward. If Paul's memory served, one of the names over the pub entrance had been 'Neil'; he'd presumed it had referred to the landlady's husband, but by the looks of this, it was her son. Either way, Neil wore the placid expression of a man who wouldn't recognise that something was wrong even if someone walked in with a stocking on his head and a gun in his hand. He gave them another drowsy smile, then ambled off.

"Memorise the route," Paul said, unfolding the map again. "It's not as clearly obvious as some of the others we've ridden, though Des Jones tells me only a real numbskull will get lost on it."

Now it was Maxine's turn to prod Josh. She stuck out her tongue in response to his casual V-sign.

"The finishing post is here." Paul's finger moved to the extreme north end of the line. "According to the map, it's a small copse of trees called 'Bluebell Wood'."

Maxine scoffed. "'Bluebell Wood'. Can't they come up with something original?"

"You can't miss it," Paul added. "It's next to the Ribblesdale road, on a bus terminus. For the cerebrally challenged, that means a turning-zone with a bus-stop notice. You won't be able to go any further."

"So what happens if we all come shooting out of Bluebell Wood at breakneck pace, and there's this whopping great double-decker swinging round?" Josh wondered.

Paul winked at him. "Like I say, you won't be going any further."

A few moments later, their meals arrived. They ordered another round of drinks, and then tucked in. They ate contentedly for several moments, now warmed by the fire and enjoying the undeniably good food. As they did, Paul allowed his gaze to rove around this small section of the pub. Quite close to them, three sepia-toned photographs hung on the wall, one above the other. The lowest one had been taken during some long-ago summer, and depicted a number of farm-hands posed beside a hay derrick. The one above that showed a very old man in a flat cap and tweeds, leaning pensively on a dry-stone wall. The one at the top, however, was less self-explanatory. It featured a tall, brick-built tower standing in the middle of an open field; at the top of it there were four cruciform sails, at the bottom what looked like a cast-iron door with no visible handle.

Paul nodded at it. "What do you suppose that is?"

"A windmill," Josh said. "What do you think?"

"That isn't a windmill."

"Eh?"

"Where are the outbuildings, the storehouses?" Paul asked. "And look how narrow it is: there isn't room for millstones and wheels and windlasses and stuff in there. That's not a windmill, not a real one."

"Maybe it's a folly?" Maxine suggested.

Paul considered. That was easily possible. It definitely had the forlorn aspect of a folly, though perhaps it wasn't quite grandiose enough. It looked boringly functional. It was built from basic brick, with no elaborate carving or stonework, no benches arranged so that visitors could sit there and marvel at the sheer vacuousness of it. "Bloody odd-looking thing, whatever it is," he concluded.

"I can tell you what that is," came a voice. It's was Neil's; he'd now reappeared to collect their empty plates. "That's the pumping station."

"The what?" Maxine asked, sounding sceptical.

"It was a wind-powered pump," he explained. "Nothing fancy like. Just a stirrup-pump. Used to send water up to the local brewery. In olden times, you understand."

"How old is 'olden times'?" Josh wondered, amused at the quaint terminology.

"Don't know for sure." Neil scratched the side of his head at the same time as performing a remarkable balancing act: all three dishes were now arrayed along one of his arms, while in the same hand he held Josh and Paul's empty glasses. "Early twentieth century, something like that. Funny story attached to it, actually. There was a gypsy lad worked at the brewery, and he got killed in an accident there. Because he was a gypsy though, and not a local fella, the master-brewer wouldn't pay any compensation. Gypsy lad's family were right angry. Story is they put a curse on the place."

"On the brewery?" Paul asked.

"No, on the pumping station. When there was no wind, one of the lads from the brewery had to go down there and crank the pump by hand. Anyway, whatever this curse was, it stopped the station working good and proper – whether there was wind or not. First time it happened, they sent a lad down to fix it. But he was never heard of again. A few more went, same thing happened to them. In the end, they locked the station up and left it. No more water, no more brewery – went out of business, just like that."

"You're kidding?" Josh said. "They let their business run down just because they were frightened of a curse."

Neil shrugged. "Folk were more credulous in those times, I suppose."

14

"Even so, didn't they at least investigate the missing lads?"

Neil grinned. "It's only a story. I couldn't tell you if it was true or not."

"You seem to know a lot about it?" Maxine said, still sounding sceptical.

"Well, the pub's been in mum's family for a long time. Bit of local folklore we've grown up with, I suppose. Pay at the bar when you're ready, yeah?"

Neil lumbered away again, leaving them gazing at each other nonplussed.

"I knew we'd come to the back of beyond, but bloody hell," Maxine finally said.

"No, it's good," Paul replied. "Nice bit of local colour. Don't tell me there were no fairy tales where you were brought up?"

She snorted. "The only fairies I knew were the ones who packed the bars and pubs on Brighton seafront every night."

Josh sniggered. "Familiar with those haunts, are you?"

"Am I bloody hell!" she retorted, and she sank what remained of her pint. "Are we going to get going then, or what? Or are you two jerk-offs going to keep trying to delay the ass-whipping you've been asking for for the last six months?"

In many ways, the group's quad-bikes, or ATVs[1] as they were officially called, reflected if not the looks of the individual riders, certainly their personalities. Paul Grogan, Mr.-Organiser-in-Chief, was a solid, reliable sort, who always kept a cool head. Of average height but broad build, he had a strong, muscular physique. His short blonde hair and clean-cut good looks gave him a military air that was both intimidating and yet trustworthy. His particular vehicle was a 250cc Firestorm, a state-of-the-art machine with an air-cooled, four-stroke engine and glinting, steel-grey bodywork.

Josh Carter was the wild card. Always ready for a joke or a wind-up, he was also the most apt to pull some crazy stunt, though this slightly barmy streak made him a real competitor on trails that required *serious* nerve and daring. Physically, he was lean and lithe,

---

[1] All terrain vehicles.

but again highly athletic. In keeping with his rebel spirit, his dark, spiky hair was razored into a permanent flat-top, and he wore rings in both ears. His piercing, blue eyes and sharp, aquiline features would ordinarily have made him handsome, had his face not been dotted and cratered thanks to a severe bout of chicken pox in his youth. His machine was a 300cc Panther, which though older and more battered than Paul's, wore its scars — many of which were clearly visible on its jet-black bodywork – with defiant pride.

Maxine Goss liked to regard herself as a toughie. Despite being petite and rather pretty, with copper-red hair that would have been truly glorious had she ever let it grow past her ears, she'd never had any time for romance. Throughout her college years, she'd enforced her status as a ladette by going round-for-round with the boys, finding endless mirth in mickey-taking and pursuing demanding outdoor activities, which latter course had finally introduced her to off-road racing. Her vehicle was a 200cc Apache, very small and compact but with huge 'mud monster' tyres; its bodywork was painted camouflage-style in green and brown stripes.

They were all now at the start-point, the southern end of a broad meadow that sloped gently down in front of them. The rich green grass that covered it didn't fool them. They knew that, at this time of year, there'd be slick mud just below it. Not only that, the surface humped and undulated all the way down to the bottom, and was criss-crossed here and there by the deep, parallel furrows of tractor tracks. No actual race-trail was visible, but far below them, maybe three-hundred yards down, a gap was broken in the perimeter wall and beyond that a dark passage led off under arching trees.

Paul turned and looked at the others. They were all gloved and suited up, each one wearing a waterproof slicker over his or her heavy-duty coveralls, and a grimy, dented helmet. The rain meanwhile was increasing in force. It had been intermittent over the last hour or so, but since they'd left the pub, which was situated about two miles back along the narrow lane, it had grown particularly heavy. It pelted loudly on the Terrano, which Paul had parked in a grassy lay-bye on the other side of the nearby farm-gate.

"Everyone set?" he asked.

There were mumbles of agreement. Maxine pulled her visor

down. Josh's helmet didn't have a visor, but he always wore a pair of goggles and these he now lifted into place. Paul closed his own visor, and they started their engines, the low growls deep and gutsy in the saturated air. One by one, they knocked their machines into gear.

Paul then took a large, smooth stone from his pocket. He held it up so the others could see it, then lobbed it forwards. It arced maybe thirty feet before striking the ground.

The second it did, they hit the gas.

Rent turf sprayed behind as the three vehicles roared to life, all three showing immediate, hair-raising acceleration. Position-wise, Paul was in the middle, Josh to the left and Maxine on the right. Initially as they tore downhill, they bunched – risky though this was, it was never wise to move out to the flanks; the quickest route from A to B was always a straight line, though the terrain wouldn't allow this for long. As their speedos rose to forty, the slightest bumps became take-off ramps, dips and curves turned to hair-pin bends. The machines spread apart as they swerved and bounced their way down this tricky slope. Josh had taken an early lead. Lying forwards until he was nearly flat – like a MotoGP racer – he surged ahead of the other two. Towards the bottom, however, they ran into quagmire country; near-marsh conditions, which instantly slowed them all down again. Mud that had liquefied to slurry spurted in every direction as they wove their way through it, but now Maxine, whose engine was less powerful than the others, but whose tyres were easily the best, was able to seize the advantage. She veered sharply in from the right as the two lads fell behind, threading through the gap in the wall first and then hitting the firmer woodland trail on the other side with real gusto.

She whooped like an Indian, and throttled up as much as she could. The track ahead swung sharply to the left, but at least it was clear of undergrowth and forest rubble. ATV races didn't occur here every week, but this particular run was well-known on the underground circuit and was used more often than most. Josh and Paul meanwhile were catching up. Paul had taken position on the right flank and was maybe ten yards behind the girl. He too was leaning forward, throttling his machine as hard as he could. As a group they weren't far off sixty mph now, which on a course as narrow as this was pushing safety to the limit. Paul's offside wheels constantly struck the verge, ploughing through leafage, thorns and brush. Josh was also having problems. Directly behind Maxine, he repeatedly had to duck and even swerve to avoid the divots and clods of soil churning in her wake. Angry, he throttled up, planning to overtake her on the left. But a split-second later, before he could even commence the manoeuvre, the woodland suddenly thinned and the racers found themselves being funnelled down a narrow ravine. It was about two-hundred yards long, and at the far end they could see what looked like a barbed-wire fence, part of which had been cut away. The space this allowed was narrow in the extreme: a chicane through which only one vehicle could pass at a time.

Determined to keep her advantage, Maxine accelerated hard. The rain having slackened off again, the rocky ground here was relatively dry, but it was also rutted and uneven, and soon she was jolting and bouncing, and Josh, as only Josh could, was still trying to overtake. She swore as he came abreast of her. His Panther simply had too much power. On the right, meanwhile, Paul had also come level. All three were now hurtling at sixty-plus towards a gap that only one could pass through.

Suddenly it had become a game of 'Chicken'.

Maxine hated this. She knew it meant Josh would grab back the lead. He was the only one mad enough to ever see this sort of thing to the bitter end. Of course, it was likely there'd be other muddy hollows further ahead, in which case she could overtake him again. So rather than risk life and limb purely for the sake of temporary bragging-rights, she throttled down a little. With a wild laugh, Josh hove in front of her. But then something totally unexpected happened – Paul tried to do the same thing. Normally more prudent than Josh, Paul also tended to lose out to him when a race turned dangerous, but perhaps he'd finally got fed up with this. After this season's races so far, he was three points behind Josh. If he came second today, it would be six points. If he came last, it would be nine – he'd be a basement-dweller.

So he swung in too, and now the duo were neck-and-neck.

This drew a startled, sideways glance from Josh. He throttled up again. Paul copied him. Only fifty yards remained, and they were travelling at close to seventy. For an incredible moment, Maxine thought the guys were going to start bullocking each other. Josh again tried to swerve ahead. Paul did the same thing. Now there was only thirty yards left. One of them shouted something to the other. The girl couldn't tell who it was. The shout was returned – it was a profanity.

They pushed on harder, still neck-and-neck.

This was madness, Maxine thought.

And then nature intervened.

A heavy stone, which, thanks to their sniping at each other, neither of the men had spotted, struck Paul's front nearside tyre. It was a massive blow and it lifted his vehicle sideways off the ground. For a second he was running on two wheels. He looked certain to topple, but fought the handlebars deftly until at last he brought himself down and back on course. He'd lost ground, however … and just in time. Josh bulleted through the gap in the barbed-wire, Paul only inches behind him. Maxine brought up the rear.

None of the trio expected the next development.

The ground fell away in front of them.

In the blink of an eye, the gentle slope became a steep embankment, and they dropped down it like stones. Still disoriented from the chaos of the ravine, they were completely unprepared for this – and for the belt of trees at the bottom.

The trees were thinly spread, but the dirt paths winding through them were a confusing tangle, impossible to navigate at such short notice. The next thing the racers knew, trunks were coming at them from all sides. They spun left and right, skidding and fishtailing – to little avail.

Maxine was the first casualty. She'd now braked down considerably, but still sideswiped a tree with shuddering force. She was flung from the saddle, landing in a spongy mass of moss and twigs, which thankfully only winded her. Josh, the second casualty, was less fortunate. He'd had to sit upright to regain control of his machine, at which point a low branch smashed him in the face, knocking his head back, almost ripping off his helmet. Seconds later, he emerged from the trees into another meadow. He was still in the

19

saddle, but now like a drunken man, swaying from side to side. Moments later, Paul burst out in pursuit of him. Not initially aware that Josh had been hurt, Paul throttled quickly up. They were on broad grassland again. As before it sloped gently downhill, but on this occasion Paul didn't get a chance to exploit it. As he accelerated, Josh suddenly cut across his path in a sharp, diagonal manoeuvre.

Paul had to jerk his handlebars left, turning the vehicle so abruptly that its front offside tyre caught transverse against a tussock of grass, and the whole machine upended. He was thrown heavily forwards, somersaulting through the air before crashing down hard on his helmet.

Josh continued his crazy path. His speed was dropping but he was bereft of any control and heading straight towards a tall object, which neither of them had previously noticed. It was a solitary brick tower with four windmill-like sails at its apex. Maxine, now limping and carrying her helmet under one arm, materialised from the trees just in time to see him crash headlong into it. With a deafening CRUNCH, his quad struck the tower's rusted metal door, which crumpled inwards like paper. Josh, who was lolling sideways, slammed his upper body and head against the brickwork to the right-hand side of this door and was thrown violently backwards.

He hit the turf, and lay there unmoving.

The girl, already tearful with shock, gasped and had to choke back sobs as she threw her helmet down and stumbled forwards. The first of the casualties she reached was Paul. He lay on his side groaning. She dropped to her knees beside him. His visor had been torn off and blood was visible around his mouth, but his eyes were open and he seemed to be breathing relatively easily.

"Where does it hurt?" she asked.

"Everywhere," he grunted. "My neck."

"Your neck!"

"Yeah, but I don't think it's broken."

"You sure?"

"Dunno." He moved his head slightly, and winced.

"Paul, don't!"

Gingerly, he tried to sit up. "I'm okay – just a bit groggy." Then: "Ow, my shoulder!" He cringed and hunched sideways, crooking his

20

left arm. "I might've broken *this*."

"Oh God," Maxine said.

The rain started again, at first slowly but then with increasing force. Fat, icy droplets were soon hitting them like bullets. Paul glanced up at her ashen-faced. More blood trickled from the side of his mouth. "I've almost bitten my tongue in half, as well."

"Listen, just stay here." She got back to her feet. "I've got to check on Josh, okay?"

He nodded, then cringed again. He looked as though he was about to be sick.

Maxine turned and hurried on down the slope towards the tower. At that moment it barely registered that this tower was the pumping station they'd seen in the photo on the pub wall. Its iron door had completely caved in, and Josh's Panther had gone clean inside. Josh himself lay half in and half out of the doorway. He still wasn't moving.

Maxine was dreading what she might find: namely an imploded chest, a mangled face, eyes that were glazed in death. It was with some surprise, and no little relief, therefore, that she found him relatively unscathed... at least visibly. His goggles had been yanked down and his helmet bashed in all around the faceplate rim, but though one of his eyebrows was cut and the bridge of his nose deeply bruised, he was otherwise unmarked. Dirt and brick-dust covered the front of his slicker, particularly the upper-chest portion, but when she touched him there, pressing gently with her finger-tips, his ribs, shoulders and collar-bone seemed to be intact.

He was deeply unconscious, however.

When she spoke to him, she got no response. She put an ear to his lips. He was breathing. She spoke to him again, but his eyelids didn't so much as flicker.

Feeling utterly helpless, Maxine stood up. She glanced into the interior of the pumping station. It was a dank, black recess, in which she could just make out the twisted shape of the quad-bike. It lay upside-down on the far side, in the midst of cluttered bricks. There was a strong smell of petrol, and dust was still pluming down around it: the impact on the entire structure had clearly been colossal. But there was no succour to be found in there.

21

As she hurried back up the hill to Paul, the rain strengthened even more. Soon it was sheeting over her, turning her hair to a soaked mop. Half-drowned, she finally reached him and dropped to her knees. "Josh has been knocked out," she stammered. "I don't know bad it is, but we've got to get help."

Again Paul nodded. He seemed unable to speak he was in so much pain. His pallor had faded to grey, and despite the fact he was well packaged against the cold, he was shivering. The rain thudded on his helmet, dripping incessantly from the end of his nose.

"Paul?" Maxine said, raising her voice, fearing that he was about to pass out. "Paul, I haven't got my mobile with me, and Josh doesn't have one. Where's yours?"

A second passed, then Paul pushed the zip down the front of his slicker, reached inside it, winced again as he encountered more bruises, and finally brought something out from an internal pocket. It was his mobile. Or rather, it had *once* been his mobile. The small appliance had split down one side; wires and bits of circuit hung out.

"Okay, okay… I'll go and get help," she said. "Have you got the car keys?"

Again Paul reached under his waterproof, but this time torturous moments passed before he was able to find what he was looking for. At last he extricated the keys, and handed them over.

"Okay Paul – I know it's bad that I'm leaving you, but I've no choice. Can you just hang on here?"

Paul made a vague gesture with his hand. It seemed to imply that he'd be okay, but the rain was now slashing into them. All Maxine's instincts screamed at her that to abandon injured friends in these conditions was insanity. She stood up and glanced around, on the off-chance there'd be somebody in sight – but there was no one. The March sky was now lead-grey; it seemed to have leached all colour from the world. The grassland was turning slowly to mush. The trees were wet, leafless husks, tossing in the droning wind. It was as bleak and desolate a scene as she had ever laid eyes on.

She choked back another sob, but, determined to pull herself together, went over to Paul's Firestorm… only to find it lying on its side with its front offside wheel buckled. After that, she thought about going back to see if she could drag Josh's Panther out of the pumping station, though from the petrol she'd smelled in there, she doubted that would be driveable either. Besides – she gazed towards the drear edifice: its ancient brickwork was covered with scabrous lichen; only threads of brown material hung from the black lattice frames of its sails. It was an eerie, derelict shell, which even on a bright summer's day she could easily believe had some sort of hex upon it; despite the circumstances, she felt no inclination to return there.

She turned and began stumbling uphill towards the trees. She was in pain herself: one hip was hurting and her right arm felt numb from the elbow down. On top of that, the slope was steeper than she'd realised and it quickly started sapping her strength. Soon, only the sense of urgency was keeping her going. When she eventually re-entered the wood, the shadows under its naked branches had darkened. For a few moments she felt as though she was in a different place, but at last she spotted her Apache. It was standing skew-whiff alongside a sycamore trunk, the bark of which had been gashed so deeply that soft white wood was visible beneath. She climbed thankfully into the saddle and when she saw the key was still in the ignition, offered a silent prayer of gratitude.

But the Apache wouldn't start.

The key wouldn't even turn, nor could she pull the handle-bars around. The whole steering block had apparently jammed.

Whimpering with frustration, she dismounted and circled the vehicle. It had sustained a lot of what she'd first thought was superficial damage – dents, grazes and such. But clearly something else was also broken, something *inside*.

Maxine knew she had no choice but to continue on foot.

It wasn't long before the rain became oppressive. For all Paul's layers of cladding, it was soon seeping down the back of his neck. It seemed to roar in his ears.

Though nauseous with shock, he managed to clamber to his feet. When he was upright, a moment passed during which everything shifted out of focus. He had to steady himself by holding out his arms like a scarecrow. After that, he slowly and painfully removed his helmet. His neck was incredibly stiff and sore; the act of just rotating it a little sent him dizzy again. And the cold rain didn't help. Now it was hammering on the top of his bare skull instead of his helmet, running from his hair in rivulets. The obvious thing next thing to do was find some shelter.

As he hobbled downhill towards the pumping station, Paul's eyes fixed on the inert form of Josh lying in its open doorway, and suddenly the reality of the situation struck home. At times Josh was an idiot, a bloody lunatic. His reckless behaviour was responsible for this disaster, but he was also a close buddy. Just how badly hurt was he?

When Paul reached his friend, he saw the same thing Maxine had: the guy was out cold, which was even more worrying than before considering that ten minutes had now elapsed. The rain had failed to revive him. In fact, water was pooling in the hollows of Josh's eyes, and there was still no sign of life.

Paul glanced up. The pumping station was a black monolith lowering overhead. Its skeletal sails, from the ends of which torrents of water were gushing, stood cross-like against a terrible sky. There was no sign at all of the rain letting up. Another gust of downhill wind blew it spitefully against them. That decided the matter. Despite the ill-advisability of moving an accident victim, it was inconceivable to leave Josh lying exposed to elements like these.

It was musty inside the windmill structure, and there was a strong stench of petrol. Paul could smell something else in there as well; something odious, like fungus or mildew. But none of that was relevant. It was shelter, and at this moment shelter was the only thing that mattered.

Maxine was half way up the ravine, when she got the peculiar feeling that someone was watching her.

She halted and turned. Nobody had entered the ravine behind her. Likewise, there was no one visible ahead. She glanced up the sides, first the left and then the right, and was startled to glimpse what looked like someone in a blue hood stepping quickly out of sight. Under normal circumstances this might have unnerved her, but not now.

"Hello?" she called. "Hello up there?" But her voice was lost in the wind and rain.

24

Frantic, she began to scramble up the slope, having to do it on all fours because it was basically wet soil and loose stones, and it slid and cracked beneath her booted feet.

"Can you help us please?" she called again, breathless with exertion.

It didn't occur to her that what she was doing might actually be dangerous until she was about fifteen feet from the top. She stopped and gazed up again. Whoever it was, there was no sign of them now. Were they keeping out of sight? If so, why?

"Hello?" she said again, this time warily. "There's been an accident. Can you help?"

Still there was no reply. It was tempting to scramble back down and hurry on up the ravine, but for all Maxine knew Josh was dying back there, and whoever this person was, he or she might have a mobile phone. She cursed herself for leaving her helmet behind. If nothing else it might have made a useful weapon, while it would certainly have served as protection if someone attacked her. But then why would someone want to attack her all the way out here? Rapists and such hunted in areas where they were likely to encounter victims. Emboldened, she thus continued, again on all fours, until she at last got to the top. When she got there, she stood up … and stared blank-faced at the 'person' who'd been watching her.

It was a tall mass of thorns growing around a concrete post at the very end of a wall dividing two areas of deserted pasture. What she'd actually seen 'ducking out of sight' was not someone in a hood, but a blue plastic bag snagged on the edge of the thorns. It flipped back and forth in the wind, the movement of which she'd just caught in the corner of her eye as she'd traversed the path below.

At that moment, Maxine wanted to fall down in a heap and cry. The rain swept across her in drenching gusts, however, and then the bag detached itself and flew straight at her face, half-wrapping itself around her head. Angrily, she batted it away, turned and trotted back down the slope. But again the slick soil gave way and this time she fell, landing first on her backside – a blow which winded her even more than before – and then rolling forwards, tumbling all the way to the bottom, bruising herself anew and streaking her face, hair and waterproofs with thick, black mud.

After that, it was agony just getting back to her feet. She tottered on up the ravine, stumbling and falling twice before she reached the far end. When she finally got there, she had to double-over she was so tired. She took several wheezing breaths before proceeding into the next belt of woodland. This too was wringing wet and whipping back and forth in the gale. At least the trail they'd followed through it was clear, but there was still a long way to go.

Josh still hadn't regained consciousness. He'd muttered a few feeble groans, however, which Paul took as a good sign.

They were both now inside the cylindrical shell of the pumping station. Paul had made Josh as comfortable as he could, though it hadn't been easy. By the looks of it, once the old building had ceased functioning, it had had the bulk of its mechanical guts ripped out, leaving it largely empty. The underground tanks and the pipes leading down to the aquifer, meanwhile, were now buried beneath a mass of decayed rubble that had presumably collapsed from above during the previous century of disuse. Paul had thus had to lay the casualty on broken bricks and masonry. The air in there was truly rank; even the smell of petrol from the shattered quad-bike was lost in a musty fetor which reminded Paul of an animal pen that hadn't been cleaned out for some time.

He was currently standing by the doorway, gazing out over the weather-ravaged meadow. The rain was easing up a little, thankfully, but the sky was still slate-grey and strong draughts continued to shrill in the upper portions of the tower. Paul glanced upwards. He'd been inside the thing for five minutes and his eyes had attuned well to the darkness. The tower was entirely hollow, and though various layers of dust-thick cobweb spanned it from one side to the other, he could see almost to the top, though the very highest section – presumably where the sails mechanism was affixed – was hidden in a blot of shadow. Here and there timber struts lay across it, and a rusted steel pole hung down one side – all that remained of the central spindle, he supposed. Dotted around the interior walls were lumps of broken and corroded metal; relics of the pumping apparatus, which had evidently been removed quickly and without delicacy. It wasn't the most salubrious environment, but at least it was dry.

Paul walked back over to Josh. He hadn't taken off the casualty's helmet – he knew better than that – but he'd slipped out of his slicker, folded it and pushed it under Josh's head as a pillow. Aside from that, there wasn't a lot else he'd been able to do, except wait. Josh mumbled something again. It was almost inaudible, but as before, Paul took it as a good sign – which was more than he could say for the stiffness in his neck and shoulder; this was now spreading down his back and chest and into his left arm. Whenever he attempted any undue movement, it hurt abominably; he was even starting to feel a tingling in the fingertips on his left hand.

He was just ruminating on this, wondering how problematic it might turn out to be insurance-wise, when he thought he heard something. It was very soft and it lasted barely a second; it had been a *slithering* – like old cloth on a hard surface.

He glanced down at Josh. Was the guy coming round, had he just changed position?

But Josh hadn't. He lay exactly as he had done before.

There was another sound: softer, shorter, but again a *slithering*.

Paul looked around puzzled. The interior of the tower was maybe twelve feet in diameter. It was still dim and dusty, but he was sure there was nothing else in there that could have moved… unless rubble had shifted under his own feet? He looked down, but saw nothing. And then he heard the sound a third time, and this time it was neither soft nor short; in fact it lasted for several moments, which gave Paul a much better idea where it was coming from.

Slowly, amazedly, he gazed upwards again.

Above the canopies of dust-web, something seemed to be stirring in the darkness at the top. Paul felt a dull creep at his neck, but hastily told himself that if there was anything up there, it could only be bats. However, he then heard the sound a fourth time, and it clearly wasn't the rustle of small, furry bodies or slight, leathery wings. It was something more substantial, something heavy and awkward, and maybe – if he could actually allow himself to believe it – something that was now *descending*.

* * *

27

The last hundred yards was easily the worst.

The rain had all but stopped, but Maxine was already drenched through. She'd had to unzip her slicker because sweat had soaked her as much on the inside as the weather had on the out. When she crested the final hill, and came to the point where they'd started the race, the breath was like a dagger in her lungs. She toppled towards the farm-gate and fell bodily against it, only hanging on by crooking her arm over the top rung. With leaden limbs, she then clambered up and across it, falling heavily down the other side, landing on her back in a patch of nettles. None of this mattered. Three yards away stood the Terrano, now, having been washed, gleaming brightly as shafts of pale sunlight broke through the turgid clouds.

Still gasping, Maxine worked her way around the vehicle to the driver's door. She took out the key, opened it and then climbed wearily behind the steering-wheel. For several seconds she had to fight off the temptation to simply lay her head back and close her eyes. But no – Josh! God alone knew what state he was in.

She fitted the key in the ignition, switched the engine on and swung the Terrano round in a tight three-point turn. A minute later, she was accelerating back up the country lane, in the direction of *The Gauntlet*.

Paul's first instinct was to run for his life.

With unashamed cowardice he dashed out into the meadow. But only when the cold, moist air hit him, and the sudden fresh sweat that had broken on his face froze, did he realise what he was actually doing. Josh was still inside, unconscious, totally helpless.

Paul now knew that he'd fractured something, probably his left shoulder. But somehow or other he had to get Josh out of there, and in the next few seconds. He pivoted stiffly around, then forced himself back in through the narrow door, trying not to glance up at the hefty, ungainly shape working its way down through the layers of dust-web. Dirt and debris cascaded below it, old timber joists and fragments of aged metal squealed beneath its weight. But still Paul didn't look.

Without thinking, he grabbed at Josh with both hands, trying to lift him by his arm-pits. And instantly, agony like he'd never known went down through his left side. He dropped the casualty, twisted where he stood and could barely suppress an animal-like howl. And still those noises overhead, getting closer every second. The stench of fetor in the place was thickening, becoming unbearable.

Instead of trying to lift him, Paul now grabbed Josh by the foot. Using only one hand, he would drag him out. It was inelegant, it might do Josh more harm than good, but what choice was there? Josh was not light, however, and Paul was still sick and dizzy from the crash. He tugged with all his might, but only slowly did the injured man start to shift. Bricks rolled sluggishly beneath him. Then he gave another low groan.

"Josh!" Paul shouted with desperate hope. "Josh, wake up!"

And then there was an explosive impact at the back of his head. It was so hard that he didn't initially feel it, just heard it – it sounded like a volcanic eruption. A glaring blue flash almost blinded him, and the next thing he knew he was on his knees alongside his friend. His hair, which had previously been wet and cold, was now wet and warm. A hot trickle ran down his nose. Then he slumped forwards onto his face. As he did, something landed beside him with a clatter – it was an old section of rusted pipe; mid-way down, it had cracked and bent at a right angle from the force of the blow it had just administered.

"Dirty, cheating basta…" Paul mumbled, but further words failed him.

Maxine staggered into the pub, and made a footsore bee-line for the bar.

The landlady, who was mopping the counter, stopped what she was doing and stared in amazement. "Neil!" she said. "Come in here please."

A split-second later, the young guy, Neil, emerged from a back room.

"Help," Maxine stammered, almost falling against the bar-top. "Please, you've got to help… can I use your phone?"

"What's happened?" the landlady asked tautly.

"We… we had a… my friends …"

"Calm down, love," Neil put in. "You had some sort of accident?"

Maxine nodded. She was only vaguely aware how wet, filthy and dishevelled she was. Their aghast expressions at first puzzled her. "That... that building you told us about, the windmill thing..."

"The pumping station?" he said.

She nodded feverishly. "Josh has... Josh and Paul... Josh crashed into it."

"How do you mean crashed into it?" the landlady asked. She looked genuinely confused, but also frightened.

Maxine swallowed spittle. She could still barely get her breath. "We were quad-bike racing... on the field. Josh hit it, straight through the door. He's hurt..."

"Straight through the door?" the landlady repeated, now with a tone that suggested her very worst fears had suddenly been realised.

"He's hurt, please!" Maxine's voice rose. Why were they just standing there like a pair of tombstones? "Please... I can't wake him up!"

"Alright, alright," the landlady said. "Neil, get the Land Rover. Some blankets as well, and the first-aid kit."

"No!" Maxine shook her head. "We need an ambulance!"

"Where do you think the nearest ambulance station is, love?" the landlady asked her. "It'll take them half an hour minimum."

"We'll get your friend," Neil said in a reassuring voice. "We'll have him at hospital in fifteen minutes flat."

The landlady put on an overcoat, then tied her hair in a scarf. Her son went hurriedly into the back room. Maxine lowered her head for a moment, too weary to feel relief that help was at last at hand.

A second later, she glanced up again. Only one other person was in the pub, a local by the looks of him: an elderly countryman type, in a waistcoat, a leather-patched jacket and a flat cap. He was seated in a corner with a Guinness on the table in front of him and a pipe in his hand. He'd been reading a newspaper, though he'd now lowered it and was regarding her steadily, the eyes like blue marbles in his plump, pink face. He was obviously a kindly man; his expression was one of extreme pity.

* * *

30

Paul was dimly aware that somebody was crouching over him; either over him or over Josh, it wasn't entirely clear. The stench of this person was eye-watering, but perhaps that was understandable. Through tear-blurred eyes, Paul caught glimpses of an old suit of clothes – very old, antiquated even; and though maybe once they'd been smart and fashionable, now they were ragged and covered in dirt and mildew and streaks of what looked like orange fungus, and they were stretched over a huge, misshapen form which had more affinity with an ape than a human.

Josh was then lifted bodily up.

It was as simple as that.

One minute he was lying alongside Paul, the next he was hoisted up and out of sight with no difficulty at all. In Paul's fragmented mind, he pictured a man scooping up a life-size rag doll and throwing it with ease over his shoulder.

Then it was his own turn.

A pair of bare feet shuffled into view: crippled, lumpen feet, with broken, dirt-encrusted toenails and thick mats of curling black hair on their upper parts. The next thing, a hand the size of a shovel had grabbed at Paul's chest with such force that its jagged fingernails tore clean through his many layers of material, and scored the flesh over his ribs. Then Paul too was yanked upwards.

At this point, the swamp-like stink of putrescence was so awful that it filled his nose and throat; he virtually gagged on it, was ready to vomit... but not before he realised that two eyes were peering directly into his. Two eyes set in a dark, square, shaggy head; two eyes that were beady and yellow and malevolent beyond all comprehension.

Paul might have briefly fainted. All he knew after that was that he was ascending the inside of the tower. He hung helpless as he did, broken and bloody, an arm as thick as a tree-trunk encompassing his waist. When he caught sight of the brick-strewn floor diminishing below, a perilous sense of vertigo struck him – but he couldn't give voice even to this horror. Foul draperies of dust-web, filled with slime and rot and multi-legged scuttling things, now fell over him, coating his nostrils and mouth.

Above, the impenetrable blackness waited.

Maxine journeyed back to the scene of the accident by a different route.

She sat in the rear of the Land Rover, which Neil was driving; his mother occupied the front passenger seat. The girl was still so shaken and tired that she only half listened to her rescuers' conversation. From what she could gather, the pub landlady was on her mobile, talking to someone called Jack Probert.

"We could use your tractor, Jack," she was saying. "Sounds like a there's quite a bit of clearing up to do. The quad-bikes'll need moving for a start."

"To hell with the quad-bikes," Maxine said under her breath. "I'll be happy if I never see one again." She spoke up: "I'm more concerned about Josh and Paul."

"Don't worry, love, we're almost there," Neil replied over his shoulder.

They were following an even narrower lane than the one before, this one banked to either side by thick hedgerows. It looped and curved alarmingly, and was so tight that if they'd met traffic coming from the other direction, they'd have had to reverse for hundreds of yards. But they met nothing, and eventually the road ended at a farm-gate. Neil jumped out, unchained the gate and pushed it open. Then he drove though onto rough and open pasture. Maxine realised they were in the same meadow where the accident had occurred. She sat upright.

They drove on for several minutes, cresting one hump after another, the vehicle occasionally sliding even though it had now shifted into four-wheel-drive. At last however, the windmill outline of the pumping station came into view. There was nobody beside or even near it. Paul's overturned Firestorm was still visible about sixty yards to the north, but Paul himself was nowhere to be seen, and neither was Josh.

"Where are they?" Maxine wondered aloud.

"Maybe they weren't as badly hurt as you thought," the landlady replied. "Could they be walking back?"

"No way."

"Well it's not raining any more," Neil pointed out. "But it only stopped a few moments ago. Perhaps they've gone into the station for shelter?"

"Yeah," Maxine nodded. "That's what they'll have done."

They pulled up about thirty yards from the tall structure. Maxine jumped out and hurried over. The wind had now eased as well as the rain; the sky was still clotted with cloud, but bands of blue were at last showing. She could even hear a bird twittering.

"Paul!" she shouted, heading straight for the door. "Paul, I'm back."

There was no response … which caused her to slow down and stop.

Suddenly the stillness and silence that surrounded that gaunt shell of a building seemed eerie. Maxine gazed in through its doorway, initially seeing only opaque shadow. As before, some sixth sense was trying to dissuade her from venturing inside.

The landlady appeared beside her. "No luck?"

"I don't suppose someone else could've helped them?" Maxine replied.

"I wouldn't have thought so. Did you speak to anyone else?"

"No."

"In which case I don't see how. So … shall we take a look?"

"Yes. Yes, of course."

Maxine shook off her foolish notions. These were her friends, she was talking about; and they were both injured. Steeling herself, she stepped in through the tower door. Several moments then passed as her eyes got used to the dark. She scanned its rubble-littered floor, pausing briefly on the wreck of the Panther. The reek of petrol seemed to have subsided a little now, to be replaced by something else – something pungent and rather rancid. There was no sign of the two men, however.

At least, that was what she thought – until her gaze alighted on several reddish dots spattered over a particular jumble of bricks. She fell to a crouch beside them.

"They've been here," she finally said in a strained voice. "They *have* been in here, definitely."

But the landlady wasn't listening. She was still outside, now talking to her son, who appeared to have backed his Land Rover

33

right up to the tower door. He was in the process of knotting one end of a rope to the vehicle's rear tow-bar. Maxine glanced around, saw what they were doing and stood up. She was about to repeat what she'd just said, when she heard something overhead. She glanced upwards, startled. The building's cylindrical interior rose into total darkness, but suddenly trickles of dust were descending from it. She heard the noise again; it sounded like faint movement.

"Paul?" she breathed, incredulous.

Then she noticed something else strange. The landlady had taken the rope her son had tied to his tow-bar, and having made a lasso at the other end of it, was now kneeling and fitting it over the top of the broken-down metal door. Maxine watched, astonished, as the woman pulled it to about a third of the way down the door's length, cinched it tight, then got back to her feet. "That'll be fine," she said, stepping outside again.

Her son nodded and climbed into the Land Rover. He started its engine.

"Hey!" Maxine said. "What are you doing?"

No one replied. The Land Rover began to inch forwards, and the door, though still bent and buckled, was slowly lifted upright.

"The locks have all gone," the landlady was now saying, "but this should do it, until Jack Probert gets here. I'll tell him to put a new door on."

"Hey, wait!" Maxine said, trying to sidle out past the door, but it was now rising back into place and suddenly there was no room for her to get around it. "Hey!" she shouted. "Wait … I'm still in here! Hey, what are you doing?"

The Land Rover ground to a halt, almost as though the driver had heard her. Neil climbed out and came back towards the door, but it was his mother's face that filled the narrow gap. "I'm sorry, my dear," she said, "but you *have* been told the story."

"What?" Maxine asked, genuinely bewildered. She wasn't sure what was going on here, but suddenly the matter of her missing buddies seemed much less important.

"Neil himself told you. About this place."

"I don't understand. You mean the curse … you're talking about the gypsy curse?"

34

The woman nodded solemnly.

"Okay, yeah. I know it ... what about it?"

"Dear me, you are slow on the uptake for a college girl." The woman pondered for a moment, then added: "The brewery it was attached to used to belong to my family. It sat next door to the pub, where the car park is now."

Maxine wanted to reply, but heard sounds overhead again: scuffling, scraping sounds. With the door almost closed on her, she was in near-complete darkness.

"What happened here is our shame," the landlady stated. "But it's in the past, and there it must stay."

"Okay, I'm frightened!" Maxine jabbered. "Are you happy now? It's worked. I'm sorry for what we did, I've learned my lesson. Now let me out, for Christ's sake!"

The woman merely stared at her.

"You're a bunch of cretins," Maxine blurted, suddenly tearful. "Don't you think we've been punished enough? Josh might be dead, for God's sake! Look, you can't lock me in here just because we were trespassing." The woman moved out of sight. "You fucking yokels!" Maxine screamed. "You can't do this! Are you stupid or just mad!"

Another face appeared. It was Neil's; he looked sad but resolute. "We'd certainly be mad to let you walk away," he tried to explain. "You tell the authorities, they come and pull this place down. But the curse won't leave. It'll be visited on us personal. Not just the pub, our home, who knows?"

"Please!" Maxine shrieked. She grabbed at the edge of the door and tried to drag it down again, but it was held fast by the rope tied to the Land Rover.

This didn't put her off. She went at it like a thing demented. So frantic were her efforts that she didn't at first notice Neil slide something through the gap at just about chest-height. When she finally did, the breath caught in her throat. She stared, goggle-eyed.

It was the muzzle of a double-barrelled shotgun.

It fired.

The detonation echoed and re-echoed in the tall confines of the tower, only falling silent when the smoke had cleared and the gun itself had been withdrawn. A moment afterwards, the Land Rover engine re-started.

"I'm sorry for that, dear," came the landlady's voice through the gap, which was now narrowing to an infinitesimal crack of light; though even if anyone had been listening, it was unlikely they'd have heard her over the creaks and slithers as something heavy now clambered back down from above. "But trust me – you'll be glad we did it."

WFTG

An ex-police officer and journalist, Paul Finch is now a full-time TV and movie script-writer. He cut his literary teeth penning episodes of the popular British crime drama, *The Bill*, but he's no stranger to prose. To date, he has had six books and nearly 300 stories and novellas published on both sides of the Atlantic, mostly in the horror, fantasy and sci-fi fields. His first collection, *Aftershocks*, won the British Fantasy Award for 2002, his novella *Kid* won the British Fantasy Award for 2007, and his short story *The Old North Road* won the International Horror Guild Award for 2007. He is currently working on two big-screen adaptations of his own stories, *Cape Wrath* and *Lore Of The Jungle*. Paul lives in Lancashire, northern England, with his wife Cathy and his two children, Eleanor and Harry.

"The idea for The Pumping Station *came from a story I made up to entertain my young son Harry with, while driving him home from infant school. We regularly followed a woodland road, which went close by an old pumping-house that had once been attached to a local brewery, though the brewery itself was long gone. The derelict building had always had an eerie reputation, probably because of its remote location, but also because adults told spooky tales about it to keep their youngsters from going too near. Harry was fascinated by it, and was always asking about the ghosts that were supposed to haunt it. One day, on the spur of the moment, I told him that it wasn't a ghost but a monster - a kind of apeman, who lived in the top of the tower. Anyone he caught trespassing would be taken up there, and never seen again. I don't know where the idea came from, I*

literally plucked it out of the air, but Harry was a little unnerved by it, so I didn't mention it again. However, we continued to drive past it every day and about a week later I had a nightmare about it, which, though it lacked rhyme or reason, was one of the most intense and vivid that I've ever had. A judgement on me I suppose, but a fruitful one nevertheless. A week or so later, I'd written this story."

B L I S S

Stuart Young

"The secret of happiness is to face the fact that life is horrible, horrible, horrible." – *Bertrand Russell*

It should have been raining.

A gunmetal sky, clouds as black as God's wrath and raindrops hammering at Lee like a million tiny fists.

But the weather has no respect for loss or grieving.

Instead the sky was blue, with tiny white wisps of cloud as delicate as God's whimsy and the only liquid was the sweat on Lee's brow.

So he walked along the street, the sun hanging in the sky, a blasphemous golden orb.

Normally he would have basked in the sunshine, especially as it was actually cooler than the searing heat he had endured recently. But not today. Today he wanted rain.

Thoughts churned his mind, recent events souring his mood. Most people would remember July 2006 for the heat wave. Lee's memories would be infinitely darker.

He spotted a trio of teenagers swaggering towards him. About eighteen - ten years younger than him – but two metres tall, towering over him by a good seven inches like some freakish race of gangly mutants. Barechested, showing off their tans and their skinny muscles. Lee knew that beneath his T-shirt he had them beat on both counts.

There was plenty of room on the pavement for them to go round him but still they walked straight for him. Lee stepped aside, just enough to be polite, not enough to look intimidated. At the same time he shifted his rucksack so it wouldn't brush against the teenagers.

Then he was jerked backwards as one of the teenagers tried to yank the rucksack from his hand.

Even caught by surprise Lee had strength and weight on the kid. He heaved on the rucksack, stopping the kid in his tracks. Realising he was on to a loser the kid abandoned the rucksack and legged it.

The sudden exit of his tug-of-war partner threw Lee offbalance and he nearly fell. Steadying himself he was about to run after the kid and his mates when he realised only two of them had run. The third still stood there, chuckling as he filmed the whole thing on his cameraphone. Bloody happy slapper.

Lee snatched the phone from the kid's hand.

"Oy! Give it back!"

Lee pocketed the phone. "Finders keepers."

"Give it back or I'll get the police on you."

"Go ahead. I'll just show them the video of you and your mates trying to nick my rucksack."

The video wasn't conclusive proof, the kids could probably pass it off as a prank, say they had mistaken Lee for one of their mates. But that didn't occur to the thwarted mugger. His IQ wasn't exactly Mensa level. In fact Lee doubted if he could even spell Mensa. Or IQ.

"Give it back," snarled the kid. "Or I'll have you."

Lee glanced round, checking the odds. One of the mugger's mates was still running, almost a dot on the horizon by now. The other stood at a distance, smiling, too far away to help his mate if things kicked off.

Lee turned back to the mugger, fighting the urge to beat him to a bloody pulp. "Listen, you long streak of piss, if you're going to threaten me then at least have the decency to look as if you can back it up. In your case that would mean aiming a cruise missile at my head but at least you could pull a knife or something."

The kid reached for his pocket. "Okay, smartarse."

Shit.

Lee lunged forward, one hand grabbing the kid's wrist, trapping the knife in the pocket. At the same time his forearm smashed into the kid's chest, slamming him against the nearest wall, knocking the wind out of him. Lee's forearm jammed up against the kid's throat, pinning him to the wall.

"You are *really* starting to piss me off. I see you or your mates round here again I'll shove that knife so far up your arse it'll give you a tongue-piercing." Lee torqued his forearm, grinding the bone against the kid's windpipe. "Understand?"

The kid's face turned purple as he coughed out a reply. "Yes."

"Good." Lee pulled the kid's hand free of the pocket and gave it a vicious twist. Metal clattered on the pavement. Lee stepped back, letting the kid go. "Now piss off."

The kid backed away, rubbing his throat. "I'll fucking have you for this!"

"Yeah, yeah, yeah." Lee waved a dismissive hand. "I'm losing control of my bowels just thinking about it."

Lee watched the kid go, catching up with his mate, the one who had stood watching with a big smile on his face. The kid kept going but his mate remained still, just smiling as if he was simple. Or as if he was wise beyond measure and was laughing at the foolishness of the rest of the world.

His idiot savant stare burned into Lee.

Lee returned his gaze, just to let the kid know that he knew he was there so he'd better not try anything. Then Lee turned and walked off.

The kid watched him go.

Still smiling.

The doorbell jingled merrily.

The door opened and Lee saw his mum standing there. Pale, face drawn, eyes red.

Her lip quivered when she saw him. "Oh, Lee."

She hugged him, her embrace tight, fierce. They stood for an eternity, arms locked about each other.

41

Finally she released him. He knew the effort that cost her because it cost him the same. "I should've been here sooner…"

Mum shook her head. "No, no, I understand."

Lee stepped inside the house, followed Mum into the lounge. It was as immaculate as he remembered it. The three-piece suite with all the cushions arranged just so, the furniture positioned neatly around the widescreen television. The coffee table varnished to a brilliant sheen. The shelves covered with model sailing ships. And the large gleaming mirror on the wall, capturing the room's image, reflecting back its perfection.

When it came to housekeeping his mum reigned supreme.

Spoiling the whole effect was the lanky nineteen-year-old sprawled across the sofa, his face all zits and gloom.

Mum tutted. "Sit up straight, Adam. You'll crease the cushions."

She had worked hard to help pay for this house, she wasn't about to let it get messed up.

Lee held out his hand. "All right, bruv?"

Adam stood, accepting the handshake. Lee went for a straight buddy grip but Adam continued into an intricate handshake that he thought gave him street cred but just made it look as if he was playing a particularly complicated game of paper, scissors, stone.

They untangled their hands and stood in hesitant silence. Then they gave each other an awkward hug.

As they sat on the sofa Lee noticed the blonde highlights in Adam's hair. Lee's own highlights were natural, his hair and eyebrows bleached by the desert sun.

"You should have called us when you got to the station," said Mum. "We could've picked you up."

"Nah, I needed to stretch my legs after being cooped up on the train." Lee decided not to mention the muggers. It would only upset Mum. And he had already dumped the knife and the mobile down a drain.

"I hired you a suit like you asked," said Mum.

"Ta. What with the travelling I wouldn't have had time to sort out a new one before … before the funeral."

Lee popped a cigarette into his mouth. He was about to light it when he caught Mum's disapproving glare. Cigarette ash was a definite no-no in her house. He put the cigarette back in the packet.

He opened his mouth, hesitated. "The phones in Iraq are rubbish, can only make out every other word. So I'm still not quite clear on what happened."

Mum bowed her head, took a deep breath before she relived it all. "There's not much to tell. Your dad was coming home from the pub. Someone ran him over. Killed him."

"And it was hit-and-run? The driver didn't stop?"

"Oh, they stopped all right. Stopped and reversed over him. Did it about half a dozen times to make sure he was dead."

Lee felt his body tighten, the muscles crushing down on his rage, transforming it to diamond-hard hatred. "The police still not caught them?"

"They found the car for all the good it did. Stolen. The driver was a joy-rider."

"Fucking kids."

Mum shook her head. "According to the witnesses it was some old dear in her sixties. Maybe even older."

Lee stared at her.

"That's not all." Mum's jaw tightened. "The bitch was laughing the whole time."

Lee didn't sleep well. Not because he had been stuck in the spare room. When you're used to sleeping in a barracks full of sweaty, snoring, farting squaddies then a change of environment isn't a problem.

It was the idea of his dad's killer running loose that kept him tossing and turning. Thoughts of revenge kept running through his mind, images of his hands about the murderer's throat.

He was glad when the morning came and he could distract himself with the hustle and bustle of preparing for the funeral. He helped Mum with the food; tossing salad, slicing quiche, popping sausage rolls in the oven. Even Adam helped despite his culinary skills normally only extending to heating up Pot Noodles. Poor kid was doing his best to hold it together for Mum's sake but the strain was starting to show.

Lee felt a sudden surge of resentment that his return home had been delayed whilst the army untangled the red tape that would authorise his compassionate leave. He should have been here, supporting his family, not out in Basra waiting for some poxy paperwork to be cleared.

He tried to make up for it now by keeping everyone's spirits up and making sure everything ran smoothly this morning. That was him; the life and soul of the party, everyone's best friend. While he was around nothing would go wrong.

"Shit," said Mum. "I forgot to buy the pizza!"

Angry tears pricked her eyes. "There's got to be pizza. Your dad loved pizza."

Lee stroked her shoulder. "It's okay. I'll just nip down the grocers and get some. I'll be ten minutes, okay?"

He started down the road, glad of an excuse to get out of the house so he could finally have a cigarette. Lighting a fag he turned the corner and walked down the street opposite the park.

A cat wandered out of the front garden of a nearby house. It gazed up at him, miaowing expectantly, a hungry look in its eyes.

"Sorry, mate, I ain't got nothing for you. Try me on the way back."

The cat gave him a dirty look as if to say that this just wasn't good enough. Then it suddenly screeched in pain, its body twisting wildly. It fled down the street, a streak of black fur.

Lee whirled round and saw a couple of kids at the far end of the park. One of them aimed an air rifle at the fleeing cat, ready to take another shot.

Lee's face twisted in rage as he sprinted towards the kids, the fag flying from his mouth. "You little cunts!"

The kid holding the air rifle just laughed and fired again. At Lee. The pellet whizzed by his head.

He kept running.

He was close enough now that he could see the air rifle was a fancy, hi-tech model, designed to look like an assault rifle. He wished he had his SA 80 with him, then he'd show the little shits how to shoot.

But he had nothing. No weapons. No cover. And by running

towards the kids he was just giving them an easier target.

Shit. He had survived Iraq and now some snot-nosed little tosser was going to nail him with an air rifle. He imagined the pellet hitting his eye, pulping the flesh, blinding him.

The kid squinted down the sights, laughed, and pulled the trigger.

The pellet missed. The kid had jerked the trigger, not squeezing it like you're supposed to, ruining his aim.

The kids turned and ran. They shouted as they went. "Ease the pain! Ease the pain!"

They ran laughing down an alley. Lee dashed after them but they had vanished. All that remained was the last faint echo of their shouted taunt.

"Ease the pain!"

The wake was in full swing. People crowded round the buffet, picking at the food like vultures.

Faces crowded Lee, some familiar, some complete strangers, all offering their condolences. He nodded at their advice, laughed at their anecdotes about his dad and cracked the odd joke to make them think their words had somehow helped mend his heartbreak, had given him the strength to go on.

He knew one of the family had to keep the guests happy and Mum was in no state to handle it. Earlier she had started the funeral with dignified grief but by the end of the service she completely lost it; weeping, her legs buckling beneath her. Lee and Adam had to practically carry her back to the car.

Adam hadn't been too steady himself, only able to use one hand to support Mum as he used the other to wipe away the tears that filled his eyes.

Lee felt the loss too but he had a little more experience at dealing with it. He had fought in a war, this wasn't the first time someone he cared about had died needlessly.

And as someone who had fought in a war he knew there was a question that everyone wanted to ask him. Sometimes the person asking was nervous, sometimes envious, sometimes accusing. But the question was always there. Inevitable. Inescapable.

"Did you kill anyone?"

He wanted to scream at them – "I've buried my dad today! Isn't that enough death for you?"

Instead he just threw them a wink. "Only some bloke who owed me money."

He could tell the answer didn't satisfy them. Tough. It was the only one they were getting.

He looked over to where Mum sat sobbing, her sister Joan next to her, an arm around her shoulder. Lee wished he knew what to say, what to do.

He wished his dad were here.

Dad always remained in command of any situation. A solid, dependable man who never stood for any nonsense or frivolities unless it was nonsense for which he himself had a passion, like his love of the model ships he painstakingly constructed and which were now dotted around the lounge.

Dad would know how to comfort Mum. He was the only one who ever could. And now he was the only one who couldn't.

All because some pensioner went mental, reversing her car over Dad again and again. Splintering his ribcage, mashing his internal organs, crushing his skull. The funeral directors had to work overtime patching up his body until it was presentable enough to be displayed in the chapel of rest.

Lee noticed Adam hiding in the corner of the lounge. Adam hated family get-togethers at the best of times. Right now he stood watching Mum and her sister, scowling fiercely.

Lee stepped over to Adam. "All right, bruv?"

"Fucking brilliant. Burying my dad always cheers me up."

"Sorry. Stupid question."

"You see the way Aunt Joan's sucking up to Mum, acting all concerned? Cow wouldn't even cut short her holiday last week when she heard about Dad and now she's acting like she's Mother fucking Teresa."

"Nah, she ain't got the looks to pass for Mother Teresa."

"She only ever makes an effort with Mum when she's after something. Probably wants to borrow more money."

They stood in silence, the wake swirling about them, the guests moving in a slow waltz of commiseration.

46

Lee offered a sad smile. "You remember the time Dad built that model of the Cutty Sark? Took him hours putting it all together. He finally finishes it, got everything perfect, the best model he's ever built. Then he goes to pick it up and he realises he's superglued it to the coffee table."

Adam nodded. "Mum went mental."

"Especially after Dad salvaged the model by chopping up the coffee table to use as a plinth for the ship."

The phone rang, severing their shared reminiscence. Lee squeezed Adam's shoulder. "Back in a sec."

Heading out of the lounge he scooped up the phone. "Hello?"

Laughter greeted him, a hysterical cackling.

"Who is this?"

More laughter.

He really didn't need this. "Whoever you are, just fuck off."

The laughter stopped. But the voice that answered him still rippled with glee. "Ease the pain."

Lee frowned. It was the kids with the air rifle. Except the voice sounded older, female.

"Ease the pain. That's what I did with your father. Eased his pain. Shattered his body to let the pain spill out, oozing across the pavement, red and glistening in the sunlight."

"Who are you?" His knuckles turned white as they gripped the phone. "Who the fuck are you?"

No answer. Just more laughter.

Then the line went dead.

The Guinness was cold, just the way Lee liked it. Adam sat opposite him. They had been lucky to get a table, the Friday night crowd was filling up the pub, people dancing to the records the DJ was spinning, the pub morphing into a nightclub.

The summer sun still shone, filling the night with a suffocating heat. Even after swapping their suits for jeans and short-sleeved designer shirts Lee and Adam still dripped with sweat.

Adam took a swig of Tennents Super. "I can't believe you let Aunt Joan take Mum home with her. You know she's going to tap Mum for money."

Lee wasn't exactly ecstatic about it either but when he spoke to the police they said there was a chance the murderer might phone again to inflict further torment. Lee couldn't stand the idea of Mum receiving one of the calls. Normally she was a tower of strength but right now she was fragile, broken. That's why he had jumped at the chance to get her out of the house even if it was to stay with that cow Joan.

"Don't worry. I made sure Mum hasn't got her chequebook or credit cards on her. The sponging cow's not getting a penny."

But Mum wasn't the only problem. Lee knew Adam wouldn't be able to handle receiving one of the calls either. If he heard the old dear babbling on about easing the pain he would freak. That's why Lee had dragged him to the pub.

Right now Lee had the answerphone switched on, ready to record any messages the sicko sent so he could pass them on to the police. He had wanted to bring the phone with him but the handset's range only extended 300 metres so it was the answerphone or risk Adam getting to the phone before he did.

Lighting a cigarette Lee looked round the pub. Some of the people on the dance floor already had the glazed eyes and manic grins of the deeply inebriated. The weekend was here so they could forget about work, about responsibility, about everything. The outside world might still have problems but they couldn't care less. They bounced around the dance floor with a feverish abandon, a group of happy idiots.

Lee watched them, simultaneously envious and resentful.

Adam leaned over to borrow Lee's lighter. "So anyway, how's playing peacekeeper in Iraq treating you?"

"Not great. Sometimes I wish the war was still on. I had less people shooting at me."

"So when you coming home?"

"Dunno. If we leave it's like we're fucking off and leaving the country in a mess. But if we stay we're just winding up the locals. I think some of them liked being Saddam's slaves."

"We're *all* slaves. It's just that some of us are more comfortable in our cages."

"Very profound."

"Seriously, it's like Chomsky said, all the supposedly free societies just have more sophisticated systems of thought control."

"Chomski? Well, he would say that, being Russian."

"Chomsky isn't …" Adam sighed. "Never mind."

Lee noticed a couple of girls at the bar giving him the eye. A blonde and a brunette. Both sunbed addicts with microscopic skirts and tiny tops to show off their bronzed curves. Very nice.

Lee forced himself to turn back to Adam. "Anyway, Mr Poncey College Student, I hope you're not wasting all your time studying when you should be focusing on more important things like shagging all the female students."

Adam shook his head. "There's only one girl I'm interested in. And I've been taking things slowly."

"So who's the lucky lady?"

"Her name's Joanne. She's in my sociology class. We've been hanging out together for a while now, going for drinks, chilling out round each other's house. Then last week she invited me round while her parents were away."

"Result!"

"Exactly. So I've gone round there expecting some red hot love action. But when I got there she says she's got other ideas. You know our local MP, Malcolm McKenna? He'd made some speech up at the Houses of Parliament supporting the British involvement in Iraq. Got right up Joanne's nose. So she wanted to stick this huge protest poster across the front of his house. Only she needed some help."

Lee could guess where this was going. Adam was a big believer in non-violent protest, he was in love with the idea of being the next Gandhi. And if there was a girl involved he loved the idea even more.

"Anyway," said Adam, "once it's dark we've gone round McKenna's house. The lights are off, no one's home so we start stringing up the poster. I'm pressed up against the window and I can see into the lounge. Got the shock of my life. McKenna's got this big bald bloke bent over the sofa and is giving him one up the arse."

Lee nearly spilt his Guinness in surprise. Only his finely honed drinker's reflexes saved him from wasting the precious liquid.

49

"McKenna's grinning away and this other bloke is just out of it. Drunk or drugged or something. And then McKenna looks up and sees me and Joanne standing at the window. Stared straight at us. So we just dropped the poster and ran."

Lee shook with laughter. "Please tell me that after all that Joanne let you have your wicked way with her."

"Funnily enough the sight of McKenna sodomising an unconscious man didn't exactly put her in a romantic mood. She sent me packing and I haven't seen her since."

"Tough luck, bruv. You could've finally lost your cherry."

Adam scowled. "Fuck off."

"I was only joking. I didn't – Hang on, are you *really* still a virgin?"

"Keep your voice down!"

"But you're nineteen!"

"I've also got a face full of zits, a body that looks like it's made of matchsticks and a brother who's a fanny magnet so even when I do find a girl who likes me she likes you even more."

Lee nodded in sympathy. Having nine years on Adam meant that to girls of Adam's age he came across as wiser, edgier, sexier. Consequently most of Adam's female friends developed a crush on him.

Adam stubbed his cigarette out in the ashtray, mashing it harder than was strictly necessary. "And now I've blown it with Joanne. Fuck, I never have any luck with girls."

Lee looked over at the two girls at the bar. They gyrated to the music, their bodies bouncing in all the right places. And they were still giving him the eye.

He winked at Adam. "Stick with me, bruv. I'll sort you out."

The taxi pulled up to the kerb. Lee paid the driver as Adam and the two girls spilled out onto the pavement, giggling.

Wendy, the blonde, cast an appreciative eye over the house. "Very nice."

Rachel, the brunette, nodded. "Must have set you back a bit."

Lee made the decision not to tell them that he was just a guest at the exact same moment Adam made the decision not to tell them he lived with his mum.

Coiling his arm around Rachel's waist Lee sauntered up the front path. Darkness had finally descended but the night was still hot and sticky. And if things went according to plan soon Lee would be too.

Behind him Adam draped one arm around Wendy's shoulders while his other hand patted his jeans pocket, checking the condoms were still there.

Lee had insisted on the condoms. He even went into the gents with Adam to make sure his little brother really did buy them. "You do *not* want to get this girl pregnant."

"Right, right." Adam reached for the condom machine's selection button.

"Not the extra sensitive. You're so horny you'll shoot your load before you've slid your cock halfway into her fanny."

"Right, right." Adam studied the instructions on how to remove the condoms from the machine. "'Pull out fully.' Fuck, if I did that I wouldn't need the bloody condoms!"

Adam was having the time of his life, even if Lee had been surreptitiously swapping his Tennents Super for shandies. Adam was already trying way too hard to impress the girls, he'd be even worse if he got properly drunk.

Fortunately Adam was a halfway decent dancer so Lee advised him to keep the chat to a minimum, especially the intellectual college bollocks, just concentrate on busting moves on the dance floor. Lee would handle the chat for both of them. Safer that way.

Even so Lee nearly blew it.

He was chatting to Rachel, the prettier of the two girls, when he let slip that he had fought in the Gulf. Immediately she asked the dreaded question. "Did you kill anyone?"

Lee's guts tightened. Normally he could shrug the question off but Dad's death and the murderer's phone calls had his nerves on edge.

He forced a smile. "Only with my cooking."

Shortly afterwards he ordered the taxi home, before she could say anything else that might put him off shagging her.

He unlocked the front door. "Welcome to our humble abode."

Pocketing the door key he flicked on the light switch and then stopped dead.

A man stood before him in the front hall, smiling at him.

Before Lee could ask what the hell the stranger was doing there the man stepped forward and punched him in the gut.

Pain exploded in Lee's midsection. He fell to his knees, gasping for breath. He tried to stand but the pain short-circuited his legs.

Bastard knew how to punch. It felt as if someone had buried an axe in his gut.

"What the fuck?" Adam stared down at Lee then up at the stranger, unsure of what to do.

This time the man didn't even bother with a punch, he just slapped Adam round the face. Still, the slap carried the full weight of the man's stocky frame. Adam's head snapped round and he staggered back, too stunned to do anything except try to remain upright.

Still smiling the man lunged forward, grabbing the girls by the wrists. He dragged them screaming over to the downstairs bathroom, shoved them inside and then locked the door. He turned back to face the brothers, light reflecting off his bald head. His thuggish features made him look like a shaved gorilla; King Kong in a T-shirt. Only not as good-looking.

Get up, thought Lee. Get up and fight. And he would. Just as soon as his innards returned to their original shape.

"Does it hurt?"

It wasn't the man who spoke. The voice was too gentle, too refined. Lee glanced over as another figure stepped from the shadows.

Malcolm McKenna. The local MP.

Lee tried to figure out what he was doing here but being in total agony didn't exactly help his thought processes. He clutched his stomach, grimacing.

"Let me help," said McKenna, smiling broadly. "Let me ease the pain."

He clamped a damp cloth over Lee's face. Lee caught a faint whiff of chemicals.

The world blurred. Wavered. Then finally plunged into blackness.

The sun blazing down on the Iraqi desert. A heat haze stretching across the horizon, the air shimmering like an army of ghosts. Civilians smiling before exploding into fireballs as they detonated their suicide bombs. Blood and shattered bone raining down upon Lee. Some of it belonging to his friends and some of it belonging to his enemies.

Screams mingling with the snaps and pops of ragged gunfire. Bullets churning the desert up around him, plumes of sand spiking the ground, each shot creating a mini-sandstorm. His rifle juddering against his shoulder as he returned fire. Bullets slicing through flesh, tearing apart hearts and lungs.

Figures crumpling. He couldn't make out faces, didn't know their names. He didn't want to. They were strangers. Enemies.

All he had to do was kill them.

The memory faded as Lee drifted back to consciousness. He awoke to find himself in the backseat of a car. Adam slumped beside him, still unconscious. McKenna sat in the passenger seat. Kong was driving.

Lee shook his head and instantly regretted it. Dizziness swirled around his skull, bouncing off his throbbing temples. Groaning, he nudged Adam. "Bruv? You okay?"

Adam stirred. "That's it, Wendy. You like it like that, don't you?"

Lee nudged him again. Adam opened his eyes, then jerked upright, scared. "What's going on?"

"No idea. You okay?"

"I think so … Yeah."

Lee glanced over at McKenna and Kong. They both knew he and Adam were awake but neither of them spoke.

Dazed, Lee fumbled for his mobile. Gone. He reached for the shirt pocket where Adam kept his mobile. Empty. So much for calling for help.

He looked out the window. They were still in town. A couple of late night revellers stumbled down otherwise deserted streets, laughing and singing. Lee wondered if he could shout to them for help but they were too drunk to pay any attention to him, lost in their own little world of drunken joy.

The car pulled into the car park for the town hall. The dark brick of the building blended with the night, giving the building an ethereal air, as if it didn't really exist, it was just an image that had filtered through from another world. The only parts of it that appeared to have any substance were the three empty flagpoles jutting from the roof, a trio of bone-white talons clawing at the heavens.

The car came to a stop. The engine died and then the lights. McKenna and Kong got out, made their way to the rear of the car.

This was it, Lee's chance to smash the door into Kong's balls and then bounce his head off the bonnet a few times. After that McKenna would be a walkover.

Kong opened the door and Lee slammed his shoulder into it. But he was still too dizzy; he didn't catch the door solidly, instead sliding down the side of it and falling halfway out the car, his head dangling just above the pavement.

Shit.

Kong grabbed him, hauling him out of the car and slamming him against the boot. Wincing, Lee raised his hands in surrender.

McKenna grabbed Adam by the scruff of the neck and yanked him out of the car, over toward the town hall. Kong followed, dragging Lee with him.

Up close the building looked a little more solid but no more reassuring. Lee's flesh crawled. He didn't want to go in. Once inside everything was lost.

McKenna and Kong shoved them into the town hall. The doors slammed shut behind them, swallowing them.

Two more of McKenna's cronies stood in the town hall's reception area. One of them bulky, his belly straining against his waistband; the other leaner, with an overbite and a weak chin.

Lee's heart sank. No way could he take on all four of them.

Kong alone would be difficult enough to handle. Lee didn't need to have taken a beating from him to know that. One look at the craggy ruins of Kong's face told Lee he was no pushover. Cauliflower ears, scar tissue mingling with his eyebrows, a broken nose zig-zagging down the centre of his face. Even without the war wounds he could give Mike Tyson nightmares, his bald head growing straight out of his shoulders without any apparent need for a neck. The kind of person you could spend hours punching them in the face and the only thing you'd get for your troubles would be broken knuckles.

And Lee couldn't expect much help from Adam. He was still groggy from the doping. Even at his best the kid had a big mouth but nothing to back it up.

Lee might have felt better if the kidnappers didn't keep smiling. He hadn't really noticed it in the gloom of the car but now he got a clear view of them he saw that none of the kidnappers ever changed their expression, their faces locked into relentless smiles.

Tubby's face crumpled into a mass of flabby creases as laughter lines etched themselves across his features. Chinless showed off his overbite, the jutting teeth emphasising the weakness of his jaw. Meanwhile Kong's smile looked like someone had slashed open his face, gaps showing in his gums where teeth had been knocked out in long forgotten brawls.

And McKenna, his lips pulled back tight, dimples gouged into his cheeks. But it was his eyes that really chilled. Grey orbs, the pupils black pinpoints, twinkling, full of mirth, happier than seemed humanly possible, especially given the current situation. They blazed with a glee only possible in the delusional, the insane.

Drugs, guessed Lee. Ecstasy, ketamine or some new weird chemical concoction he'd never even heard of. Whatever it was McKenna and his pals were higher than the International Space Station.

Great.

McKenna released his grip on Adam and the two newcomers took hold of Adam instead, each taking an arm. McKenna took the lead, striding towards the stairs.

Adam shook his head, straightening up slightly as he finally shook off the effects of the doping. He called to McKenna. "Where are Wendy and Rachel?"

Lee blinked. He had forgotten all about the girls. Right now he had problems of his own.

McKenna ignored Adam's question. Scowling, Adam tried again. "Oy, Fuckface, I'm talking to you. Tell me what you and your boyfriend did to the girls."

Jesus. Full marks for diplomacy. It was one thing to put on a brave face, it was another to give your kidnapper an excuse to beat the living shit out of you.

Adam tried to make his voice strong, confident, but it kept cracking, veering between octaves as though he had just started puberty. "Tell me what you've done, you cunt!"

McKenna stopped walking. He turned and faced Adam, his eyes still twinkling, his lips still parted in a smile. He leaned in, his face an inch from Adam's.

Adam shrank back. "I'm not scared of you."

McKenna lifted a finger and put it to his lips.

Trembling, Adam fell silent.

McKenna turned and continued over to the stairs. The others followed.

Lee's brain whirred. Adam had called Kong McKenna's boyfriend, which meant Kong was the man Adam had seen McKenna fucking. The pieces fell into place. McKenna wanted to keep his love life out of the papers. He'd tracked Adam down and brought out the heavies to make sure he kept his mouth shut.

But how far was he prepared to go? Was all this just to put the frighteners on Adam or to shut him up for good?

Reaching the top of the stairs they started along a corridor. Lights shone from one of the offices ahead of them. Lee could hear muffled voices; low, urgent.

A man: shocked, gasping. "I wasn't expecting this. I thought you brought me here to dish more dirt on McKenna. Not that I'm complaining."

A girl: equally breathless. "Less talking. More fucking."

Gasps filtered through the door. Along with the odd squelching sound.

McKenna opened the door. A man lay on the floor; a girl straddled him, bouncing up and down energetically.

A bag lay on the floor beside them, its contents spilling out onto the floor: a notepad, a dictaphone, a press card with the man's photo on it.

The man's head jerked up as he spotted the newcomers. "Shit!"

The girl kept bouncing up and down.

The man tapped her thigh. "Er, we've got company."

"Yeah." Still the girl kept bouncing. "I know."

"You *know*? Look, I'm not into this kinky stuff. I don't want people watching me while I'm –" The man broke off, gawping as he caught a clear view of McKenna's face. "McKenna! Shit! This is some kind of set-up!"

He tried to squirm his way free from under the girl but she clamped her thighs tight about him so that the only way to escape would be to leave his dick behind.

Adam's mouth hung open as he stared at the girl. "Jesus. That's Joanne."

Lee raised an eyebrow. "*Your* Joanne?"

Adam nodded, speechless.

Lee looked back at the girl. Young and slender, her face pretty despite the sharp point of her long nose, her short blonde hair bouncing with each thrust of her hips, her jeans and knickers down around her ankles as she continued to fuck her unwilling partner.

Lee shrugged. "Seems like a nice girl."

The man was still struggling to get free. "Get off me, you crazy bitch!"

Joanne looked down at him. She smiled, her eyes blazing. "Ease the pain."

Lee started. Joanne was one of *them*.

The man tried shoving her off but McKenna and Chinless stepped forward, pinning his arms to the floor. Tears leaked from the man's face as Joanne kept thrusting away. "Ease the pain. Ease the pain. Ease the pain."

With each thrust of her hips the man uttered a pitiful sob. He screwed his eyes up tight, shutting out the view of her smile.

Then Joanne stopped thrusting. She just sat there smiling down at the man.

The man lay still.

Slowly, he opened his eyes.

And he was smiling too.

The smell of sex hung in the air.

Even now Joanne and the man had pulled their trousers back on

57

the musky odour still tickled Lee's nostrils. He eyed the two lovebirds as they stood lined up against the office's cramped walls along with Kong and the other Smilies. Except now the smiles had faded, as if all their energy had been drained out of them, drawn to some central source.

Only McKenna still flashed his teeth. He stood in front of Lee and Adam, his eyes flicking back and forth between them. Lee and Adam sat on the chairs they had been dumped on, a desk at their backs.

Lee didn't like this set-up one little bit. In the past he had been hauled in by the military police after various indiscretions; the red caps would ask him questions, sometimes bawling them out like a sergeant major, sometimes chuckling like they were his best mate. But whatever the approach, there were always questions.

Here there was nothing but silence.

That should be his trick; keeping his lip buttoned, avoiding incriminating himself by refusing to answer any questions until he knew the score.

McKenna remained still, silent.

Lee flicked a nervous tongue over his lips. Trying to hold his nerve, fighting the desire to say something, anything, to fill the silence. It didn't help that his only experience of interrogation was with the red caps; professionals shackled by the same rules and regulations that they accused him of breaking. Here there were no rules. Anything could happen. Violence. Torture. Death.

He glanced over at Adam to see how he was holding up. Adam stared at Joanne, betrayal and disappointment etched upon his face. Soppy sod was still more concerned with getting his end away than in getting out of here alive.

Finally McKenna asked a question. He stepped forward, leaning over Adam. "Did you tell anyone?"

"What?" Adam looked shocked to have his view of Joanne replaced by McKenna's leering features.

"Did you tell anyone what you saw?"

Adam tore his gaze away from McKenna to glance at Kong. Then his eyes snapped back to McKenna. "N-no. I didn't tell anyone."

58

Without turning McKenna raised his arm behind him, pointing an accusing finger back at Joanne. "*She* did."

Of course. Joanne had spilled the beans to the journalist in order to smear McKenna's name. But McKenna had traced Joanne, turned her into a Smiley, told her to call the newshound, get him here before he submitted his story.

Lee wasn't quite sure what Joanne had done to Newshound, probably given him the same drug as the others had taken.

It had to be drugs. It had to be.

Adam began to tremble. "I didn't tell anyone. I never said anything."

McKenna cupped Adam's jaw in his hand. There was no violence in his grip, his fingers merely brushing Adam's face in a gentle caress. Still the gesture seemed obscene. "Are you sure? You were more difficult to find. You had more time to tell people."

Lee half-rose from his chair. "He said he didn't tell anyone."

Kong's smile flicked back on. So did that of his companions. As one they all took a step towards Lee.

He sat down. Stupid. He shouldn't antagonise them. They could do whatever they wanted and no one would ever find the bodies.

McKenna released his grip on Adam's face, turned to smile at Lee. "Ah, yes. The warrior. Home from the wars."

Reaching in his pocket McKenna pulled out a knife. Light glistened off the blade as he placed it against Lee's throat.

"Tell me," beamed McKenna. "Have you ever killed anyone?"

The blade felt cold against Lee's skin, cooling him from the humidity of the hot summer night.

Fear surged through him. He seized it, harnessing it, using it to focus his alertness.

If McKenna looked away, if only for a second, Lee could knock the knife aside, maybe even take it off McKenna, allowing him to take control of the situation. All he needed was for McKenna's concentration to slip, just a fraction.

McKenna didn't even blink.

"Again," said McKenna. "During the war: did you kill anyone?"

"...Yes."

59

McKenna nodded, pleased. "How did that make you feel?"

Lee hated McKenna for the question, hated him for making him examine his own soul. Lee was a soldier, each time he killed someone he did so with pragmatic, ruthless professionalism. But afterwards, as the fear faded, along with the relief that he killed an enemy soldier before the bastard got him, the guilt would kick in.

He would run from it, try to deny it, seeking solace in the arms of Lieutenant Phillipa Hyde-Wright. It wasn't a real relationship but she liked a bit of rough and he needed the comfort, losing himself in the thrusting and groaning, pretending he was happy. And he had attempted the same thing after Dad's funeral, pulling Wendy and Rachel, aiming to drown his guilt in a sea of lust.

Sometimes that's all his life seemed to consist of. Sex and death.

Impatient for a reply McKenna increased the pressure on the blade. "The killing. How does it make you feel?"

Lee gave him his best hard-man glare. "I probably don't enjoy it as much as you."

McKenna chuckled. "You'd be surprised."

He obviously wanted to say more but he paused. Although individual sentences came easily enough prolonged conversation seemed something of an effort, as if he was playing a game of chess in his head whilst talking.

As Lee waited for McKenna to continue he felt a bead of sweat trickle down his neck. It reached the knife blade, changing path, sliding along the blade to the handle then dripped down onto his shoulder.

Finally McKenna spoke again. "Killing is a last resort. I avoid it whenever possible."

That was a relief. Assuming Lee believed him.

It *could* be true. Lee had read somewhere that in wartime most of the killing is performed by only a handful of the soldiers. Most of the troops can't bring themselves to kill another human being so they deliberately fire their weapons over the heads of their enemies, never actually shooting anyone. Another, smaller, group enjoy the killing – the psychos, the murderers, the sociopaths. And then there is that rare handful, the troops who take no pleasure in killing but do it anyway because it's the only way to save themselves and their comrades from a bloody death. Lee didn't entirely trust these studies, war is too chaotic a thing to be dissected and analysed; weapons malfunction, orders get muddled, training is forgotten, strategies go to hell. Ultimately each individual's motives for killing or not killing would remain their own.

Still, Lee didn't like to think about which category his own wartime exploits would fall under.

As for McKenna – the odds suggested that he was in the group that couldn't bring themselves to kill. Except he radiated a cheerful malevolence. Lee had him pegged as one of the crazies.

McKenna stared at Lee. "But sometimes killing is necessary. I need someone to kill for me. Someone who can do it quickly and efficiently." McKenna tilted his head to one side. "Someone like you."

Lee's jaw dropped. This evening just kept getting more surreal. Any second now Osama Bin Laden would stroll in singing 'Rule Britannia.'

McKenna leaned into him. "You've seen death. You understand it."

He was only half-right. Lee had seen death but he would never understand it. He had too many memories of ambushes and suicide bombers, of snipers putting bullets through the heads of soldiers who were just trying to help. But it wasn't clear if the Iraqis even wanted their help. Some welcomed them as conquering heroes, liberators of the enslaved and oppressed. Others spat at them, hurled stones at them, wouldn't be happy until they were dead.

Lee sometimes wondered if the army's presence was just making things worse. On his last leave he had drunkenly remarked to Adam that he was thinking about quitting the army, becoming an aid worker instead, see if that allowed him to be of more use in the war zones he had fought in – Iraq, or maybe Sierra Leone.

Adam had pulled a face. "Yeah, right. Before you got posted there you thought Sierra Leone was some bloke who directed spaghetti westerns."

Much as Lee hated to admit it maybe Adam was right. Maybe he wasn't cut out to help people. Maybe fighting was all he was good for.

Lee looked up at McKenna. "You want me to do your dirty work for you?"

"You could do it?"

"Yeah. I could do it. There's just one problem." Lee glared at him. "You killed my dad."

"He killed Dad?" Adam jumped up, heading for McKenna. "You bastard!"

McKenna pressed the knife against Lee's throat. "Stop!"

Adam froze.

McKenna's eyes twinkled. "Just because I dislike killing doesn't mean I am incapable of it."

Adam stood seething, his pacifist principles temporarily forgotten, torn between keeping Lee alive and battering the bastard who had murdered their dad. Everyone in the room could see him wondering if he was fast enough to do both.

Lee knew he wasn't. He just prayed Adam realised it too. Lee sat, waiting, his pulse hammering against the blade that rested just above his carotid artery, hoping that Adam didn't do anything stupid.

Adam clenched his fists. Unclenched them. Slowly, he sank back down onto his seat.

The pressure on the knife relaxed and Lee started breathing again.

McKenna tilted his head to one side. "I didn't kill your father." He toyed with the knife. "But I can give you the person who did."

Silence greeted McKenna's words as the two brothers absorbed what he had just told them.

Lee nodded grimly. "So the old dear that killed our dad works for you?"

"No. She was not under my control."

"And I suppose the kids with the air rifle weren't working for you either?"

"No."

"Bollocks. All these people sniffing around my family, going mental, jabbering on about easing the pain, that's one hell of a fucking coincidence."

"Not really." McKenna waved his hand at Kong and the other

62

Smilies. "These are not my only recruits. I have spread my influence across the town. But my control is imperfect, imprecise. In some cases it is non-existent. So it is with your father's killer. And with those others you encountered."

"The drugs were too much for them?"

McKenna shook his head. "There are no drugs."

"If you say so. Go back to the part where you give us Dad's killer."

"My disciples hunted her. They bring her here. She slipped from my control. She tries to fulfil my mission but she does not understand it."

Lee's eyes narrowed. "Mission?"

"I am here to make things better. Life is suffering. Sorrow. Fear. Hate. Disease. I wish to ease that pain. As do my disciples. But in some instances the intent becomes confused, garbled. They know life is pain – therefore if they end life, they end pain."

Lee couldn't believe he was hearing this. McKenna was crazy, deranged, madder than a box of frogs. But Lee needed to go along with it in order to keep himself and Adam alive. "Okay, McKenna – "

"He's not McKenna."

Lee gaped at Adam. "What?"

"He's not McKenna. I've seen McKenna make speeches, give interviews, I even met him once. This isn't how he speaks, how he acts. Him turning out to be a closet homosexual was hard enough to swallow. But this? No, bollocks, it's not him. Same as that isn't Joanne over there. There's something inside them, something making them do things they wouldn't normally do."

McKenna smiled at him. "You are right. And you are wrong."

"For fuck's sake, bruv, get a grip." Lee was beginning to feel like the only sane person left on the face of the planet. Adam's infatuation with Joanne was making him clutch at any excuse, no matter how crazy, to explain why she would rather shag a complete stranger instead of him.

Adam ignored Lee, instead eyeing McKenna coldly. "Who *are* you?"

"Someone who wants to help."

"You want to help?" Adam blinked back tears of rage. "Give me back my dad."

"That is beyond my power in this dimension. All I can offer is his killer." McKenna suddenly stiffened, his back arching and his eyes closing. He held the pose for a long moment then relaxed, opening his eyes. "She is here."

Despite himself Lee felt a tiny thrill of anticipation. He *wanted* the bitch to be here, wanted to make her pay for what she had done.

McKenna looked at Lee. "My control is weak. I must go to my disciples and guide them to this room. But first tell me that you can kill. That you can harness this impulse. That you can eliminate those who have slipped beyond my control. Who kill without rhyme or reason."

Lee felt McKenna's gaze burning into him, piercing to the very heart of his being. No, that was bullshit, McKenna couldn't see anything that Lee didn't show him. All he had to do was tell McKenna anything the nutter wanted to hear until he could figure a way out of this mess. Anything to stop them getting pumped full of drugs and turned into smiley-faced zombies. If that happened they could kiss any chance of escaping goodbye.

His face hardened. "Bring me the bitch who killed my dad and I'll show you some real killing."

McKenna's smile broadened. Perhaps at Lee's words or perhaps at something he thought he saw within him.

Placing the knife back in his pocket McKenna glanced round the office then nodded to Kong. "This room lacks space. Take the boy into the next office. Keep his brother here."

He made to leave the office; paused in the doorway.

"Convert them."

Adam struggled as he was dragged to the door. A wasted effort, he couldn't escape the grip Joanne and Newshound had on his arms.

Lee's mouth flapped wordlessly. He thought agreeing to McKenna's crazy scheme would buy them some time, not speed things up.

His mind flailed desperately for a new plan. Newshound had been turned into a Smiley through sex – if that was the only method of transmission then he and Adam were safe provided neither of them shagged Joanne. Shouldn't be too difficult, this wasn't exactly the most romantic setting.

Even as he thought this Joanne leaned towards Adam, her tongue caressing his ear. He gave a little gasp of pleasure, horny teenage hormones overwhelming his fear. Joanne's hand strayed to Adam's groin, stroking it. Adam's eyes bulged. So did the front of his trousers.

Shit.

Joanne and Newshound led Adam from the office.

Lee started after them but Kong, Tubby and Chinless blocked his path. He called out to Adam. "Don't let her shag you! She can't infect you if she doesn't shag you!"

He hoped.

Kong and the other two continued to bar the exit. Lee stepped back, desperately scanning the office for any escape routes. He had to find a way out before Joanne came back for him. Fighting his way out was a last resort; even with the odds reduced to three against one he didn't fancy his chances. But if he could somehow lure Kong outside the office he was pretty sure he could handle the other two.

Before he could figure out a way to do that Tubby and Chinless grabbed his arms, holding him tight. Kong stepped forward, smiling, shoving the chairs out of his way, tipping them over. He bunched his fist for a punch.

Lee twisted his body, trying to dodge Kong's huge fist. With Tubby and Chinless dragging on his arms he couldn't completely avoid the punch but at least he managed to reduce it to a glancing blow, bouncing off muscle instead of burying into soft internal organs. Even so it staggered him and he sagged in Tubby and Chinless's arms.

Squatting, Kong undid Lee's trousers. He yanked them down around Lee's ankles and then did the same with Lee's boxers.

A coldness erupted in Lee's stomach, spreading across the rest of his body. He writhed in his captors' grip, trying to pull himself free, but they held him fast.

Kong stepped back, unzipped his fly, freeing a short stubby cock. Bulging purple veins wrapped around it, the swollen helmet peeping forth from the taut foreskin.

Lee's own cock shrivelled, his balls withering away to nothing. This couldn't be happening.

Tubby and Chinless dragged Lee round and forced his head forward, bending him over the desk.

He swore and cursed then he begged and pleaded, anything to stop them doing this. They remained silent, just held him in place, smiling those obscene fucking smiles.

His head pinned to the desk Lee could see nothing but what lay directly before him; the grain of the wood, a pencil sharpener and a ruler. Then tears filled his eyes, blurring his vision, and he could no longer even see that.

But he could hear.

Could hear his heart pounding, could hear his own desperate sobs, could hear Kong's approaching footsteps.

He felt his sphincter tighten. God no, that would make it worse. Tense muscles ripping, tissue tearing, the only lubricant his own blood.

And yet afterwards, once he was under McKenna's control, he would smile about it.

One final sob then rough hands seized his buttocks, spreading his cheeks apart.

The office door burst open.

Lee managed to twist his head round just far enough to catch a glimpse of Adam standing in the door, trembling with fear and rage, a folded metal tripod clutched in his hands. "Get away from him!"

Adam charged into the room, swinging the tripod like a club.

Kong turned to meet Adam's attack, ducking under his wild swing with dismissive ease. He lunged forward, his body slamming against Adam in a rugby tackle. They crashed to the ground and the tripod went flying. They both scrambled wildly, trying to regain their feet.

Lee gasped, stunned by his sudden reprieve. But he knew that unless he moved fast it would be only temporary. Adam wouldn't last five seconds against Kong.

Fortunately Tubby and Chinless had turned to watch the fight, the grip on his arms slackening slightly. This was his chance.

66

Yelling, he shoved himself up from the desk. The sudden movement weakened Chinless's grip on his right arm even further and Lee twisted it free, lashing out in a backhand strike at Chinless's face.

Even before the punch landed he knew he had blown it. He'd panicked, didn't aim properly, didn't get his hips behind the blow, didn't even clench his hand into a proper fist.

Then blind luck took over, the edge of his hand clipping Chinless's windpipe. Chinless staggered back, gagging, clutching at his throat.

Spinning round Lee grabbed Tubby around the back of the neck, yanking him onto a vicious headbutt. A sickening crunch sounded as bone and cartilage shattered beneath the impact; Tubby's nose and maybe one of his cheekbones. Blood spewing from his ruined face Tubby crashed to the ground then lay still.

Lee turned back to see Chinless kneeling before the desk, still coughing and clutching his throat; effectively out of action for at least a few minutes.

Still, Lee wasn't about to take chances. Grabbing Chinless he rammed his head into the desk. Chinless's skull *thunked* off the wood then he sprawled across the floor, unconscious.

Lee looked up to see how Adam was doing. Just in time to see Kong nail him with a body shot. The blow lifted Adam clear off his feet; Lee expected Kong's fist to burst through Adam's back, along with a shower of blood and spine fragments. As Adam crumpled to the floor Kong turned to face Lee. Smiling, Kong walked towards him, slowly, purposefully, his hard-on still poking out from his fly.

Lee hesitated, fear suddenly freezing him in place. Kong was in a whole different class to the two wimps he had just decked. He would soak up Lee's punches whilst delivering his own bone-shattering blows.

And it wasn't just the fight that scared Lee. It was what Kong would do to him afterwards.

Lee couldn't even try to run, his trousers remained bunched up around his ankles, ensnaring his feet. And there was no time to pull them back up; Kong was nearly within striking distance. Kong didn't have the same problem, his trousers were still fastened, his cock jutting out from his open fly, eager to finish the job from which it had been interrupted.

A shudder of revulsion ran through Lee, shocking him back into action. Lunging across the desk he snatched up the ruler and whipped its edge into Kong's erect penis.

Lee expected Kong to crash to his knees, his face contorted in pain. Instead he flinched slightly then kept moving, still smiling.

Flinging the ruler to one side Lee seized one of the overturned chairs by the leg and swung it at Kong's head. Kong twisted away, shielding his skull with his arm. As the chair struck him his forearm snapped and he stumbled a little. Then he continued advancing towards Lee.

Lee didn't have room to lift the chair for another swing. Snarling, he thrust the chair straight at Kong's face, aiming to ram the top edge through the back of his head.

He missed, hitting him in the chest, but the impact still knocked Kong backwards. Lee pressed his advantage, shoving forward, keeping Kong offbalance, forcing him back across the room and pinning him against a filing cabinet.

The problem was that with his trousers slowing him down Lee didn't have the speed to slam Kong into the cabinet hard enough to wind him. On the plus side the chair put distance between them, Kong couldn't connect with his flailing punches. On the downside Lee couldn't pull the chair back to hit Kong again without giving him enough room to escape.

Stalemate.

Except Lee needed to KO Kong so he and Adam could escape. Kong only needed to keep Lee here long enough for McKenna and the rest of his cronies to return.

Lee leaned his weight on the chair, the chair's edge sinking into Kong's flesh like a blunt knife. Grunting, Kong shoved against the back of the chair with his good hand. Feeling the chair shift back towards him Lee redoubled his efforts. Kong had the muscle but he had two hands plus leverage.

Even so the chair started to slide off Kong's chest. Lee wrestled against Kong's grip, his muscles straining, tearing, as he forced them beyond their limits. Still the chair continued to slide upwards.

One inch.

Two inches.

Three.

Kong beamed a triumphant smile.

At the last second Lee changed tactics, pushing with Kong instead of against him. The chair shot off Kong's chest and onto his throat, the edge jamming up against his windpipe.

Spluttering, Kong clawed at the chair. Lee increased the pressure. Kong's eyes bulged, his face turning red, then purple. One last burst of frantic struggling and then he was still.

Lee eased up on the chair and Kong slumped to the ground.

Sagging, Lee dropped the chair. He gazed down at Kong's inert form. His cock still protruded from his fly; flaccid now, harmless, just a mass of wrinkled skin with a huge red welt where the ruler had struck.

Lee wanted to vomit but his stomach wouldn't cooperate, instead tying itself into knots. Wiping away his tears he turned to face Adam. Then he lurched forward, panic gripping him.

Adam still lay facedown upon the floor. He wasn't moving.

Worse, it didn't look like he was breathing.

The problem with CPR is that it isn't as effective as people think.

It takes more than a couple of quick puffs and a few chest compressions to revive someone who has stopped breathing. The CPR just keeps oxygenated blood flowing through the casualty's body until someone can apply a defibrillator. *That's* what saves the person's life.

"Adam! Wake up!"

Lee had used CPR on five separate occasions during his time in the army. Only once had the casualty survived long enough to receive medical attention.

"C'mon, bruv. *Please.*"

The procedure had changed since then. Go straight to the chest compressions instead of mouth-to-mouth, and double the amount of compressions from the old system.

But before he started he had to find out if he needed to call an ambulance. Without medical attention all the CPR in the world wouldn't save Adam.

Okay, find the pulse. No, forget the pulse, people had died whilst would-be rescuers fumbled about trying to find that elusive double-thump. Just check the breathing. He leaned forward, placing his ear next to Adam's nose and mouth, praying for the gentle caress of air against his cheek.

Nothing.

Oh God, oh God, oh God.

Then his skin tingled, quivering at the touch of a tiny breeze as Adam exhaled. Lee's face crumpled in relief.

Adam's eyes flickered open and he rolled onto his back, groaning. He stared at the unconscious bodies strewn across the office. "Fuck, did *I* do that?"

"No. But you had a bloody good try."

"Pity. I was hoping I'd managed to lamp at least one of the bastards." Adam clambered to his feet. Then he noticed Lee's half-mast jeans. "What's with your trousers?"

"Nothing." Lee yanked his trousers back up. He didn't want to talk about what had happened. Not now. Maybe not ever.

He headed over to the desk and snatched up the phone. "Line's dead. Check these wankers' pockets, see if they're carrying mobiles." Dropping to his knees he started to pat down Kong. "Anyway, what happened to you?"

"You were right, I was safe so long as I didn't shag Joanne."

"You managed to resist her charms then?"

Adam blushed. "Not exactly. When she knelt down to undo my trousers I got a bit ... overexcited."

"Eh?"

"I shot my load all over her face."

"You're kidding."

"It went right in her eye. Stung her like crazy. I'm surprised she didn't scream."

Lee started to frisk Chinless. "Right in her eye? Blimey, that's one hell of a shot. We'll have to start calling you Dead-eye Dick."

"Anyway, she's fallen back, clutching her eye and that gave me a chance to grab the tripod and clobber that journalist bloke. I tied them up with the cable from the overhead projector then I came back for you."

Lee felt a little glow of pride. Most people would have legged it without so much as a backward glance. But not his kid brother. Daft git had balls of steel and didn't even realise it. "Cheers, bruv. I owe you one."

Lee finished patting down Chinless. "None of them have mobiles. Looks like they even ditched our ones after they nicked them. That doesn't make sense – how are they supposed to keep in touch with each other?"

"They don't need phones. McKenna knows what they're thinking. He can just call them whenever he likes."

"You didn't believe all that rubbish did you? The bloke's nuttier than a fruitcake."

"He meant every word he said."

"Just 'cos he meant it doesn't mean it's true. Besides, he's a politician, when's the last time you trusted anything one of them said? If you don't watch it your mates won't invite you along to their next anti-government rally."

Adam set his jaw, stubborn. "He's not McKenna."

"Whatever. Either way we better move it. He's going to be back any second. We don't know how many of his mates he's bringing with him."

He glanced over at Kong and the others, checking they were still out for the count. As he did so he realised how he had positioned them as he frisked them. Tilting a head here, bending an arm there – he had put them all in the recovery position. He hadn't even noticed himself doing it. His numbed mind had just operated on autopilot, still in first aid mode after his scare with Adam.

Scowling, he took a half-step forward, intending to roll them onto their backs, let their tongues fall back down their throats, slowly choking them to death. It was what they deserved.

He stopped. McKenna would be back soon. Every second counted. Besides, wounded troops sometimes slowed the enemy down more than dead ones. Injured troops had to be carried, given medical treatment – dead troops could just be left. Lee wasn't sure how loyal McKenna would be to his drones but anything that might hinder him had to be worth a try.

Snatching up the tripod he tossed it to Adam. "You see anyone,

71

whack 'em one."

Okay, they were ready to roll. Lee bounced up and down on his toes, psyching himself up.   Provided they managed to avoid McKenna all they had to do was make it to the front door. After that they were free. Piece of piss.

He marched across the office, eased open the door and peeked outside. All clear. He gave Adam the thumbs-up then stepped through the door.

Just as Joanne stepped out of the shadows and plunged a pair of scissors deep into his gut.

Lee stared down at the scissors embedded in his stomach. The suddenness of the attack stunned him, rendering it unreal. It didn't even hurt much. Just felt like she'd punched him in the gut. Weird.

Joanne yanked on the scissors, drawing them sideways across his belly, trying to slice open as many of his internal organs as possible.

Snapping back to reality Lee grabbed her wrist with both hands, locking the scissors in place before they got moving, stopping them doing even more damage. He heard Adam yell but it was faint, distant. Then there was silence. All that existed was him, Joanne and the scissors.

They wrestled for control of the blades. Lee's hands were slick with sweat, he felt his grip slipping. Joanne smiled at him; a sexy come-to-bed smile. But her eyes blazed with fear and bloodlust.

Lee shifted his grip, taking a tighter hold, his superior strength coming into play. Now there was no way Joanne could drag the scissors across his innards.

So she leaned her weight onto them instead, plunging them deeper into his gut.

Lee gasped. Then he slammed his fist into Joanne's jaw, sending her flying backwards. She still had hold of the scissors and they jerked free of Lee's stomach to clatter on the floor alongside her. Blood sprayed from Lee's wound and he clasped his hands over it, trying to stem the flow. His legs crumpled beneath him and he slumped to an awkward sitting position upon the floor.

Adam ran over to him. "Are you okay? I tried to help but you were blocking the doorway. God, I tried to help."

Adam's face was pale, practically bone-white. Lee guessed his own face looked worse. And he felt cold, freezing. All evening he had been sweating in the summer heat and now he was shivering like he was sitting in a freezer. He felt himself begin to panic, his thoughts speeding up, crashing into each other, sending shards of hysteria spinning across his mind.

Cold – should be warm – freezing – blood was warm and he was covered in that – going into shock – blood – been in shock before, deal with it – was this how that Iraqi soldier felt when Lee rammed his bayonet in his gut? – blood everywhere – how could anyone do this to another person? – blood, *his* blood!

He gulped down huge mouthfuls of air. Hold it together for fuck's sake. He was no use to anyone like this.

Trembling, he checked his wound. He needed to stop the bleeding.

"Get my wallet." He turned, allowing Adam to get at the back pocket of his jeans.

"What?"

"*Get my fucking wallet.*"

Baffled, Adam fumbled the wallet from his pocket.

"Give me a credit card."

Adam opened the wallet, handed him a card. Lee took it, silently ordering his quivering fingers not to drop it. He ripped open the bottom half of his shirt, buttons scattering across the floor. Then he slid the card over his gut, sealing the wound.

"Go to the desk. Get some cellotape."

Adam ran to the desk, yanked open the drawers then ran back, cellotape dispenser in his hands. "Now what?"

"Hold it steady." Lee tore off a strip of cellotape and stuck it to the card, sealing one of its edges to his stomach. Five more strips and he had the card held firmly in place.

He wanted to crack a joke to reassure Adam – to reassure himself – but the words wouldn't come. He was too worried about whether his stomach was filling with blood, whether it would bloat and swell, whether he would die screaming in agony, drowning in his own blood.

Adam stared at him, shaking. "Are you okay?"

73

The poor kid was scared shitless. Time for Lee to stop feeling sorry for himself. He managed a wink that didn't look too much like a grimace of pain. "I'm fine. Let's go."

Lee clambered to his feet and hobbled towards the door. Adam followed.

Joanne still lay out in the corridor, unconscious. Adam went to kneel beside her.

"Leave her."

"She might be hurt –"

"I said leave her."

Adam straightened. A last backward glance at Joanne and then he followed Lee down the corridor.

They had only gone two paces when they stopped. Footsteps echoed around the corridor. Lots of footsteps. Heading towards them.

McKenna was back.

And he wasn't alone.

The brothers turned and ran.

At least they tried to. Lee was still unsteady on his feet, he couldn't manage anything more than a fast stumble.

He spotted a set of double doors at the end of the corridor. If they could just make it through them and round the corner they would be safe. He and Adam could slip away into the night whilst McKenna stood ranting and raving over the mess Kong and the others had made.

Gritting his teeth Lee stumbled towards the doors, Adam supporting him, practically dragging him along.

Behind them Lee heard the footsteps growing louder, drowning out their own footfalls. Any second now McKenna and his cronies would come dashing around the corner.

The doors at the end of the corridor seemed a mile away. He didn't think he could make it.

Fuck it, he had made tougher runs than this. Desperate dashes for cover whilst bullets zipped through the air about him. Compared to that, this was nothing.

His ankle buckled beneath him and he nearly fell.

The pursuing footsteps were deafening now, the impacts blurring together like automatic gunfire.

Oh God, he had doomed them both. Sorry, Adam, so sorry —

Adam threw open the door to the nearest office and dragged him inside. Pushing the door shut Adam squatted down beside Lee as he slumped against the wall. They huddled there, cowering, chests heaving from their exertions.

Outside the footsteps stopped.

Slowly, painfully, Lee eased himself to his feet to peep through the small window at the top of the door.

He was taking a huge risk but he needed to see what was going on. And with the office lights off he was obscured by darkness, giving him a better view out than McKenna had in. As he peeked out he tried to remember what he had been told about stealth techniques the time he got chatting to a couple of blokes from the SAS.

Shut down your sense of self, let yourself fade into your surroundings. If you're hiding behind a rock *become* the rock, if you're hiding behind a tree *become* the tree.

Lee tried to let himself fade away, to become a door.

Outside in the corridor McKenna stood over Joanne's unconscious body. His head tilted to one side as he gazed at her yet he looked surprisingly unruffled by her condition. As he studied her Joanne stirred and McKenna helped her to her feet where she stood, tottering.

Behind McKenna stood three more of his cronies — a spotty teenager, a middle-aged black woman, a large bearded man — all wearing that same creepy smile. The teenager and Beardie held a fourth person; an elderly lady. She gazed around in ecstasy, her dentures glistening. "Ease the pain."

Lee stiffened. It was the woman who had phoned him. Dad's killer.

McKenna surveyed the corridor; empty apart from himself and the Smilies. He spoke, raising his voice, projecting like an actor upon a stage. "I apologise for Miss Harrigan's attack. My control slipped, her bliss became incomplete and she panicked, fearing you would do to her what you did to her colleagues. Consequently she acted to

75

defend herself."

McKenna paused, waiting for a reply. Lee didn't give him one. McKenna was bluffing, he didn't know they were still within earshot; they could be anywhere in the building.

"No need to be shy," said McKenna. "I know you can hear me. You didn't pass by us and the doors at the end of this corridor are locked."

Lee dipped his head, exchanging glances with Adam through the gloom. They were trapped.

Lee desperately tried to remember if they'd left a trail. Blood had soaked into his shirt and covered his hands but he didn't think any of it had dripped onto the floor. And the office door was clean, Adam had opened it not him, and Adam only carried bloodstains on his torso from where Lee had clung to him, not on his hands.

No blood trail. That bought them some time. At least until McKenna started searching the offices.

Lee peeped back out the window, became one with the door again.

"It's in your best interests to surrender." McKenna spread his hands. "I can heal your wound. After all, an abdominal puncture is never pleasant."

Lee frowned. How did McKenna know Joanne had stabbed him in the stomach?

"I confess, I didn't expect your brother to be capable of overpowering Mr Connor." McKenna nodded to the teenager who opened one of the office doors and returned a few moments later with the groggy Newshound.

"But that pales beside your own vanquishing of Mr Brandon. I have seen him defeat foes twice your size, three at a time. But he lacks your special gift – the eagerness with which you kill."

As McKenna spoke the teenager helped Kong, Tubby and Chinless out of the other office. Dazed and clutching at their injuries but the bastards were still smiling.

Again McKenna knew the facts before speaking to anyone, before he even saw any clues as to what had taken place. Suddenly Adam's theory about McKenna having a telepathic link to the Smilies didn't sound quite so crazy.

McKenna held out his hand to the old lady, drawing her to him. "Killing is something you share with Mrs Taylor."

Lee stared at the woman. She looked so innocent, so harmless.

McKenna cocked his head to one side. "You said if I bought you Mrs Taylor you would show me something. So show me."

McKenna must think he was stupid. If he went out there he and Adam were fucked. Literally.

"You're thinking that if you show yourself I will convert you. But as a gift to you I'll allow you to kill Mrs Taylor before you change. You'll be able to savour her death."

Lee trembled. What would it matter if he surrendered to McKenna? They were going to get caught anyway. At least this way he knew he would avenge Dad's death.

"I know you want to. I could smell it on you." Pulling his knife from his pocket McKenna held the point directly before the woman's eye. She didn't even flinch, just kept beaming her insane smile.

"You will settle for nothing less than an eye for an eye."

McKenna drew the knife across the woman's eyeball; slowly, deliberately. The outer surface split, gelatinous liquid running down her cheek, dribbling into her smiling mouth.

Lee's stomach churned. He had seen people beaten by mobs, shot, blown to pieces, but he'd never witnessed torture.

McKenna traced the point of the knife down the woman's cheek, along the line of her jaw. The knife came to rest with its blade pressing against her trachea. "If you wish to kill her show yourself. Otherwise lose your chance of revenge forever."

Lee's hands twitched. Almost as if they were closing around someone's throat.

"We both know my killing her will not satisfy you. Your body burns to commit the deed."

The hell with it. The wound in his gut was probably going to kill him anyway. Might as well take the bitch out first.

Lee straightened, ready to give himself up.

Adam caught Lee's arm. Staring down at him through the darkness Lee could just about make out Adam shaking his head. He was right.

77

Lee might be a dead man but Adam still had a chance to get out of here.

Outside McKenna grew impatient. "Very well. Dishonour your father's memory."

He slashed the knife across the woman's throat.

At least he tried to. The blade moved less than an inch before halting. Trembling, McKenna attempted to force the blade forward. It refused to move.

A thin line of blood dripped from the tiny cut McKenna had made on the woman's throat. She smiled. "Ease the pain."

McKenna continued wrestling with the knife. Still it remained stationary.

Lee frowned, trying to figure out what McKenna was playing at.

A white light began to emanate from McKenna's chest, bathing him in its glow. His smile faded and he spoke through gritted teeth. "No! You can't make me do this!"

The glow grew more fierce. "You *must*."

"Get out of my body, you bastard."

Lee's jaw dropped. Adam had been right, something was possessing McKenna, controlling his mind. If McKenna could fight it, reclaim his body, then maybe there was a way out of this after all.

The glow intensified, first creating shadows along the corridor then obliterating them, reducing everything to the same bleak radiance. Lee had to squint to make out any details.

The woman giggled. "Ease the pain."

The knife trembled in McKenna's hand.

Lee held his breath. Come on, you fucker. Fight it.

"Ease the pain." The woman's voice became a chant. "Ease the pain. Ease the pain. Ease the – "

The glow suddenly vanished. Lee blinked, spots dancing before his eyes. His vision slowly cleared and he spied McKenna, his smile restored. Beside him stood the woman. She too had gained a smile, a thin crimson arc sweeping across her throat, mirroring the curve of her lips. Blood bubbled from the wound, snaking down her neck; trickling at first, then flowing, cascading. She fell to the floor, her body folding up beneath her.

Lee closed his eyes. His father's killer was dead. He didn't know whether to curse or rejoice.

Holding up the knife McKenna sent his voice booming along the corridor. "Make no mistake. *I* am the master here. If you will not join me willingly then I will take you by force."

He nodded to the Smilies and they each strode towards a different office, ready to search them.

Chinless chose the office in which Lee and Adam were hiding. Lee shrank back in horror as Chinless reached for the door handle.

The handle began to turn.

Lee tensed. Beside him Adam drew back the tripod, ready to take a swing. They both knew they would lose but they would go down fighting.

The door began to open.

Then it clicked shut again.

Footsteps padded away from the door.

Confused, Lee directed a questioning glance at Adam. Adam shrugged, equally baffled.

They waited. Nothing.

Lee risked a cautious peep out the window. The Smilies stood gathered around McKenna. McKenna himself held open one of the double doors at the end of the corridor. They hadn't been locked after all.

McKenna regarded the door wryly. "Well, this changes things."

The Smilies filed through the door. Once they had gone Lee and Adam would have a free run at the front door.

McKenna and all the Smilies were through the door now. Only Chinless remained. Lee waited for him to follow.

Chinless stayed where he was.

Fuck, McKenna was posting a bloody sentry. As soon as Lee and Adam moved Chinless would call McKenna. Bastard probably had him on telepathic speed dial.

Chinless shouldn't even be mobile. After the beating Lee gave him he should be off whimpering in a corner somewhere. But nothing short of unconsciousness seemed to stop the Smilies. Lee guessed that whatever put that smile on their faces also flooded them with endorphins, nature's painkillers.

79

Even sneaking up on Chinless and knocking him out – which was pretty doubtful given Lee's wound – would probably alert McKenna. He would sense the broken connection as soon as he stopped receiving info from Chinless.

Violence wouldn't work here. Lee needed strategy.

It took him several minutes to decide on a course of action. He actually came up with the idea within the first thirty seconds but it was such a stupid plan he wanted to make sure there were no other options.

Slipping a coin from his pocket he placed it on the floor, lining it up with the gap beneath the door. A flick of his wrist and the coin shot through the gap, *thunking* against a door further down the corridor.

Chinless followed the sound. Opening the door the coin had struck he went inside, flicking on the light.

Instantly Lee sneaked out into the corridor, Adam close behind him. They crept towards the body of Dad's killer. Blood seeped from her throat, forming a dark pool upon the floor. They tiptoed past her corpse, then down the stairs and towards the front door.

Adam hesitated, whispering to Lee. "We should go back for Joanne."

Lee pointed at his stab wound. "Don't know if you noticed but me and her ain't exactly at the top of each other's Christmas card list."

"That wasn't her. It was whatever's controlling her. She can fight it, same as McKenna did."

"Yeah, 'cos he did a really brilliant job."

"He's the main carrier; she's just a drone. She can snap out of it, I know she can. Please, she won't hurt anyone."

Lee sighed. Adam had always scored top marks for naivety. Even after what had happened to Dad he honestly didn't believe killing was part of human nature. He thought war was an aberration created by politics and imperialism; ancient Sumerians and Romans spreading their empires, conquering, killing, all in the name of civilisation. This behaviour was so alien to ancient cultures they needed to overcome their warriors' fear of both killing and dying by demonising their foes and promising their own fallen warriors eternal happiness in Valhalla, paradise or heaven.

Lee always countered this argument by pointing out that modern-day tribes that had remained hidden away, untouched by civilisation's corrupting influence, had managed to develop murder and warfare just fine by themselves. Adam wasn't the only one who could quote anthropological theories, Adam might have all his fancy books but Lee had the Discovery Channel.

"Listen, bruv, right now Joanne's safe. McKenna won't hurt one of his own."

"He killed that woman."

"Because she was a killer. And you just said Joanne's not a killer so everything's sorted. Now come on."

Adam frowned, trapped by his own arguments. Reluctantly he followed Lee over to the door.

Lee eased the door open. It was on a push-bar, easy enough to open from the inside but impossible to open from the outside unless you had a key. "Wait here. I'm going to check there isn't a welcoming committee hiding out in the car park."

"I'll do it. If they are waiting for us there's no way you can outrun them the state you're in."

Now it was Lee's turn to frown. Eventually he nodded. "Okay."

He watched anxiously as Adam slipped out the door, heading over to the car park in a low crouching run. Ducking behind a rubbish bin Adam swept his gaze back and forth across the car park. Turning back to Lee he gave a thumb's-up.

A relieved grin touched Lee's lips and he stepped forward to join Adam.

Then he gasped as strong hands grabbed him, dragging him back inside.

He struggled, trying to break free, but there were too many of them. They clawed at him, smothering him, fingers tearing at his hair, fists smashing into his face.

Somewhere in the middle of it all he saw Adam, tripod raised above his head, charging to the rescue.

No! Run away, you idiot!

Just before Adam reached the door Lee grabbed it, slamming it shut, sealing himself in the building alone with the Smilies.

81

* * *

"I trust you are feeling better?"

McKenna sounded sincere in his query. Ever since the Smilies had marched Lee back into the office, dumping him on a chair, a look of mild concern had touched McKenna's face. As much as it could past his ever-present smile.

Lee spoke through gritted teeth. "Yeah, out of all the near-fatal injuries I've ever had this is definitely the most fun."

He winced as Joanne applied a bandage to his wound. Her fingers moved gently, delicately, but she couldn't help aggravating the tender injury. In fact Lee's whole body throbbed with pain; aching muscles wrapped tight about a skeleton that had fused into a sculpture of solid bone. "You got anyone else who could do this? I keep expecting Joanne's idea of playing Florence Nightingale to be setting fire to me with her lamp."

"You have nothing to fear. As I told you before she only stabbed you because she felt threatened."

Lee remembered the look in Joanne's eyes when she attacked him. "Threatened? By me or by you?"

"She has no reason to fear me. She knows I'm creating a happier world."

"McKenna didn't seem to think so."

"His reluctance was understandable, even welcome. Killing is not part of my plan."

"But you're willing to make exceptions."

"Unfortunately sacrifices must be made."

Joanne finished dressing Lee's wound. Closing the first aid box she joined the circle of Smilies that surrounded Lee. They stared at him, glassy-eyed and smiling. He noticed that the teenager and the bloke with the beard were missing from the circle. They had run out of the building, chasing Adam. Hopefully the fact they were still out there was a good sign.

Another good sign might be the slight tremor in McKenna's hands. Maybe he was starting to tire, the strain of controlling the Smilies finally getting to him.

"Something I've noticed about sacrifices," said Lee. "They're always easier to accept when someone else has to make them."

"Unlike your sacrifice for your brother." McKenna chuckled. "A foolish gesture. All you've done is delay the inevitable. He has at best a few more hours of his muddled, painful existence before he enters into bliss."

"So you still haven't caught him?"

"Not yet. But it's a matter of hours at most."

"Still, pretty sloppy not being able to hold onto him. Especially when that was the point of the whole evening."

"The situation is in hand. Besides, you are the one I want."

Lee had guessed as much. He just wanted to keep McKenna talking, delay the inevitable violation of his body. Even with Joanne there he knew he wouldn't be the one doing the penetrating, he was too battered and bruised for that. Kong or one of the others would get to do the honours.

He tried not to shudder at the thought. Just keep McKenna talking.

"Yeah, that's right. You need me to deal with those exceptions you were talking about."

"Precisely. In comparison your brother is of little consequence."

An ear-splitting screech cut through the night, sounding like an army of demons unleashed from hell. McKenna spun round, bewildered by the hideous racket.

The fire alarm. It had to be Adam's handiwork. Lee grinned. His little brother was just full of surprises.

"Fire brigade'll be here soon. Once they see the dead body the police won't be far behind." Lee leaned back in his chair. "Looks like Adam's of more consequence than you thought."

"Indeed." McKenna didn't look as worried as Lee had hoped.

McKenna nodded to the Smilies and they ran out of the office, eager to begin their hunt.

Taking Lee's arm McKenna led him over to the window. "You have your reinforcements. I have mine."

Frowning, Lee peered out the window. His jaw dropped as he spied a horde of figures striding across the car park.

Smilies.

Hundreds of them.

The Smilies moved towards the town hall, their course inexorable, relentless. They made a macabre sight. Some fully clothed, some in nightdresses and pyjamas, some naked. Men with semi-rigid cocks flapping before them, women with semen dribbling down their legs, hardening, encrusting their flesh. Young and old, black and white, Indian and Chinese, they all marched forward, united by their smiles. Children walked among the adults, beaming merrily. Lee didn't like to think about how they had been recruited.

McKenna cocked his head to one side. "Impressed?"

The sheer number of Smilies boggled Lee's mind. They must have been just grabbing people, fucking them in the street, the whole town descending into an orgy of rape and blissful delirium. No, that didn't make sense. They couldn't all have been infected in a single night. The infection wouldn't spread quickly enough, the Smilies would have been spotted, stopped. Some of them must have already been Smilies.

Lee thought of Joanne luring Newshound to the town hall. The Smilies must be able to pass for normal, for short periods at least. He looked at McKenna's hands, trembling with the strain of controlling all those Smilies. That's it, normally McKenna only exercised minimal control, probably with one simple order – Ease the pain. Only when McKenna took full control did it become clear that someone was a Smiley.

The revelation stunned Lee. Smilies could be hidden anywhere. Friends, families, colleagues. Colleagues – Jesus, McKenna could have spread the infection across Westminster; half the government could be under his control.

Outside the Smilies continued their advance, their shadows stretching before them, elongated limbs and torsos mingling together to create a writhing mass of infinite blackness.

McKenna leaned against the window frame, gazing lovingly at the Smilies. As he did so the alarm stopped screeching, a sudden silence rushing to fill the void. "Ah, not long now until your brother is found."

Not if Lee had anything to do with it. Turning, he limped

towards the door.

McKenna stepped past him, blocking his path. "Join me."

Lee shoved him aside. "You're not fucking raping me."

Staggering out into the corridor Lee headed for the stairs. McKenna overtook him, keeping pace with him as he stumbled along. "No rape. Total mind transfer. Difficult – I only use it in special cases. McKenna when I first entered this dimension. And now you. I need a corporeal body in order to function in this reality. McKenna is too weak. But you, you are –"

"I know. I'm a killer, a murderer, an unfeeling killing machine."

"No. You had the chance to kill Mrs Taylor, to give in to your bloodlust. But you controlled it. You passed the test." McKenna stopped walking, stared Lee straight in the eye. "You only kill from necessity, not from bloodlust. That is why I have nothing to fear from you."

Lee punched him in the face.

It wasn't a great punch, just giving McKenna a cut beneath his eye without even coming close to knocking him out. But that was okay, it meant that Lee got to hit him again.

He started another swing, ignoring the screams from his tortured muscles and the sharp sting in his knuckles where he'd screwed up the first punch. This time he was going to take the bastard's head off.

Before his punch could land McKenna lashed out. It was a feeble blow, no power behind it, but it landed right on the knife wound in Lee's gut. Pain lanced through his body, doubling him over. His legs wobbled and only the wall beside him prevented him from crashing to the ground.

Gritting his teeth he flashed a defiant glare at McKenna. Then he gasped as the cut beneath McKenna's eye faded, healing at incredible speed, leaving unmarked skin.

McKenna cocked his fist. "The less injuries I have to heal once I take over your body the better. But I'm prepared to do a little work."

His fist slammed into Lee's wound.

Lee ordered his body to ignore the pain. His body didn't listen. Agony and exhaustion swept through him – legs giving out, vision blurring, arms dead.

Don't quit. Adam's out there somewhere. Just get down those stairs and find him.

But McKenna stood between him and the stairs, throwing punch after punch at his butchered stomach.

Lee had lost. He would become McKenna's slave. So would Adam, and Mum and the rest of the world. And it was all his fault.

No! Lee lunged forward, shoving McKenna hard in the chest, sending him tumbling backwards down the stairs.

McKenna's limbs windmilled wildly as he fell, the thuds of his fall counterpointed by a series of vicious snaps. Then he hit the ground; spread-eagled, his neck twisted at an unnatural angle.

Lee stood at the top of the stairs, clutching the banister for support. Numbness swept over him. Later he might feel joy or triumph or even disgust over what he had done. Right now he felt nothing.

Slowly he staggered down the stairs to stand over McKenna. McKenna's dead eyes stared out unseeingly. He had finally stopped smiling.

"Ease the pain now, you bastard."

McKenna's hand shot out, grabbing Lee's ankle.

Fingers dug deep into his flesh, holding him tight. As he stared down McKenna smiled up at him, a series of pops and crunches sounding as McKenna's neck straightened, the shattered vertebrae weaving themselves back together.

But that wasn't the most frightening part of McKenna's resurrection. The most frightening part was the alien consciousness Lee felt enveloping his mind, taking control of his will.

He screamed, clutching at his head.

Then he fell into madness.

Pain. Streams of unintelligible gibberish spiralling about each other, pleating together to form a braid of insanity. *Agony.* A writhing maelstrom of chaos, growing, spreading, multiplying beyond all control. *Torture.* Deranged concepts swirling about in a nightmarish whirlpool, currents mingling, blurring together to form ever more terrifying unions.

Lee tried to clear his head, get his bearings. The town hall had vanished. Now he stood at the centre of an alien landscape; ground and sky indistinguishable from each other, both of them a purple blur slashed by savage sparks of lightning. Jagged scalpel-like sculptures towered above him, not quite moving yet not quite still. Everything wavered, out of focus, with two or three multicoloured outlines that refused to resolve into a cohesive whole.

The painful confusion of this strange new world began to dissolve into a soothing caress, a calming rapture. The rapture wanted to help him. He just had to surrender to it.

Slowly he realised where he was. Inside McKenna's mind.

He looked around, searching for a way out. The world churned around him, morphing into hundreds of bizarre tableaux. Worlds where the laws of physics didn't exist, where reality was just a dream. One realm was inhabited by creatures composed entirely of colours, another realm homed beings of intelligent silica. Countless other species spread across this cosmic vista. Joy emanated from all of them. It didn't matter that they were all slaves to the sinister force that controlled McKenna, serving its will, providing the unquestioning love that helped sustain it. They were all happy. Some were as gods, others were less significant than bacteria yet now they were all equal, all united. A cosmos composed entirely of bliss.

Lee shook his head. He didn't understand how he knew all this.

Then he spotted McKenna. Not the real McKenna; the creature that had possessed him, the extra-dimensional parasite. It was silent, invisible, yet somehow he could still see it, hanging like a cloak over the multitude of worlds. It twitched awkwardly, as though in pain. He sensed that the mind transfer had hurt the parasite almost as much as it had hurt him. No wonder it only used it when absolutely necessary.

As he watched tendrils unfurled from the parasite, reaching forth to ensnare all the different worlds, joining all its minions together in an intricate web. In this plane of being the parasite had a physical form. Or perhaps nothing did, Lee wasn't quite sure.

He guessed he only knew as much as he did because the parasite was feeding information into his mind, preparing for the moment when he faded into its consciousness.

But that didn't explain why it needed him. In these other dimensions the parasite effortlessly enslaved gods; on Earth it needed to beg, cajole and trick people into becoming its lackeys. It didn't make sense.

He felt the parasite enfolding itself about him. He tried to resist, to pull free, and somehow his struggling shook loose another piece of information. One that the parasite planned to keep hidden.

Earth was not its natural habitat, away from its energy source its powers were diminished. That's how McKenna had managed to resist it, if only briefly. It could be fought. Defeated.

Lee tensed himself for battle. The parasite had made a big mistake leaving its home turf. It should never have invaded his world.

More information leaked into his head. Intentionally this time.

He paled. It couldn't be true. But it was.

The parasite's arrival on Earth wasn't an invasion. It was the acceptance of an invitation.

Humanity couldn't cope with the reality of life; the death and the unhappiness. They just wanted to be told everything was all right; to be comforted, even if it was by a lie. Countless prayers and wishes and daydreams had floated out into the ether where the parasite had heeded them. Now it had arrived, a joyous saviour.

Humanity couldn't survive without it.

To prove its point the parasite extinguished its rapture, leaving Lee at the mercy of harsh reality.

Life is pain.

That single concept hammered at him again and again, beating him into submission. Life was just pain and suffering and endless struggle. Genes battled against each other, striving to become the dominant factor in shaping his physical form. And within his own mind was a battlefield, thoughts cascading across his consciousness, all vying for supremacy, all wishing to control his actions, to define him. Teachers and leaders fought to mould his mind even further, sculpting it into the shape they desired. Then he had been dumped into the same mess as the rest of humanity, fighting against each other, constantly sniping and back-stabbing, their squabbles constantly escalating into evermore deadly conflicts – riots, wars, genocide.

Lee hated life. Hated his unhappiness. He just wanted it to end.

The rapture rose again, reaching for him, seeking to embrace him.

This time he didn't even try fighting it.

Waves of joy swept over Lee, permeating his being. The sensation soothed him, replenished him, filled him with a strength greater than anything he had ever experienced. He didn't know how he'd ever been able to survive without it.

Love wrapped itself about him, flowing through him, connecting him to the whole of creation. His love went out to everything in existence and the cosmos's love was reflected back at him; an endless feedback loop of love, harmony and elation.

He wallowed in the sensation.

This was Heaven. This was Paradise. This was Bliss.

So much better to end things this way, to cease his pointless struggle. He knew that now. Even if he had won the victory would have cost him too much. Caging the parasite's power within him, fighting it for all eternity, would bring him nothing but pain. The energies flowing through his body would keep his physical self safe from harm – would even grant him eternal life – but they would not save his mind. His sanity would crumble as he remained forever young while his loved ones withered and died. He would be hunted by doctors and scientists eager to unlock the secrets of his immortality, forcing him to live in the shadows, shedding old identities and donning new ones as the years passed. And as humanity gradually scaled the evolutionary ladder he would be left far behind, ridiculed as a sub-human ape, unable to function in the world of the future. Eventually even these new strands of humanity would perish, leaving him to wander the Earth, alone and insane, a deranged epitaph to the human race. Perhaps he might even survive the demise of the sun, a supernova blazing across the solar system, obliterating the Earth, leaving him floating in space awaiting the heat death of the universe, wondering if he might somehow survive even that.

With his newfound joy he could endure all those horrors, could actually relish them. He would watch Mum and Adam die without shedding even a single tear.

He should not fight.

He had to.

Straining, he pushed against the rapture, trying to squash it, constrain it. In return it tried to smother him, to seduce him. He ignored its promises. Adam needed him, Mum needed him – he refused to let them down.

The parasite appealed to his conscience; if he defeated it the Smilies would be forced to confront the atrocities inflicted upon them when they became infected. The violation by strangers, the betrayal by loved ones; the ordeal would leave them traumatised, unhinged. Lee gritted his teeth, he knew he had no right to condemn them to this fate. But the parasite had been responsible for Dad's death and now it wanted to enslave the rest of his family, the rest of his planet.

Rage seethed within him.

A glow began to radiate from his chest, the same glow that had shone from McKenna when he defied the parasite. The glow flared, engulfing Lee's entire torso. He shielded his eyes against the blaze. He sensed the glow was a doorway to infinity, a cosmic abyss. The parasite's access to other worlds. He could send it back. No, it would just gather its strength and attack Earth on another front. He needed to ensnare it in the doorway, trapping it between worlds. If he could concentrate – centring the doorway so that it remained fixed in his consciousness – his mind could form a prison for the parasite.

He focused on the glow, allowed the vortex to fill his mind. The edges of the surrounding landscape took on a shining luminescence.

He felt the parasite's fear. It was no longer coaxing him. Now it was begging, pleading.

Laughing, he dragged it closer. The glow blazed, incandescent.

Now the parasite threatened him. He could not stand the strain of containing cosmic forces within his human mind. His psyche would shatter, it would destroy him. He could not possibly live with the strain of attempting to balance happiness with pain, life with

90

death, pleasure with guilt.

Bollocks, thought Lee. He dealt with that shit every day of his life.

The glow swallowed him.

The parasite screamed.

Everything went white.

When his vision cleared Lee found himself back in the town hall. He fell back against the wall, drained. But his muscles no longer ached, his bruises had faded, his stab wound healed.

He looked around him. The world shimmered. A new form of vision overlaid his regular eyesight, allowing him to see deeper, clearer, cutting straight to the centre of things: protons, neutrons, electrons, atoms, all weaving together to create solid matter. He had never realised the world was so fragile.

He stumbled over to McKenna. The MP was alive. Unconscious. And not smiling.

Lee dropped to his knees. He had done it. Had won. All he had to do now was pay the price.

Footsteps sounded along the hall and Adam came running into view, his body glittering beneath Lee's newfound visual abilities.

Adam stopped when he saw Lee. "Lee! You're okay!"

Adam ran over to him, hugged him. "All of McKenna's goons are back to normal. Whatever was controlling them has gone."

Lee said nothing.

"It's over. Everyone's going to be okay." Adam noticed McKenna's body, the blood on Lee's hands. His face dropped. "Oh God. Did you kill anyone?"

"No." Lee looked at Adam; already he could see his brother's cells dying, the organs deteriorating. Lee blinked away a tear. "No one's dead. Not yet."

W F T G

Stuart Young has had over fifty stories published in various magazines and anthologies such as *Enigmatic Tales*, *Darkness Rising*, *Nasty Piece of Work* and *The Mammoth Book of Future Cops*. He has published three short story collections; *Spare Parts*, *Shards of Dreams* and, most recently, *The Mask Behind the Face*, the title story of which won the British Fantasy Award for Best Novella. His hobbies include shagging supermodels, wrestling giant squids at the bottom of the ocean and telling fibs to make his author's bio sound more interesting.

"'I want horror,' said Gary McMahon. 'Real horror, not this namby-pamby 'quiet horror' rubbish. Half our readers should die of fright and the other half should end up as gibbering wrecks who have to be dragged off to the nearest loony bin. That's how scary I want these stories to be. They're going to be pure horror, you understand me? Horror, horror, horror!'

'Right,' I said. 'Horror. Got it.'

So then I went away and wrote a science fiction thriller.

I tried not to. But I was reading a lot of thrillers at the time so, for a laugh, I started adding in a fistfight here and a chase scene there. And, well, I got a bit carried away.

Fortunately Gary didn't notice. He was probably too busy downing beer and curry to actually read the story before accepting it. In fact he probably still hasn't read it even now.

So if you ever happen to run into him and he asks you what you thought of 'Bliss' just tell him it's the scariest thing you've ever read. And if you really want to impress him you might want to say something about it examining humanity's age-old anxieties about territory and tribalism as well as delving into the ultimate paradox of the human spirit: the urge to create and the urge to destroy.

That's complete bollocks of course but he'll like the sound of it.

But for God's sake whatever you do don't tell him I was just having a laugh."

H E A D S
Gary McMahon

"On horror's head horrors accumulate." - William Shakespeare, Othello

If this were a film (probably a cheap exploitative horror flick), there would be a disclaimer before the opening credits, a brief, sober message to the audience that might run something like this:

Based on a true story.

But the tale that follows isn't just *based* on actual events; it *is* a true story. It is my story. The only one I know.

Every last aching word of it.

The ground was hard, but I was harder, and determined to break through.

I leaned heavily on the spade, pressing down with a big mud-encrusted work boot, transferring my weight through the sturdy shaft of the tool and into the resisting earth. The top layer suddenly crumbled away, but the soil beneath was rocky and tightly compacted: as hard and unmoveable as concrete. I paused in my labour, wiping sweat from my brow. Then I put down the spade and picked up the large pickaxe, hefting it to get the feel of the thing in my undersized, office-soft hands. At school, my nickname had been Ladyhands because they were so small, and even as an adult I was constantly ashamed of them, convinced that they were not the hands of a real man.

93

I glanced back at the house, catching sight of Helen through the kitchen window. She was washing dishes at the sink and staring into mid-air, weak sunlight caressing her face and encasing it in a vague golden cup. I waited until she noticed me, and then stuck out my tongue. Helen smiled; she always looked so beautiful when she was happy, but these days she was so rarely in a cheerful frame of mind.

The pickaxe felt good in my grip; my short stubby fingers wrapped easily around the wooden shaft as if it were a natural act - or perhaps the axe was more like a physical extension of my persona. When I swung the thing, the motion sent a tremor of excitement along my arm and deep into the muscle of my shoulder, where it spread and blossomed warmly in my chest like a shot of good whisky. The pointed tip penetrated the crusted topsoil with a dull, heavy thud, and when I wrenched it free for yet another swing, I felt stronger than I had in months. Maybe even years.

Soon the labour became hypnotic, like a ritual in praise of human mechanics. I swung my arms like pistons, the pickaxe rising and falling in true syncopation with my heartbeat, and the soil broke away in clumps. The early July air was cool, but still I sweated. My mind drifted free of everyday worries and concerns, the simple act of digging becoming all that I was able to focus upon. I realised, somewhere deep inside, that this feeling was why men - even tired middle-aged men like me - were in love with physical activity: while the body worked, the mind shook off its fleshy shackles and was free to soar with eagles.

As if on cue, a large hawk picked that exact moment to fly overhead, dipping through the high, hazy sky to hover over unseen prey. The sun shifted, pale clouds churned like butter. I was momentarily lost in the task, and began to feel close to nature in a way that I'd never before understood or appreciated. I also felt a bit like whatever unseen prey that hawk was stalking, and the sensation unnerved me.

"Would you like a drink, He-man?" Helen stood a yard away, her bare feet unsettling the loose stones at the edge of the shallow hole I'd managed to scrape in the dry, featureless lump of a garden. "That looks like thirsty work." She held out a can of lager, fridge-fresh, its sides dripping with condensation.

I put down the pickaxe and mopped my brow with the back of my hand. The smile I offered Helen was tired but genuine. My shirt was sticking to my back with sweat, so I pulled it off over my sodden head and tossed it to her.

Helen made an appreciative wolf-whistle, and giggled. It was the first time she'd laughed in a long time – longer than I cared to remember - and I was almost afraid to respond in case anything I said made her self-conscious and ruined the purity of the moment. So I just took the can and drank from it.

"Good?"

"God, yes. Very." And it was, all of it: the little two-storey house that we'd managed to buy here in Henley, the surrounding fields and the woods beyond; and the simple fact that away from the city we were finally beginning to allow ourselves to stop grieving for the children we'd not been allowed to have.

A shadow crossed Helen's soft, round face, as if she'd been reading my thoughts. I gently placed my hand on her bare forearm; the skin was striated with gooseflesh. Helen's smile took on a nervous aspect, and she pulled away, back-pedalling from the hole in the ground as if it contained unfathomable horrors.

"You okay?" I asked, rather redundantly.

Helen tried to smile, but it was difficult for her. Instead, she gave a little half-shake of the head.

I waited, not wanting to push her. On the rare occasions that we spoke – I mean, *really* spoke, and not just flirted around the issue like trainee ballet dances – I was always conscious of not pushing too hard.

"I don't think I'm ever going to feel fixed," she said, unable to meet my gaze. She shuffled her feet in the dirt, like a naughty schoolgirl waiting to be scolded. "I mean, whatever is broken inside of me...what if it never mends?"

"The doctor said –"

"I know what the *doctor* said." Her tone was hard, but there was an apologetic note hidden beneath the words. "What he said was, basically, 'third time lucky.' What the hell does he know about my body?"

"Just because you lost one –"

She interrupted me again; I felt that she was making a habit of it. "Two, Morris. I lost two babies. God, how I hate that word 'lost'. It makes me sound so damned clumsy…"

I waited again, fearful of agitating her further. I had to keep reminding myself that however bad I felt, Helen felt so much worse.

I sensed that she was perched on the edge of some great abyss – a hole in the earth far greater and much deeper than any shallow trench I could ever dig.

"I'll have the ground works done soon", I said, changing tack, trying to divert whatever storm I had sensed on the horizon. "Then we can start to plant. You might even get that herb garden you keep asking for."

This time Helen's timid smile regained a hint of its former warmth, and she moved closer to me, drawn by some intangible and unnameable force that exists only between people who have suffered through great hardships together. "I'd like that," she said, rubbing her arms and hugging her heartbreakingly empty abdomen.

"Then consider it done." I finished off the lager and handed her the empty can; she crumpled it in her dainty fist, pulling a deranged face and causing me to laugh. She could always make me do that, at least.

I paused for a moment before returning to work, watching her closely as she crossed the patchy garden, the plain white dress she wore becoming transparent in the dusty sunlight, giving me a glimpse of her still-slim figure, her gentle curves. For a moment, I forgot about whatever shadows had recently fallen across our relationship, and remembered how much I loved her. Tears sprang into my eyes, but I quickly wiped them away, wondering what obscure and complex combination of emotions had summoned them in the first place. Then I got back to work.

We'd bought the house in Henley as a way of trying to get over everything that had happened: call it relocation therapy. Living in the countryside had been a dream we'd shared, but only now could we afford to pursue it. Driving through Henley early last summer, after we'd left the motorway on a whim on the way back to Leeds from a fraught visit Helen's aged parents at the nursing home in Edinburgh, we'd both been amazed by its beauty. The road had wound forever through fields of bright yellow rapeseed, before the flat Northumbrian scenery gradually became less repetitive and opened out into mile upon mile of untrammelled green and small, irregular clutches of woodland that rose along the horizon to greet us like old friends.

Henley itself is a tiny village, comprising mostly of the remnants of a dead North Eastern coal mining community. The area has somehow managed to throw off the curse of mass pit closures in the 1980s, inflicted by a grasping Tory government, and gradually transform itself into a quiet refuge for those fleeing the hue and cry of the city. The locals are slightly stand-offish, quietly resenting the infiltration by outsiders, but after a while they tend to grudgingly accept newcomers. The village sits in a gorgeous location and both Helen and I fell in love with the place at first sight - the small church surrounded by leaning gravestones, the cute little market in the Village Square, the quaint buildings constructed from rugged locally quarried stone. We thought it was like a picture postcard come to life, and without really discussing it at any great length, we soon decided to sell up and move there.

The hole had turned into a series of channels. I was studiously turning the earth to reveal the decent stuff that lay hidden beneath the decidedly unhealthy topsoil. After discarding the pick once more in favour of the spade, I was delighted to see how easily it sunk in after the top was scabbled away.

When the blade made contact with something hard, I assumed it was just another of the many rocks I'd initially encountered when I'd begun my labours. Then, when loose slivers of dark grey slate appeared through the dirty brown soil, I realised that I'd possibly found something a lot more interesting than a simple indigenous geological deposit.

I dropped the spade and got down on my knees, dusting away loose earth with my bare hands. My lady hands. Several thin flinty shards were exposed, and I carefully picked them out of the hole and laid them down by the tools I'd found in the garden shed when we'd moved in, along with an old wooden bucket, a huge axe, and a strange, half-rusted metal device that looked like an old bear trap. As I dug in with my fingers, I was surprised to find that the soil around

97

the spot crumbled away easily and rapidly, to reveal what looked like a badly assembled box. My spade had obviously cracked the lid, and I could see that the contents seemed to be wrapped in some sort of animal hide or a similar coarse, heavy material.

Mindful of causing any further damage, I gently lifted the bundle out of the earth. Then, sitting down and shuffling clumsily backwards on my arse, I lay my prize on the ground between my legs.

Helen had disappeared from the kitchen window, but I caught sight of her in an upstairs bedroom, changing bed linen and scowling at something that seemed to have displeased her – possibly a stubborn stain on the sheets.

Even the everyday stuff of life weighed heavily on her mind these days; every little thing was a chore. I sometimes thought that the real Helen had been scooped out and deposited in a dark and lonely place, leaving only a hollow replica to carry on sleepwalking through life, mouthing meaningless phrases and making empty gestures. Simply going through the motions.

I watched as she paused in her ask, staring into space. Her hands fluttered at her belly, fingers stiffening, and for a moment I thought she might cry.

Helen hadn't wept since the night she'd returned home from hospital, and even then she had broken down only that one time; her tears had been hard and brief and angry.

I gazed back down at the bundle I'd unearthed. It looked like leather, but was certainly untreated; perhaps merely dried in the sun after being flayed from whatever animal had once worn it. Someone had hidden this here a very long time ago, I was sure of it. They'd wrapped it up and jammed it between rectangular slivers of flint before burying it, perhaps with the intention of recovering it later.

I peeled back the wrapping, using only my fingertips, as if, subconsciously, I feared some kind of infection or contamination. When at last I uncovered the booty, at first I didn't understand exactly what I was looking at. Then, the objects resolved into definite shapes. Three roughly egg-shaped stones, each one slightly smaller than a tennis ball, or more or less the size of a child's fist; smooth and weathered but with subtle indentations in their surface…but no, these were *carvings* and not, as I'd first thought, the result of weathering.

The objects were clearly manmade.

Then, finally, I realised what I held in my grubby little hands.

Three small sculpted heads, the carefully etched facial features smoothed-out by the passage of time and the pressure of the earth around them, but still recognisable as such. I folded them up inside the shirt I'd discarded earlier and carried the bundle inside, calling out loudly to Helen so that she might share in my wonder.

"I don't like the look of them," Helen said, frowning, her long, narrow nose wrinkling in distaste. Back when we'd first met, I'd loved the way she did that, but now I merely found it irritating. It's amazing how, over the passage of time, the little idiosyncrasies and eccentricities that we first treasure in the people we love soon turn into mild annoyances.

I stared at my find; I'd placed the heads in the middle of the dining table so that we could study them better. In the dim light of the kitchen, beneath a flickering fluorescent bulb, the faces looked slightly more complete than they had done outside in the open air. One seemed to represent a woman, with wide flat eyes and pouting lips; the second was possibly male, with a broader face and pinched aquiline nose. The third and slightly smaller face was less easy to define; its narrow features were blurred and insubstantial. I have to admit that its vaguely lupine quality freaked me out a little.

"I think they're Celtic." I moved away, examining them from a distance as I leaned against the sink.

"And what makes you think that, Professor?" Helen smiled, teasing me mercilessly.

"Remember that old church I was working on last year, the one near Doncaster? Well, I told you about the old remains we discovered during the site investigation, didn't I? That we had to halt work and call out some bloke from the museum?"

Helen looked pensive. "Yes. I think so."

"Well, there were some weird artefacts among all that stuff, stone carvings of animals; and these things remind me of them. I think it's the *animalistic* qualities…they're not meant to be human."

99

"Shit, Morris. Are you trying to scare me? 'Because it's bloody working."

I walked across the room and draped an arm around her shoulders, my hand resting against the side of one breast; the muscles there were hard, tensed. Even after several seconds, she did not relax, so I took away my arm, feeling slightly rebuked. "Don't be silly. They're just bits of old stone."

"Maybe," Helen said, lowering her voice as if she feared being overhead. "But there's *something*...something about them. Something that I don't think I like."

Helen moved through into the living room, dismissing the heads, but I remained where I was, fascinated by the crude workmanship, however worn away it might be by the subtle shifting of the earth's strata. Someone had loved these things enough to bury them for safekeeping: perhaps they were even religious icons, stashed in the ground to prevent their theft. History has never been my strong point, but in that moment I had the sense that these weird little heads were valuable in some way – if not in terms of money, then certainly as a record of whoever had lived in this land before us - before *all* of us.

I carefully wrapped up the heads in their protective covering and placed them on a narrow timber shelf near the door, ensuring that they were pushed well back from the edge. The last thing I wanted was to break or damage them. Then I went to the fridge and took out the makings of a tomato and garlic pasta.

Soon the house was filled with the aroma of cooking – fresh garlic, garden-grown basil, and frying onions. Helen emerged from her latest sulk, smiling coyly and slipping her arms around my waist from behind.

"Your favourite," I said, turning my head slightly to the side and blowing her an air-kiss.

"I know. And so are you." She squeezed me tightly – too tightly; enough that the embrace soon became uncomfortable, born more out of desperation that genuine affection. Then, just as suddenly and unpredictably, she released her grip, spun away from me, and began to set the table. Those mood swings, they happened all the time now, and I was just about beginning to get used to them.

"Have you got rid of those awful things?" she said, her voice pensive.

I kept stirring the onions. "Yes. I've put them away."

"What are you going to do with them?" A fork clattered on the stone floor; Helen sighed as she bent to pick it up.

"Dunno. I was thinking of calling into the village tomorrow, perhaps to have a chat with that guy who runs the antique shop on the high street. Is it Mr Cunningham?"

"Yes, that's him." Helen poured two glasses of wine, taking a sip from one of them and setting the other down by the cooker.

"Thanks," I said, distracted. "Yeah, Cunningham. Seems like an interesting old chap. He might know something about them."

Helen fell silent, her thoughts occupied elsewhere. I knew exactly what she was thinking – after twenty-one years together, it was sometimes difficult not to. She was mulling over the conversation we'd had the previous evening, the one about trying again for a baby. I hadn't the heart to deny her, but deep down I was afraid that the same thing would happen as had twice before.

I served the pasta in shallow dishes, topping each off with a sprig of fresh parsley. Helen touched my hand briefly when I placed her bowl on the table, the tips of her fingers gently brushing my thumb. I smiled. Sat down opposite her and began to eat. We finished our meal in silence, each in our own little world yet, at the same time, sharing the same physical space.

Later that evening, lying together in bed, Helen moved in close, her hands caressing my hot skin. She obviously wanted to make love, but I was unsure. I lay back and closed my eyes, aroused and confused by the attention. When Helen climbed astride me, arching her back and guiding me inside, I saw in her eyes what she really wanted. The sex was perfunctory, almost mechanical: a means to an end. Instead of an expression of our relationship, it was simply another attempted impregnation.

I tried to ignore the sounds of the house settling around us, but when a loud scratching started up somewhere low down and behind the walls I felt my erection dwindle inside her. Helen grabbed my hair, riding me more fiercely, and when I responded favourably she whispered breathy encouragement into my ear.

101

Afterwards, as Helen's cold fingers drew unseen patterns on my belly, I stared into the dark. A scavenging fox screamed in the road outside; an owl answered with its own midnight call. Something shifted under the floorboards. Rats? Mice? The old wooden structure settling beneath the weight of our new King-sized bed? For some reason I felt like weeping, but instead I held onto my wife as if she might slip away in the night and leave me, alone and afraid and with no one to turn to for comfort.

I woke early the following morning, long before Helen had even stirred. I washed in the cramped upstairs bathroom and went down to the kitchen to prepare breakfast. While I waited for the grill to heat up, I took down the heads from their shelf and placed them on the counter. Then, moving quickly in case Helen appeared and caught me in the act, I rummaged in a drawer and brought out my digital camera. I took two quick shots in case the first one failed, and then put the heads back on the shelf before returning my attention to the food. I still don't know why I acted so secretively. Perhaps, even at that early stage, I sensed that something was not quite right about the situation.

The cooking chores often fell to me; I genuinely enjoyed spending time in the kitchen, making even simple recipes and clearing my mind of the clutter of a workaday existence. My mother had taught me to be self-reliant from an early age, ensuring that I shouldered my burden as man-of-the-house whenever my father ran off on one of his scouting missions for the local football club. When my dad died from a heart attack at the relatively young age of fifty-three, I took on the role full-time until I managed to escape to University in London where I studied Architecture, coming away with a decent degree and a brighter future.

My student dinner parties were legendary.

Grinning at the memories, I slid several slices of bacon under the grill and used a fork to whisk together eggs and milk for the omelettes. I cracked the huge farm-fresh eggs on the side of the bowl, watching the luxuriously yellow yolks as they drooled into the mixture – such is the beauty of local free-range dairy products. Then, when I cracked the third and final shell, I was appalled to see something thick and red pulse out of the fracture. Dropping the broken egg onto the counter, I took an involuntary step backwards and grabbed a tea towel. The contents of the shell oozed out onto the work surface.

A chick, I thought. Nothing but the messy remains of a chicken foetus contained in an egg that had been mistakenly fertilised before being collected from the chicken coop. But the shape did not look like any kind of bird; it looked more like a mammal: four folded limbs instead of wings, a longish face with a mouth instead of a beak, and between thin lips that were curled back into a post-natal scowl, there was the suggestion of tiny teeth.

I scooped the disgusting mess into a paper napkin and threw the whole lot into a carrier bag that I found in a drawer. Tying a tight knot in the top of the bag, I pushed it as far down into the kitchen bin as I could manage and covered it with other garbage.

When I returned to the stove, my appetite had vanished.

"I'm such a lucky girl," said Helen, creeping up behind me to peer over my shoulder.

"Yes," I said, shaking of the repulsion caused by what I'd found in the egg. "You are." Helen enjoyed her breakfast immensely, but I left mine untouched on the plate and nibbled instead on a slice of toast.

After we'd eaten I drove into Henley, leaving Helen to potter around the house and tidy up in the vague manner she habitually employed – vacuuming random patches of carpet, dusting the TV but not any of the ornaments, leafing through bookshelves before finally quitting to read something that suddenly took her fancy. It wasn't laziness, she claimed, more like energy conservation.

The day was overcast, the sky low and wide, like a heavy-duty mesh being lowered across the land. Thick clouds buffeted one another, and rain was threatened more and more with each successive grey mile that I covered in our little Ford Fiesta that was coming apart at the seams. I left the open fields and joined the narrow track that ran through the northern edge of Idle Woods, shivering inwardly as deep shadows began to engulf the car. I tried to focus on the road ahead, struggling as my gaze drifted continually out of the side windows. Clots of darkness flitted behind the trunks of imposing pines, fooling me into thinking that I was being stalked.

Even though both Helen and I tried to act like nothing had changed, there was no doubt in my mind that things were different since the second miscarriage. Helen's need for a child was becoming an obsession, and my own feelings on the matter were at best ambiguous. When we'd first decided to try for children, I was delighted at the prospect of fatherhood – and I thought that Helen would make the perfect mother. Now, after everything that had happened, I wasn't so sure. I still wanted a family, but recently I'd been thinking that perhaps it just wasn't meant to be.

Just then something tall and dark and too fast to identify darted out in front of the car. I turned the wheel quickly and powerfully, guiding the vehicle off the track. The wheels spun, the tyres screamed, but I managed to control the skidding car and direct it into a shallow ditch that served as a makeshift passing point in the narrow road.

I sat in the silence that had suddenly replaced the sound of the engine, resting my head against the hard plastic steering wheel. When I looked up again, staring through the grubby windscreen, there was no animal in sight. The trees seemed to shuffle forward, reaching out for me; a bird clattered somewhere in the foliage above the roof of the car. The stuttering cry of an animal echoed from somewhere deep within the woods, sounding far too much like manic laughter.

Turning the key slowly, I managed to restart the car and coax it back to life, willing the wheels not to get stuck in a rut when they finally moved. My prayers were answered; the vehicle shuddered forward, and then as the treads finally bit it lurched back onto the main track. I allowed myself to relax once the woods began to thin out, the spaces between trees becoming wider and brighter. But the darkness remained, clinging to the bark like a fungus, its fingers pushed deeply into the fabric of the woods.

The Old Antiquary was an amazing place, and packed to the rafters with valuable antiques and useless tat alike. The shop was tiny, basically consisting of two rooms in front and one out the back, but every conceivable space was packed with obscure objects of desire.

104

It was a rummager's paradise, and I reflected with sorrow that my late mother would have loved to have been let loose in the place for an hour or so.

"Good morning," said a loud voice that preceded a short portly man into the room by several seconds. "You must be the new boy in this quiet little burg!"

I turned to face the proprietor, Albert Cunningham, who was dressed in a pair of black trousers that had seen far better days, a stained white shirt, and a faintly absurd pink and white polka-dot bow tie.

"Hello. I'm Morris O'Neil. My wife and I bought the place on the far side of the woods."

"Yes, yes, I know all that. Just tell me the juicy stuff: have you found any dead bodies under the floors in that old house? Trinkets? Gold doubloons from a shady past? The place has been uninhabited for donkey's years, so there must at least be something of interest in there." The man's smile was genuine, his dry humour and enthusiasm contagious.

"I'm afraid there's no hidden treasure, Mr. Cunningham. Just a load of creaky old radiators and an attic full of old religious pamphlets."

"Please, do call me Albie. We don't stand much on formality round here. Also, next time you're passing would you think about calling in with those pamphlets? You never know, they could be worth a bob or two."

The man almost rubbed his hands together like a pantomime moneylender, and I struggled to contain my laughter.

"So what can I do for you on this rather dour day? Is it a social call, or something in particular?"

"A bit of both, really." I sat down when Cunningham motioned me towards a high-backed chair, and waited while he balanced his own generous frame on the edge of a small occasional table that protested loudly at the indignity. "I *have* found something that you might be able to help me with."

"Oh, yes?" Cunningham's eyes almost lit up; he was suddenly all-business, and the front of earthy bonhomie was dropped like a mask, his face becoming stern and serious. "Please, tell me more." I sensed a deep sadness lurking behind the man's façade, something that had remained buried for such a long time, but given the right set of circumstances might come burrowing to the surface.

"It's probably best if I just show you these photographs I took this morning."

Cunningham's hand shot out like a snake going after a mongoose when I offered him the photos: a pale pink flash that took me utterly by surprise. Then he examined the photographs, taking his time and handling them with great care, as if they were the objects themselves rather than simply images of them.

"Well," he said after several minutes of utter silence, during which I had grown rather uncomfortable. "I can honestly say that I've never seen anything like these. They could, of course, be Celtic, but there have also been remains of druid shrines found in the area. And I won't even mention the Romans! Judging by the state of these little chaps they are certainly very old – so old in fact that I couldn't even begin to formulate a guess at their actual age. Where did you say you found them exactly?"

I told him how I'd discovered the artefacts, adding: "It's as if someone had tried to hide them, but not *too* hard."

"Indeed," said Cunningham, stumped for answers – or perhaps stalling for time as he tried to decide whether or not he could trust me. "These are fascinating. Do you mind if I hang on to the photographs? I could send them to a friend at the University, see if she can shed any light."

"Feel free," I said, a little bit deflated that no answers were immediately forthcoming.

"I will say one thing about them." Cunningham looked up from the photographs, his eyes hard, cold and suddenly unreadable.

"What's that?" I asked, feeling as if the temperature inside the shop had dropped by several degrees.

"Simply looking at these bloody things scares me for some reason that I just can't put my finger on."

If there was any more, the old fellow was not letting on - not just yet. But I sensed that, in time, he would open up and tell me whatever he was so obviously keeping under wraps.

* * *

A week later, and the house was at last beginning to look like a home. Helen had arranged our possessions: stacking books on shelves, unpacking framed prints, photos and qualifications, even buying some new stuff from the village store. I felt utterly comfortable surrounded by nature, and even Helen was beginning to relax. We'd made love once more since the night when I'd felt so strange about the act, and things had got better – not perfect, just better: approaching what I thought of as normal within the loose boundaries of our relationship. There was still an unpleasant edge of desperation to Helen's amorous attentions, but she was managing them, keeping the raw need that burned within her under control for now.

I had found out nothing new about the heads, but my interest in them was growing. I'd even generated three-dimensional models on my laptop, using the software that I worked on to produce the architectural plans and blueprints of the buildings I designed at the office.

It was late on a Thursday night, a full moon hanging low in the sky and peeking through the window into the spare room. I was staring at the laptop screen, studying the images of the heads, turning them through every conceivable angle in pursuit of a clue to a mystery that I doubted even existed outside my own head. I was supposed to be working on a new commercial project just outside Newcastle, but my mind kept wandering back to the heads, drawn like iron filings to a magnet. They were all that I could think about.

"What are you?" I said, muttering under my breath.

The actual stone heads stared at me blankly from their perch near my elbow.

Helen was asleep next door, the duvet thrown off her legs and the window opened wide. An early summer heat had descended over the last day or so, and the nights were growing particularly humid.

I was fascinated by the images on the screen, absorbed in the smooth surfaces that spun before my tired eyes. The faces were so vague as to be barely there at all, but I'd decided that there was definitely a woman, a rather strange looking man, and a repellent

107

hybrid of the two - something that was perhaps their offspring. The light that spilled from the screen was beginning to give me a migraine; I'd been looking at them for what felt like hours. Somewhere in the house timbers creaked and popped, and a faint and familiar scratching started up behind one of the skirting boards.

I fell into the dream without really being aware of the transition between waking and sleeping. One minute I was awake and listening to the night, the next I was wholly inside the nightmare.

I stood and approached the wall, listening to the thumping sound that was coming from behind it. The noise was rhythmic, hypnotic, possessing a strange tonal quality, like an avant-garde musical composition I'd once heard in a tiny University theatre, and it was accompanied by the sound of laboured breathing. I reached out and touched the wall; the wallpaper peeled beneath my damp fingers, rolling back like flayed skin to reveal plaster that was cracked and pitted and covered in a thin, dark layer of rot. The rich smell of decay hit me hard, causing me to take a step back from the wall. The thumping sound grew louder, more insistent.

I turned around and opened the door, moving out onto the uncarpeted landing. The door to the master bedroom was open, so I stepped inside, staring, sweating, and aching as if from a lengthy spell of exercise.

Helen was sprawled on the bed, her legs spread wide. Something lay between them, thrusting into her with savage abandon. The headboard knocked against the wall: the thumping sound that had summoned me.

The figure that lay on top of my wife was human in size and proportion, but that was where the similarity ended. Its broad back was covered with thick bristles, almost like the spines of a hedgehog, and its arms were twice the width of any man's I'd ever met. The skin beneath the porcine bristles crawled with things that resembled oversized lice, and as I looked on in terror a small swarm of them dropped down onto the floor and surged towards me.

I screamed, but the sound that emerged from between my lips was weak, pathetic. I raised my tiny, useless hands and stepped towards the thing that was so brutally defiling my sleeping wife…

And awoke with a start, aware that a sound had roused me but unsure as to the location of its source. I listened intently, mouth dry, eyes moist, ears stuffed with cotton wool. Nothing. The house was silent: even the natural settling of the structure had ceased.

I struggled to my feet and went next door, popping my head around the doorframe to check on Helen. She was lying on the bed with the duvet wrapped around her legs, perspiration shining on her inner thighs, just like in the dream. I went to her and covered her modesty, stroking her cheek, her sweat-wet hair with a shaking hand, and allowing it to trace a course down across her soft breasts.

The dream…it had been terrible, but oddly I found that the intense fear I'd felt was receding now that I was awake; the whole thing had become a blur. Briefly, confusingly, my wife repelled me; I felt this with an intensity that disturbed me, and fought the urge to pack my belongings and flee while she slept. It must have been a remnant of the nightmare that still clung to me like fine traces of brick dust. I turned my back on Helen, feeling ashamed and somehow powerless, and went back into the other room to examine the heads.

"I have something to tell you."

I glanced up from reading, at first annoyed at the interruption but then glad that Helen had entered the room to break the spell. She looked beautiful in the weak late morning sunlight, its rays cascading like water droplets in her hair. I smiled, but the gesture was not returned.

"It's happened. I'm pregnant."

I felt as if my heart had been torn loose and risen up into my throat, lodging there to prevent speech. Was I pleased, shocked, appalled even? I really didn't know quite how to feel.

"Say something." Helen's face was pale, bloodless, yet still her skin shone with a strange muted radiance.

"Are you sure?" I knew the answer before it even came.

"I've taken a home pregnancy test, but yes, they're pretty accurate. I wanted to speak to you before consulting a doctor."

Again I tried to smile, but my lips felt brittle, as if they might shatter like glass. Helen's face resembled a sculpture, a graven image on a stone head, and I felt fear gnawing in my belly like a starved dog.

"I'll call the doctor," said Helen, unconvincingly; then she left the room.

I returned my attention to the sheaf of papers that I was clasping in my hands so hard that I was afraid I might tear them. I'd searched the Internet (we'd had the foresight to have a wireless connection installed before moving into the house) and discovered something interesting - an extract from a book called *Secret Sorceries: Myths and Legends of the North East*, written in the 1930s by someone called Titus Hardacre.

read the printed pages one more time, not sure whether I should be pleased that my amateur sleuthing had paid off or terrified by what the anecdote seemed to imply:

> *Also based in the Henley area is the little-known legend of Sister Knettlefoot, a young woman accused of witchcraft in 1612.*

> *Henrietta Knettlefoot was a nineteen year-old orphan who lived in a lean-to shack near Idle Woods, eking out a living selling firewood, hand-carved "protections" and, often, sexual favours.*

> *In the late summer of that year a number of women in the area reported sightings of a prowler with "bristling hair and eyes all afire", and after the wife of a respected businessman was actually attacked, several people (mainly middle-aged females who disliked the fact that the girl was young and pretty, and probably a prostitute with whom their husbands conducted business) stepped forward with claims that Sister Knettlefoot was practising sorcery.*

> *Before a hastily convened kangaroo court it was claimed that the girl had lain with the devil, or at the very least one of his cohorts, who apparently appeared to her in the shape of a large dog walking on its hind legs and "conversing like a gentleman". These accusations were borne out when it was revealed that her month-old baby suffered from a rare birth defect: the child was born with*

patches of "hog-like bristles" on its body.

The disappearances of local cattle and livestock were also blamed on young Miss Knettlefoot, and when the recently slaughtered carcass of a sheep (its bones apparently covered in teeth marks) was found buried in a shallow pit near her shack, along with three small carved stone heads of unknown origin and sporting "fearsome looks", the jury briskly found her guilty of witchcraft.

Henrietta Knettlefoot was hanged just two weeks later, in the month of September. Her last words are confusingly recorded as being either "Cursed by the heids" or "Cursed be the heids", it is unclear which. At the time this was understandably taken to be a hex levelled upon the heads ("heids"), or leaders, of the village, but in retrospect could have meant something else entirely.

Unfortunately, there are no written records concerning the fate of her illegitimate child (probably the result of a coupling with one of her regular clients) or of the mysterious stone heads.

The heads – and surely they must be the same ones – were mentioned only fleetingly, but it was enough to intrigue me even further. How long had they been here before Sister Knettlefoot had discovered them, and what exactly, if anything, was their power?

I could barely contemplate the thoughts that ran through my mind. I was a realist, a rational, technically minded man, and didn't believe in superstition. My Gods were the scale rule and set square, and my altar was the drawing board. This silly amateur website contained nothing but nonsense and claptrap regurgitated from tabloid newspapers and supermarket magazines. There were no such things as ghosts, aliens had not landed in Roswell, New Mexico, and those damn stone heads did not emit any kind of paranormal influence.

Helen's footsteps approached the door and stopped abruptly outside. She did not enter the room. "I've spoken to the doctor in Henley. I have an appointment tomorrow morning, at ten." A beat of silence, then she said in a much lower voice: "Are you coming along?"

I nodded my head, then, realising that she could not see me, I said: "Yes."

Helen's footsteps retreated along the hallway, then slowly climbed the stairs. Buried under their hushed passage, I was certain that I could detect the sound of weeping.

The day passed in silence: Helen remained upstairs, first taking a long bath and then retiring to bed with a headache. I knew that she was avoiding me, and thought it for the best if I left her alone. I booted up my laptop and visited the website that contained the text from *Secret Sorceries* again, but there was no further mention of either the Henley witch or the stone heads. After logging off, I poured a large whisky and went upstairs to study the heads, caressing them lovingly, running my palms across their surface, feeling the intense cold at their core. I realised now that they depicted a family, but was unable to grasp what the family itself was meant to represent. I knew it would come to me eventually; all I needed was patience.

It had been dark for hours when I finally went to bed, climbing in beside Helen and lying as stiff as a board at her side. I became aware that she was not sleeping only when her hand skimmed across the mattress, her insistent fingers entwining with my own. I held my breath and waited for her to speak; her fingers unwound themselves from mine and she turned over onto her side to face the wall.

I listened to the sound of her breathing, afraid to move until it became deep and regular. When I was sure that she was soundly asleep, I shifted into a more comfortable position. Only when I was absolutely positive that Helen was not going to move did I allow myself to drift off.

When I opened my eyes it was pitch dark; blackness pressed down on me, gluing me to the bed. Helen was no longer by my side, and as I struggled to turn my head – fighting invisible restraints – I saw the proof of her absence. The curtains were drawn and the door was closed; wherever my wife was, it wasn't in the room with me.

That was when I heard it.

A faint snuffling sound, not unlike that of a housedog sniffing out food. Then, even more disconcertingly, there followed the scrabbling of claws on the old wooden floorboards. Some hunched figure was moving around on the floor, just below my eye-line but ducking in and out of sight. Whatever it was, the thing moved clumsily, awkwardly, as if unused to the position it occupied. I strained to sit up and confront the intruder. Tried to call out, but my lips were sealed tightly shut, as if they'd been stitched up in the night.

Then, like a long shadow, the thing rose up at the end of the bed, standing to its full height. I caught sight of a long lupine snout, eyes that blazed with dull yellow fire, and a bristling face that was undoubtedly that of a man, but mutated, twisted to resemble a beast. The figure drew back as if ready to pounce, long arms spreading like the boughs of a mighty tree, claws like twigs whipping in the wind. And then the bedroom door opened and Helen walked in, blinking back tears, stringy spittle on her chin bespeaking the fact that she'd obviously been vomiting in the bathroom. Watery light crept across the floor, advancing towards the creature. I opened my mouth, dry lips tearing, and the coppery taste of my own blood tickling my tongue. I cried out as Helen walked blindly into danger, but whatever horror I'd imagined was no longer there. It had vanished. Like smoke in the night.

"What is it?" Helen turned on the light and ran to my side, wiping her mouth on the sleeve of her night-dress. "What's wrong?"

I held her tight, ashamed of my previous thoughtlessness, telling myself that she was worth so much more than this. "I had a nightmare," I said between sobs. "But now I'm wide wake."

Helen was uneasy on the trip back from the doctors, and when we passed the village store she asked me to stop so that she could buy something for dinner. I remained in the car and waited while she shopped, my feelings churning in the pit of my stomach. There was no doubt that she was pregnant: the quiet, professional doctor Smailes had confirmed it. We were to be parents…but only if this one was strong enough to reach full term.

113

I remembered the agony of the previous two failed pregnancies, the grief and the blame and the ultimate acceptance. We couldn't go through it all again, and I certainly could not allow Helen to be hurt in the same way as before. I doubted that she could survive any further heartbreak.

Albie Cunningham was arranging a display in his shop window, creeping around like a cripple, his back bent, legs shaking. I raised a hand in greeting, and Cunningham returned the silent salute. I had planned to visit him again - if only to see if his University friend had turned up any info regarding the heads, but other things kept getting in the way. First I had to offer Helen support, to help her through this testing time and provide the necessary strength to carry us both, whatever happened and into whatever darkness we were lead.

It was strange, but whenever I was away from the house – or more specifically, from *the heads* – I could see what needed to be done, as if a mist was clearing before my eyes. But when I was in their proximity, things became a lot more complicated. A lesser man would have blamed supernatural forces, demons and monsters, but I still could not bear to accept anything so fanciful. The forces acting upon my marriage, threatening to tear it down to the ground, were purely psychological in origin.

Staring blankly through the windscreen and out into the almost empty street, a previously unnoticed detail suddenly caught my eye. Everywhere I looked – on lampposts, fence posts and in dusty shop windows – were pasted slips of A4-sized paper. I peered at the mostly hand-drawn posters, attempting to discern what they signified. One of them was a cry for help in finding a lost dog named Rex, another asked if anyone had seen a cat answering to the name of Spike, and yet another showed a badly scanned photograph of a sad-looking German Shepherd that had gone missing only the day before. Lost pets, all of them. Vanished, or so it seemed, without a trace.

Feeling strangely disorientated, I got out of the car and headed across the street, towards Cunningham's shop. He was no longer visible through the window, but when I entered he appeared behind the counter like a ghost.

"Hello there, Morris. Have you by any chance stopped by with those religious pamphlets?"

I was caught out for a moment, then remembered our previous conversation. "No, I'm sorry. Forgot about them. I saw you from over the road, and thought I'd ask if your friend had managed to take a look at those photos."

He came round from behind the counter, his movements slow and cumbersome. He looked older than the last time we'd met. "No, not yet. She said she'd ring me."

I nodded my head, and shrugged my shoulders. "Okay, just let me know when she does."

"I've been meaning to ask you something. Something about that house you bought." His face looked grey, as if he'd suddenly fallen ill. "Quite some time ago – fifty years to be exact – there was a young woman who rented the place for a short spell. She lived alone, and made few friends in the village. Bit of a loner, you see."

Just as during our last discussion, I sensed that so much was being left unsaid.

"She… well, she came into town once every two weeks, to pick up supplies. Often, she would come in here to browse. Never bought anything; just looked.

"Anyway, she told me about these noises she sometimes heard in the night. Like wild animals, but coming from the room next to hers, or downstairs in the kitchen. She was afraid. She thought the place was haunted."

"Do you think this has anything to do with the heads I found?" This was getting interesting; I willed him to go on, to give me more to go on.

"I don't think anything, Morris; I'm just telling you a story, some colourful local history."

I thought he might stop then –that I'd upset him in some way; there was an unfamiliar bitterness in his voice – but he didn't. He continued.

"She was six weeks pregnant when she moved into the house. I've heard that pregnant women go a bit funny – that they see things and hear things, and often get a little paranoid. That's what I thought was wrong with this girl. I thought she was paranoid, so I didn't go up there to check."

115

Then he did stop, as if he was suddenly aware of how much he'd said. He looked embarrassed, and I could've grabbed him around the throat to shake the rest of the story from his lips. I followed him with my gaze as he walked to the window; he stared out into the street, and eventually I did too, realising that he'd finished, he was spent.

Helen came out of the grocers' shop, walking slowly towards the car. Her face was ashen. I left without saying another word; Cunningham didn't even watch me go. When I finally turned around to look at him, he had his face buried in his hands, as if he were weeping.

Helen was leaning against the car bonnet, looking pale and tired. I made a vow to help restore her health as I guided her into the passenger seat; she wasn't even eating properly, and I'd been to obsessed with those stupid stone heads to notice.

"What did you buy?" I said, nodding at the bag that was balanced on her lap as we drove away from the kerb.

"Just food. Meat and stuff." She did not look me in the eye when she spoke; unresolved guilt hung over her like a shroud.

I chose not to pursue the matter, but when the car rounded a bend just after that creepy unmade road through Idle Woods, I managed to peek inside the bag as the top flapped open. It was filled with meat, fresh red cuts directly from the butcher's block.

Helen went immediately into the kitchen when we arrived back at the house, hefting her bag and saying nothing. I felt the familiar mental mist descending, and the urge to see the heads fell upon me like a dead weight. I climbed the stairs to the spare room, and closed the door behind me. I could hear Helen chopping meat on the wooden block in the kitchen, a loud thwacking of sharpened steel on worn timber.

I went to the cupboard that now served as home to the heads, drawing open the double doors and preparing to grab what was inside. But the cupboard was empty; the heads were not there.

Panic gripped me like a giant fist, kneading my flesh, crushing my bones, and sending me into a fugue of paranoia. The heads. I had to find them. Rushing around the room like a mad dog, I pulled books and newspapers from shelves and out of drawers, searching

116

frantically for the heads. Wherever I looked and did not find them meant one less place where they could hide. Soon I'd searched the entire room, looking even into nooks and corners that were obviously far too small to contain them.

"Helen," I called, running full-tilt and almost tumbling down the stairs. "Helen! Where are they?"

I ran into the kitchen only to confront Helen's back. She was facing the sink, her hands not clearly visible because she was holding them up near her mouth. Her shoulders hitched in a strange sequence of movements that seemed almost sensual. Unpleasant wet noises were coming from her, as if she were washing her face, or drinking noisily straight from the tap.

I was suddenly terrified that she would turn around, and that there would be blood on her lips.

"Have you moved the sculptures? The stone heads that I found in the garden?" The words came slowly; my voice no longer sounded like my own.

Helen stopped moving, her entire body slumping forward. "No," she said, simply and with a chilling finality. Then those rapid twitching movements and weird, moist sounds resumed.

Again, I prayed that she would not turn around to face me.

I ran back out into the hallway and made for the stairs. The heads were resting on the bottom step, in a neat row. Waiting for me. I could sense, if not exactly see, their cold, eager, implacable smiles.

As summer dwindled into Autumn I made more and more flimsy excuses not to return to work. I told my partner that I was working from home and would send him some plans for the new Business Park in Newcastle as soon as I could. I felt no guilt: lying was merely an alternative route to freedom.

Helen's pregnancy looked like it might be for keeps; her belly was magnificently swollen and her health was blooming - despite the fact that her usually round face had become more angular, and now looked slightly cruel. She was surviving on a diet that consisted mostly of raw meat, but I didn't dare complain. Whatever she was doing, it seemed to be working. She'd even stopped seeing the

117

doctor, preferring to look after her own welfare.

One night in late October, I woke in the dark to see Helen crawling around the bedroom on all fours, like an animal, a feral thing that knew no social constraints. She was naked. Her pale skin looked sickly. I was instantly reminded of the time a few months ago, when I'd witnessed that huge bristly figure in the room, but the dread I experienced soon faded when I saw that my wife had turned up her face from the floor and was smiling. Or perhaps the expression constituted more of a snarl. Either way, her teeth were bared, and she certainly *looked* happy enough.

Early the next morning, on impulse, I made a panicked telephone call to *The Old Antiquary*. My hand shook as I dialled the number, and while I listened to the distant, repetitive ringing on the other end of the line, I feared that Cunningham would not answer.

"Hello, *Old Antiquary*. Can I help you?"

"Albie. Mr Cunningham. It's Morris, here. Morris O'Neil."

A lengthy pause, then: "Ah, yes. Hello Morris. How are you? And your lovely wife?"

"I have to ask you something. I'm sorry, but it's rather personal."

Nervous laughter swelled, and then died in the other man's throat. "My life is an open book, Morris. I've lived in Henley far too long to have any secrets."

"That last time we met, when I came into your shop. You mentioned a young girl who lived in my house fifty years ago. A pregnant girl."

Static on the line; a loud hissing sound that I realised could not possibly have been an animal snarling in my ear. "Albie? Mr Cunnignham? Please, this is important." And it was; I just didn't know why.

"As you've probably guessed, she was my lover. My occasional lover."

I said nothing. Simply waited. Listening to the sound of his sadness, the thing that had been buried but was now coming up for air.

"Oh, the baby wasn't mine, if that's what you're thinking. She came here from the city, a single girl who'd been taken advantage of by a married man."

118

My hand tightened on the telephone receiver; plastic creaked; my palm oozed cold sweat. "What… what happened to her?"

This time the pause seemed endless, as if I was listening to the sounds that bounced between the stars – a booming, empty silence that echoed with dread.

"I've never told anyone this, Morris, but I have the worrying feeling that I need to warn you. Does that make any sense?"

I did, but again I could not have told him why.

When he spoke again, his voice was different. Hollow, monotone: empty. "She killed herself. Dangled a length of rope from a tree in the garden. She left me a note: it said that the presence in the house had driven her to it, and not to worry, no-one could've helped her. Not even me."

"Oh God," I said, barely loud enough to hear my own voice. "I'm sorry, Albie."

"Not even *me*," he said again, his words breaking up with the static. "*Because I was too weak.*" These last words were no more than a whisper that was swallowed up by the crackling on the line.

"Albie?"

The line went dead.

I never spoke to Albert Cunningham again.

Then, late one Friday night in November, everything changed.

Everything.

Lying sleepless in bed, I rolled onto my back and stared at the ceiling. Moonlight dappled the textured plaster, making it crawl, and the longer I stared the closer I came to seeing faces on its shadowed surface - monstrous faces that leered down at me, looking for my weak spots.

I got up and went downstairs, leaving the lights off. When I entered the living room I picked up yesterday's edition of the local newspaper from the floor just inside the door. Had Helen merely discarded it after reading, or had she left it there deliberately for me to notice? The news it contained was pretty small-scale stuff: a car boot sale in the church grounds this coming weekend, a flower festival planned for next march, and three local police dogs had gone missing in a continuing spate of what the paper termed "petnapping".

I threw the tatty publication aside, bewildered by its crudity. Then I went into the kitchen to pour a drink – probably whisky and probably large: my alcohol consumption had rocketed lately, but at least when I was drunk I was able to grab a few hours' shut-eye.

I smelled it before I saw it, and as I approached the sink I hoped that I was mistaken. But no, it was there. It was real. A heap of matted fur and small, bloody bones sat in the kitchen sink. The bones had been stripped of meat and glistened in the weak light that dribbled through the small square window; as I moved in for a closer look I was horrified to see that they bore signs of what looked like teeth marks. No knife had been used to slice away the flesh: the bones had been *gnawed*.

I opened drawers and cupboards, looking for something that I'd recognise only when I found it. Just as I was about to give up, I spotted the plastic bin bag by the back door... Tearing it open with my hands, I pulled away the thin black skin of plastic to reveal what lay inside. The sight was almost comical in its inevitability, but still it chilled me, still it hit me in the chest with the force of a shotgun blast. An assortment of cat and dog collars, thin leather leashes and ID tags sporting names like "Spot" and "Rover" and "Blacky".

The sickly smile that crossed my face was more like a silent scream. I resealed the bag with masking tape and put it back where I'd found it, trying to deny its existence.

Like sunlight penetrating a dense bank of cloud, I saw for the first time that we were in real danger, and I felt a terror that I could not explain. What was happening to us in this place, and how much of it was the fault of those damn stone heads?

Shadows rushed across the walls and ceiling as if cast by someone running past the window, but when I glanced outside the garden was empty. I turned and watched the doorway, convinced that at any moment someone, or some *thing*, would come walking through it, baying for blood and ravening for flesh. Slowly, cautiously, I stepped towards that doorway, aware that something was moving beneath the cover of darkness. A heavy thud came from upstairs: the sound of a solid object falling from a height and hitting the floor. Then the object rolled across the room, slowly trundling towards a spot on the landing directly above me. Two more followed in quick succession.

I stopped moving just as the sounds ceased.

My breath caught in my throat and my bladder ached; fear grew within me like a mutant foetus, desperate to be born.

"*Helen*," I whispered.

Scrabbling at the window; scurrying across the roof; growling in the corner of the room. Something was desperate to be inside with me, but it was biding its time, toying with me. Some powerful animalistic presence that wanted me to know that it was hunting me, step by step, second by second… sniffing me out.

The sparse hair on my head bristled as if in answer to some unheard call, and my eyes grew tired, seeing nothing but darkness and the dim outline of a horror that dwelled within it. Cruel. Wolfish. Hateful. A thing that had been repressed for centuries deep within the heart of mankind: an imprisoned primal entity that was searching for a way back into the world.

I bolted for the stairs, feeling the wind-rush of claws as they barely missed my arm. The material of my T-shirt tore, and I felt the skin beneath tingle at the near miss. Taking the stairs in twos, I hared up to the first floor, heading for the master bedroom. Some invisible presence snapped at my heels as I hit the landing, and my mind was filled with the image of huge jaws containing rows of curved teeth closing on empty air. Biting back a scream, I threw myself at the bedroom door. It was locked.

I pressed my cheek against the wood, straining to hear something, anything, beyond the door. Was that the sound of long nails on bare wood, of a heavy body dragging itself across the floor? Then, quietly, softly, a woman's feeble cry? I slammed my fists against the door – my tiny inconsequential fists. Again. *Again.* Beating against the wood with my babyish hands.

Slowly the door swung open, as if moving through treacle. The air thickened; it was difficult to breathe. Something was stirring in the subtly altered atmosphere, readying itself for a final blistering assault.

"*Helen?*"

The only answer I received was a low growling, the rumbling lament of a trapped beast. I inched forward into the room, terrified

121

but unable to turn my back on my wife. I glanced quickly over my shoulder and in the direction of the spare room. The door stood open. The three stone heads were resting on the threshold. Watching. Rocking back and forth, back and forth, like forgotten wind-up figures in a dusty toy museum. Were they guardians, jailers whose job it was to watch over the presence that was struggling against its invisible bonds, or was the entity itself their protector? Even now, these questions remain unanswered.

The door slammed shut in my face, locking me in with a darkness that had previously lived only inside me, where the primal heart beats in a tiny bone chamber. I peered into the depths of the room, searching for movement. Ready to defend what was mine. Wood splintered, a heavy weight shifted nearby, causing the floorboards to buckle beneath my feet. A loud hissing filled my ears; a light spray of rancid spittle soaked my face.

Helen giggled but she sounded different, like a mad child.

"Come out, damn you!"

And she stepped forward from the shadows, passing into the grey pool of light that had gathered by the window. She was naked, her white skin glowing, giving off a faint dead light. She pushed her distended belly forward, showing it off. The skin rippled when it made contact with the meagre light, as if whatever squirmed beneath was reacting violently to the illumination.

"*It wants daddy.*" I knew the voice was Helen's — after all, I'd just watched her speak — but it sounded nothing at all like my wife.

I was certain that Helen's face had lengthened, her nose elongating into a rough kind of muzzle or snout; her eyes had spread wide apart below her ample brow, almost to the point that they were now resting on opposite sides of her enlarged head. Her mouth was so huge that it had almost cleaved the skull in two, and it was filled with pointed yellow teeth. Thick whitish spittle dripped from her protruding jaws, running down her chest and into what seemed in the poor light like a nest of matted bristles that had sprouted in the dark crease of her cleavage. Her belly swayed; the motion was horribly sensual, almost unnatural.

Another black shape loped around the perimeter of the room, making quick circles but clinging to the walls high up, near the

122

ceiling, and keeping strictly to the shadows. I tried to make out its form in the gloom, but my eyes failed to grasp its fluid geometry. The thing was massive, of that much I can be certain, and its body was covered in a thick fur that writhed with bloated parasites. Its jaws were even bigger than my wife's, and when it opened its mouth the stench was like carrion left outside to rot on a hot day.

This other thing, I realised, was somehow linked to Helen's pregnancy; whatever she carried in her womb was an extension of the vague growling presence.

I could not be certain how much of this was real and how much was my imagination. Nothing had felt solid for such a long time – since our first child had died in the womb. Was I going mad? Was I in fact lying in a hospital bed, doped up to the eyeballs and experiencing fever dreams?

Helen dropped down onto all fours, her convex belly brushing the floor like a water-filled balloon. She growled, then followed it up with yet another bout of that crazed childish giggling. I backed away, still very much aware of the thing that was doing endless laps of the room, and reached out to grab the door handle. Helen followed, her eyes on fire, bristles emerging from her face like months of beard growth recorded in time-lapse photography. Her form was growing more bestial by the second, and as she advanced her slender hands twisted into gnarled claws that left deep white runnels as they gouged the heavily varnished wooden floorboards.

For a moment I doubted everything that I was seeing: the entire room *fluttered*, like film scenery painted onto a paper background, and reality seemed to unhinge from its moorings. Then I found myself out on the landing, my wife rearing up in the doorway. Instinctively I slammed the door and turned around, but the heads were blocking my way, forming a small but somehow impassable barrier on the floor across the top of the stairs. Without thinking, I reached down and picked them up, feeling them leap and twitch like frogs in my hands. I pressed them against my chest to keep them still and turned back to face the master bedroom.

The door bulged outwards, a great and unnatural pressure being exerted from within. The wood split, shattered, and then it flew off its hinges. The thing that had once been my wife now stood before me, grinning. Its eyes were yellow and slitted, its face a vision of ravenous horror. And the teeth…oh, such teeth: like daggers in its mouth.

I raised the heads in my tiny hands and held them up for the beast to see. Then, slowly but with as much force as I could muster, I did the first thing that came into my head and brought the heads swiftly and purposefully together. The sound was like tectonic plates colliding, or boulders raining down from a mythic mountaintop. Huge. Resounding. *Deafening*. The beast reeled, going back on its heels. Its huge front paws went up to cover its ears and it fell suddenly to its knees. I slammed the heads together again, rejoicing in my new-found power. The Helen-thing's stomach distended visibly, painfully, the skin stretching like elastic as whatever was inside tried to get out and away from the terrible clashing of the stone heads.

Just as I sensed that victory was in reach, the heads slipped from my fingers, escaping the clutches of my small, clumsy hands. I stood for a moment like an amateur juggler in some cheap pier-end show, trying to stop them from hitting the floor but succeeding only in delaying their inevitable fall.

The heads tumbled from my hands and rolled towards the stairwell. The thing in the doorway began to regain its composure, dragging itself upright against the doorframe. Darkness bulged behind it, supporting its weight and shoving it forward. Urging it on.

I dived for the heads, cracking one knee against the newel post at the top of the stairs, my ridiculous fucking ladyhands snatching at the cold, cold stone. Somehow I managed to grab hold of the three unwilling objects, and using all my remaining strength I slammed them together one final time as I rolled over onto my back.

The sound was deafening, and reverberated for a long time, its timeless echo hanging like shadows in every dark corner of the house, each tiny imperfection in the structure.

Then, with little drama, the thing in the bedroom doorway slumped gently to the floor. The other entity, the one on the wall inside the room, returned quietly to darkness; its planned rebirth into the world had failed.

I struggled to my feet and descended the stairs, slowly and

hesitantly, and still hearing the echoes of that almighty clash of the ancient stone heads. The damn things were mine now, I owned them; and I could do with them whatever I pleased.

Once in the living room I flipped the lid on my laptop and Googled *Secret Sorceries*. Then I located the online text and searched for the chapter headed *Vampires, Werewolves and Demons*. I scanned the cramped lines of text until I reached the section that I was looking for – two specific paragraphs that had made an impression when I'd first read the extract I'd printed out what now seemed like years ago. The text detailed specific methods of disposal: how to kill them and what to do with the remains.

It took me ages to drag Helen's body out into the garden, manoeuvring it gracelessly down the narrow staircase and out the back door. Every so often, I was forced to stop so that I could wipe the tears from my eyes.

My wife looked as she always had; the monstrous countenance I'd glimpsed upstairs was long gone. I lay her on the ground as delicately as I could and stared down at her perfect, peaceful face, making the sign of the cross, just like they do in the movies. Then I unlocked the shed and grabbed the axe - a big old-fashioned chopper left behind by a previous resident of the property. I had a feeling that the bear trap contraption was the better tool to use but had no idea how it might work. The axe felt... *appropriate*. Traditional. Like in a fairy tale.

I possessed no wooden stake or silver bullet, but according to the book the other favoured method was decapitation.

I raised the axe, taking careful aim before closing my eyes to shut out the awful sight of my broken wife, my shattered life.

Later that night I buried four heads in the garden. One of them, the largest and most beautiful of the group, I kissed lightly on the lips before placing it in the ground.

WFTG

Gary McMahon lives, works and writes in West Yorkshire, where he shares a home with an understanding wife and their weird and wonderful boy-child. Gary's fiction has appeared in countless magazines and anthologies in both the U.K. and U.S. He is the author of the British Fantasy Award-nominated novella *Rough Cut.* Other books include *All Your Gods Are Dead*, and *Dirty Prayers* (a collection of short fiction). A novel, *Rain Dogs*, is now available from UK publisher Humdrumming. Also forthcoming, from Screaming Dreams, is a double-novella collection called *Different Skins*. In 2009 Pendragon Press will publish *To Usher, the Dead*, a collection of stories about Thomas Usher, a reluctant working class psychic detective; one of these stories has been selected by Ellen Datlow for reprint in *The Year's Best fantasy & Horror 21.*

"In 1976, when I was just seven years old, I saw something on television that probably did more than anything else to turn me into a horror writer. Nationwide was a popular early evening local news programme. The stories it ran were for the most part light-hearted (I still remember with fondness the startling claims of the "discovery" of a real, live dinosaur one April 1st) but occasionally they focused on the more unusual aspects of life.

Type the words "The Hexham Heads" into Google and you'll get the whole rather magnificent story, but what I recall vividly is a sombre news report about three stone heads – probably Celtic in origin – found buried in a garden in Hexham, Northumberland. Once uncovered, these artefacts set off a chain of events which culminated in a local woman witnessing a terrible "half man/half beast" enter her bedroom and then pad down the stairs of her suburban home "as if on its hind legs".

Understandably, I found the whole thing utterly terrifying. I still feel an odd sense of nausea whenever I think about watching the (no doubt badly) dramatised sequences accompanying the report (I even recall false scenes that were never shown, like a severed head rolling slowly down a garishly carpeted flight of stairs). But it stayed with me, and I've wanted to write a story inspired by the case ever since..."

THE MILL
Mark West

1

The trees around him were bare and there was a strong chill in the air that raked his throat as he breathed. A crow cawed loudly, as if he was getting too close to its nest.

He was in a clearing, that felt familiar though he couldn't place it. Ahead of him was a fence, splintered wooden posts set at six foot intervals, draped with barbed wire and just beyond that a rough looking hedge. Spindly trees were dotted around, the tips of their apparently hollow trunks knocking against one another in the breeze, like damped bamboo wind-chimes. To his left were more trees, thicker with dense foliage and a narrow path led between them into depths that seemed to pulse with darkness. To his right, a mound of earth rose sharply to the height of a double-decker bus and he climbed up it, so that he could get his bearings at the summit. The top of the mound was sunken, littered with the detritus of winter.

From this vantage point, he could see that he was surrounded by fields and a couple of stands of evergreen trees. Ahead, the sun was setting behind another copse, but this one was different, bigger, the branches of the trees spreading out as if they were sheltering something.

He saw movement at the copse and shielded his eyes, squinting into the dying light. There was someone there, a woman with long red hair, wearing a pale dress.

He had to reach her, to find out where he was and he started down the mound, slipping and sliding. At the base, he stumbled and felt a sharp pain in his ankle but ignored it, got to his feet and ran, as best he could, to the gap in the hedge.

"No, don't."

The voice seemed to come from all around him and he stopped, looking around. "Nic?"

"Don't go, Michael."

At that, as always, Michael Anderson started awake. Quickly, he looked at Nicola's side of the bed but, as usual, it was empty.

He closed his eyes.

2

It was a cold evening in early October and the rain, which had been threatening all day, was now falling as a drizzle.

Michael Anderson pulled into the small car park at the end of Duke Street. Broken glass glittered in his headlight beams, like a carpet of diamonds.

There were four other cars parked, the occupants barely visible behind the misted windows but he didn't glance at them as he got out, locked the car and walked to the pavement where the lights from the Duke Street Community Centre splashed across the paving slabs. He couldn't see or hear anything but knew that Drew would be inside, bustling about and setting the room up, waiting for the bereft and lonely to turn up, to try and take comfort from others, sharing a camaraderie they desperately wanted but couldn't quite give.

Michael wasn't blessed with a photographic memory but now, sometimes, he wished he was. There was one thing he remembered vividly though, from the summer before last, which had been long and hot, the temperatures breaking all previous records.

They were on the patio. His wife, Nicola, was in the sun topping up her tan whilst he was sheltering under the umbrella. He watched a bead of sweat slide from her neck into her cleavage, which

128

glistened with sun lotion.

"Isn't this great?" she asked, turning her head to look at him, shielding her eyes. "We're happy and healthy and it's a lovely day. Could life get any better?"

"No," he said and leaned over, to kiss her, "I don't think it could."

A narrow corridor led to the Community Centre's main hall, where the Tots & Toddlers group met. Small tables and chairs were stacked neatly along one wall, coat hooks above them as high as Michael's waist and the far wall was covered with impressionistic images that only the artist could identify. The floor, marked out for games of football, tennis or basketball, always looked clean but felt gritty to him, as if the kids had brought sand in from somewhere and it had shaken out of the grips of their shoes during the day. The room had a peculiar smell, at once sweet and sour and he now associated it - must and warm bodies and budget cleaning fluids - with the thought of death.

The Bereaved Partner's Group met in a small ante-room and through the open door Michael could see several people, their backs to him, making drinks. Drew was perched on the edge of a table, flicking through some papers and, as if he could feel Michael watching him, turned and smiled.

"Good evening," he said, "how are you?"

"Not brilliant," said Michael, as he went in and shook Drew's outstretched hand.

"Oh." Drew was somewhere in his early fifties, a short podgy man with thinning hair who dressed in very rich colours. Michael didn't know what had happened to Drew's partner, except that he'd been in a hospice for a long time and had died last year. "I know you don't want to hear this, but it does get easier. Never better, absolutely not, but it does get easier."

Michael felt his eyes warm with tears, as they often did at these meetings. He didn't want life to be easier to live without Nicola, that didn't seem at all right and listening to his fellow Group members, half of them felt the same way. Drew seemed to notice his discomfort and nodded, so Michael hung up his coat - the pegs set at an adult height in this room - then went over to the refreshment table to make himself a cup of tea.

"I don't know how much more I can take, I'm not sleeping, I feel awful, nothing seems important anymore."

As he grieved, Michael suffered with insomnia. Between Nicola's passing and the funeral, he'd survived on little more than cat naps but everyone told him that was natural and he felt so bad anyway, the tiredness didn't register with him.

Doctor Colbert looked at Michael through steepled fingers. "Michael, you have to accept you've suffered a massive trauma, a massive loss, at a relatively early age. You need to deal with it yourself and, I'll be frank, I'm reluctant to prescribe you too much."

His condition slowly improved after the funeral, as he moved into a new routine. He'd potter around the house, eat, go out for long walks and veg out in front of the TV. As the clock rolled past midnight, he'd go to bed and lie in the darkness, willing sleep to come. It often took a while and he'd lay and watch the lights from cars outside dance across the ceiling or listen to people as they walked by. He'd hear human life, outside the four walls of his house, going about its business whilst inside, with him, there was only silence.

"I am dealing with it, every day when I open my eyes and the other side of the bed hasn't been slept in."

"Michael, I've been your doctor for a long time, Nicola's for even longer and what happened to her was just…" Colbert paused for a moment, as if trying to decide how best to express himself. "Well, it was very aggressive and you need time to deal with that, to process your thoughts and reactions." Colbert reached for his prescription tablet and began writing. "I can give you something to deal with the insomnia and some of the feelings, a course of Mirtazapine. It'll help but not necessarily for the long term, for that I think you'll need to speak to people."

"I don't want to go to a psychiatrist."

"I was thinking more of a local group, for people who've lost partners."

"A group?"

"Just give it a chance, okay? You'll meet people in the same position, who'll know how you're feeling and might have suggestions on how to deal with your emotions. You can talk, work through issues, realise that you're not alone. The guy who runs it lost his partner and he believes it was the group that helped to pull him through the worst of it all."

Michael stared at the wall behind the doctor, where three fingerpaint drawings were tacked below his medical certificates. Below them was a framed photograph of an attractive blonde woman holding a curly haired blonde toddler.

"Okay," he said finally, "if you think it'll help, I'll go."

Michael did find the group useful, though he rarely spoke in discussions and didn't feel that he'd particularly opened up. But that didn't matter, listening to others had been helpful. Part of it was the strength these people displayed - the matter of fact way they discussed how their spouses were taken from them, some suddenly but most having succumbed to an illness that, more often than not, left them a shadow of their former selves. Not all of the attendees spoke and some of them didn't seem particularly friendly but Michael could see that by the end of each evening, their spirits were raised - however slightly - as were his, until he drove home to the empty house.

Drew did a good job, keeping the group as informal and light as he could and now, he was shooing people to their seats, checking his watch theatrically.

"Come on folks, we don't have all night."

A couple of people laughed and joked with him, calling him a control freak. For some reason, the idea of that - and looking at Drew's pretend-outraged face - made Michael smile.

"Well that's nice," said a woman beside him.

Michael turned. "Hello, Saskia," he said. "What's nice?"

"You smiling." She looked at her hands, as if suddenly embarrassed. "It's nice to see you smile, I mean."

He nodded and sat next to her. "Thank you."

"You're welcome."

He'd spoken to Saskia a couple of times and they often sat next to one another. A tall, slim, redhead, she was the only person in the group younger than he was. He didn't know the story behind her loss, since neither of them had asked the other, their conversation skirting the topic like an expert skater.

They looked at one another, not needing to ask silly questions about how the other felt. She offered him a lazy smile, as if in compensation.

"It's good to see you," he said.

"And you."

Drew finally got as close to his silence as he was likely to and sat on the edge of the desk. He ran through some news items, local events that might interest the group, but nobody took him up on any of them so he put his papers back into a folder.

"Tonight," he said, "I thought we'd discuss 'The Grief Cycle'. I know I've touched on this before, but we have some new members now," he gestured towards Michael and Saskia, "and it might be good for them to know about it."

Someone said "I found it very useful" and Michael nodded, wishing that he hadn't been singled out.

"This isn't a new concept," said Drew, "but I think it works and I like it. In essence, it states that there are sequential stages to grief, hence the idea of a cycle and, generally speaking, most of us will be affected by at least some of these stages."

Michael loved pretty much everything about Nicola and he loved looking at her. If she noticed him, she always told him to stop, said it made her self-conscious, but he couldn't help it.

Now, he could pinpoint the exact time that his world, as he loved and understood it, began to crumble around him.

It was a normal Wednesday morning and he'd just had a shower. Nicola was standing at her dresser, doing up her bra strap and he stood in the doorway, watching her. The early morning sun, diffused by the net curtains, gave her a glow, glints of light colouring her bare back and legs. Her hair was loosely pulled up, stray strands brushing the back of her neck.

"Mrs Anderson, you look beautiful."

Nicola turned to face him and fluttered her eyelids. "Flatterer."

"Will it get me anywhere?"

She smiled and raised her left eyebrow. "Often."

He laughed and walked up behind her and pulled her tight to him. She wiggled her behind against his groin and giggled. "You like that, eh?"

"Of course," he murmured, kissing her neck gently and slid his hands up her belly. Her bra wasn't clipped together and his hands ran under the cups, gently squeezing her breasts. He heard her sigh and then he felt it.

"What's that?"

"What?"

"There's something under your left boob."

"What? Where?" She pulled her breast up, feeling underneath with her fingers delicately. He guided her hand until she found the bump and looked at him. "What is it?"

He crouched down. "I don't know, sweetheart, I can't really see anything."

"It's probably nothing," Nicola said and smiled a fragile smile.

"The first stage is denial," said Drew. "When I lost Simon, it took me a long, long time to believe it and I was convinced, for ages, that he'd walk through the door at any moment, smiling his big silly grin and asking me why I looked so sad."

Drew stopped for a moment, as if to gather himself. Someone across the table from Michael coughed, but otherwise there was silence before Drew carried on.

"Anger next, aimed at either the departed, or yourself, or whichever God you happen to believe in. Or at a third party, of course, if you'll forgive me mentioning it, Bridget."

Michael glanced over at Bridget, who was staring at the table, dabbing her eyes with a tissue. What was her story, what rage did she feel?

"Then there's bargaining, which - with hindsight - is frankly silly but I did it, I begged God many times to spare Simon and take me instead. That's when I hit rock bottom, I think and that led me straight to the next stage, of depression."

"Amen," said somebody quietly.

"We all know about this and all of us will have a different reaction. There can be tears or no tears, rage or no rage, any number of feelings, but it doesn't matter if what you feel isn't what the books tell you to feel. The way I reacted, I know, isn't what happened with others."

"That's right," said a man across from Michael. "I internalised everything and made myself very poorly for a long time."

"Thank you Bill", said Drew. "From here, we move to the last stage, of acceptance, where we're ready to accept what's happened and move forward."

"Are you there, Drew?" asked Bill.

Michael watched as Drew swallowed, looked nervously around the room and touched his adam's apple gently. "Some days I am," he said finally, "but other days I'm not."

3

Michael was at work when Nicola called. She'd made an appointment but insisted on going alone and he sat at his desk, waiting for her call, trying to concentrate on his computer monitor but failing miserably. He knew it was probably nothing, perhaps even something as silly as heat-rash, but he also knew that Nicola's aunt had had a mastectomy three years ago.

"They don't know what it is," she said. "I'm being set up with an appointment at the hospital."

There were a lot more appointments and phone calls and then, three months shy of her thirty-third birthday, Nicola Anderson was diagnosed with ductal carcinoma.

Michael knew that the doctor, who didn't look old enough to have done all of his necessary training, wasn't trying to be brusque but it sounded like it - to him, it was business as usual, to the Andersons it was earth shattering news.

"What kind?" asked Nicola.

"IDC," said the doctor, "it's quite a common type." He searched his cluttered desk for an X-Ray wallet, took out the negative and slapped it onto a lightboard.

"That's the culprit, the blob with the spines coming out of it."

"What happens now?" asked Nicola. Michael noticed that her arms were crossed over her chest.

"Well judging by the size, we've hopefully caught it early enough to treat it, though people obviously react differently."

"Could you be wrong about any of this?" Michael asked.

The doctor pursed his lips and shook his head. "It's highly unlikely, the biopsy just confirms what we can see with the X-Ray."

"So what happens now?" asked Nicola again, her voice sounding a million miles away.

"We treat it, Mrs Anderson, to try to get rid of it."

But, even though Nicola was treated promptly and thoroughly, they couldn't. Within a couple of months they were sitting in a consultants office, which had a nice view of the grounds and plenty of spare desk space. Michael didn't think he'd ever felt so nervous in his life and the fact that Nicola was gripping his hand as if she was hanging off a cliff didn't help.

"Mrs Anderson," said the consultant, leaning forward, his hands pressed hard on the desk. "I'm afraid that I have bad news."

"Tell me," she said, her voice tight.

The consultant cleared his throat. "Have you ever heard the word metastasis?"

Michael had and felt his world give way, as a wave of nausea washed over him. Nicola had researched her condition on the Net and metastasis was just one of the fun new words they'd discovered.

"Yes," said Nicola. Michael squeezed her hand and swallowed back bile.

"I'm afraid, Mrs Anderson, that as we suspected, you have a very aggressive cancer and, unfortunately, the metastasis is widespread."

"Lung?" asked Nicola quietly.

The consultant nodded. "It's also showing in your bones and pancreas. I'm very sorry."

Michael looked at his wife, the tears gleaming on her cheeks and the consultant, who looked between them gravely. He couldn't take any of this in, didn't want to hear it, just wanted to be back in the bedroom, holding his wife tight.

The cancer attacked Nicola without mercy. Sometimes, Michael would go to work and, on his return home, be able to see a difference in her, even if in some undefinable way.

Too soon, she was admitted to hospital and then to the Church View hospice, where she would eventually see out her life. Michael grew to hate the place. It looked imposing as you drove towards it, with bright red bricks and brown windows and white fascia, but close-up it was like any other building where profit wins over compassion. The bricks were starting to crack, some of the double-glazing was fogged and the plastic fascia was peeling at the corners.

Nicola's room, which looked out onto the brick wall of a haulage company's yard, was small and functional, never entirely clean but not exactly dirty either. Michael called in on his way to work, spoke with the staff to find out how her night had been and then called in on his way home from work to sit by his wife's bed until they kicked him out. Then he'd pick up some food and go home, wishing his life could go back to how it was before, with Nicola by his side.

As her condition worsened, so too did the mental toll on him. Sometimes, he didn't think she was his wife, the gorgeous vivacious woman he'd married, who reached for his hand whenever they were out walking and giggled like a schoolgirl if he told her the most stupid of jokes. No, this poor wreck of a woman, who didn't move and slept a lot and smelled vaguely of antiseptic, was someone else - an impostor, imperfectly made because Nicola had never looked this frail. He couldn't hear her breathing as she slept, however close he sat and contented himself with the shush of the morphine slide, hidden under the bed covers. It wasn't the same, but it was something.

The night before she died, as he prepared to leave, he leaned down to kiss her. She moved her head slightly and their lips touched.

"Goodnight," she managed to whisper.

He smiled. "G'night, beautiful, I'll see you tomorrow." He kissed her again and went home.

Nicola passed away just after ten, on an overcast Wednesday morning. Michael stood next to her mum, who dabbed her eyes with a handkerchief. Her dad was on the other side of the bed, biting his lip and trying to remain stoical.

The attending nurse confirmed that she was gone, then opened the window. Nicola's mum burst into loud, wracking sobs and Michael and Nicola's dad looked at one another, unsure of what to do.

He drove his in-laws home, sat in the lounge with them, made strong sweet tea and poured a large slug of whiskey into his father-in-laws. He went through old photo-albums with them, which ran from the early seventies, with bright, almost Technicolor photographs of a toddler Nicola running around on the beach right up to the mid nineties, when they'd been married. Beyond that, there were only sporadic images of her, at family gatherings and various functions and Michael had a sudden, awful thought, that by marrying her he'd taken her away from her parents, something this lack of photographic history seemed to prove. But they didn't say anything and seemed grateful that he sat with them into the early hours.

He didn't cry the next day, when he went to the registry office and dealt with all of the paperwork. Or the day after that, meeting with the vicar and undertaker with his father-in-law. Or even when he was asked for Nicola's favourite song, which would play her coffin into church.

Nicola was buried the following Tuesday, in the little churchyard on the hill outside of Gaffney and Michael didn't cry at the graveside.

It took another three days for him to crack. He was making a cup of tea when he realised he couldn't see the kettle properly. In the moment it took to register the tears, they were cascading down his cheeks. He felt a sudden pressure in his chest, took a deep breath and sobbed it out. The tears came heavily then and he slid to the floor, his back to the fridge, sobbing for his wife and everything that had been taken away. He stayed like that for a long time and it never happened again.

Afterwards, he tried, as best he could, to get on with his life. He went back to work, endured conversations with people who told him they knew 'just how he felt' and was amazed he didn't throttle any of them. He let the post build up at home, not wanting to open any more sympathy cards, hating each of them for their perfectly realised pictures of doves and hearts and scrolls, alluding to a state that is serene and peaceful when, in reality, it's anything but.

And he suffered with his insomnia.

But when he did, finally, sleep, he mainly dreamt of the wood and Nicola.

4

"Please remember, folks, that if you need to have a chat about anything, you can call me at any time."

People got up, wishing their immediate neighbour all the best and went to get their coats. Michael went to wash up his cup and then got his jacket. Saskia was at the doorway, talking to Drew and Michael watched as he touched her forearm gently. Saskia looked at it, briefly, then bit her lip and wiped away a tear. Drew said something and Saskia nodded, as she pulled her coat on.

"Goodnight," said Michael as he walked by, "thank you for the talk, Drew."

"You're welcome, Michael." He touched Michael's arm to stop him, then pulled out his wallet and took a card from it. "I'm serious about ringing. This has my home and mobile numbers and my email, just in case."

Michael took the card. "Thank you."

"You can get through this, trust me." He looked around, as if to make sure that nobody was standing close. "How long has it been now, about six weeks?"

"Yes."

Drew nodded. "If you have dark thoughts, dark dreams, ignore them."

The words became a blur that Michael couldn't understand. "What does that mean?"

"Exactly what I said." Drew smiled, but it didn't touch his eyes. "Dreams are just what they are, Michael, your mind unwinding at the end of the day."

"You've lost me."

Drew smiled again and this time, his face lit up. "Ah, I'm just being silly. But ring me if you need to."

138

"I will," Michael said, nodding but confused, "thank you."

Saskia was holding the door to the corridor for him, so Michael rushed over to her. "Thanks."

Slowly, they walked to the exit, Saskia picking at her nails.

"Drew said a weird thing back there," said Michael.

"What about?"

"That I should ignore dark dreams."

Saskia looked as if she was going to laugh, then seemed to check herself. She put her fingertips to her lips and strode for the door.

"What?" Michael called, rushing to catch her up. "Do you know what he means? Is he talking about suicide or something?"

She stopped at the doorway, the yellow wash of the streetlight making her look sick and other-worldly. "I'm not sure, he said the same thing to me, after my first few meetings here. I think he believes that you'll see a place in your dreams, with your loved one guiding you there, but if you follow them, you won't come back."

Michael looked at her, trying to see if this was some kind of weird, sick joke. "Really?"

"Yes."

"What about you, do you believe it?"

"I don't know."

Something about the way she said it struck him. "Have you ever had dreams like that, with your husband?"

"No," she said and Michael knew immediately that she was lying. "People kill themselves for all manner of reasons, not just because they dreamed of a place."

"No, of course not."

"I'll see you in a fortnight," she said, turned and was gone into the darkness, her shoulders hunched against the drizzle, her right hand keeping the neck of her coat together.

Michael watched until she was safely into her car, then ran for his. He sat inside quietly, listening to the hum of rain on the roof, looking out of the soaked windscreen at the distorted world beyond.

Could the dreams that Drew meant be the ones that he'd been having, or was it all some weird coincidence?

Shaking his head, he started the engine and drove back towards the town centre.

Traffic was light and those pedestrians that had braved the weather were either hunched over or sheltering under umbrellas, rushing to get where they needed to go.

Bright lights from fast food outlets splashed primary colours across the pavement and into the gutters, making the street lights seem almost dull. The windscreen wipers, which he'd set on intermittent, struggled with the drizzle as the car picked up speed.

Michael glanced out of the window, saw the traffic lights turning amber at the pedestrian crossing and then it was too late, he was past them and a woman standing at the kerb glared at him.

He slammed on his brakes and the car shuddered to a stop on the wet tarmac. He turned in his seat and called "Sorry", though he knew the woman couldn't hear him. She was glaring at him from the kerb, her clothes soaked, her hair stuck to her head.

He hadn't seen her, his mind elsewhere.

The amber lights flashed and she hurried across the road. He unclipped his seatbelt and opened the door, then stopped. What was he going to do, chase after her to apologise? No, that would just make a bad situation worse.

As he put his seatbelt back on, he thought he saw Nicola. She was across the road, sheltering under the Pizza Plus restaurant awning and the ache of longing and nostalgia was so strong he felt it in his chest. That had been their restaurant and once, on a very rainy night, he'd been held up by traffic and arrived late, to find Nicola standing under the awning, pissed off with him.

He pulled into the kerb and got out. Glancing quickly from left to right for traffic, he ran across the road.

By the time he reached the other side, no-one was standing outside the deserted restaurant that had once been Pizza Plus. The awning was ripped and the chipboard covering the windows was plastered with bills for local bands and various graffiti.

He leaned against the wall, tears mixing with rainwater on his cheeks. He knew that he couldn't have just seen her, however much he wished he had but he missed her so much. The way she talked, the way she laughed and the way she'd say things with a totally straight face that would reduce him to fits of laughter. He missed

140

that it took her so long to get ready, that sometimes her procrastination skills would have shamed a sloth, he even missed the bunched up tissues with lipstick smears that always seemed to find their way onto his chest of drawers. He just wanted her back and wondered if that meant he was still at stage one of Drew's cycle.

5

He was standing on top of the mound, the naked trees making their strange knocking sound.

He looked towards the other copse and saw the woman with red hair again and tried desperately to remember where this place was. He'd been here before, he was sure of it, he and Nicola had...

He started down the mound, slipping and sliding, trying to get a grip to slow himself down but only succeeding in skinning his palms. He stumbled at the base, his ankle shrieking with pain.

"Please, Michael." The voice seemed to come from every direction. "Don't go."

He looked around but he was on his own. "Nic? Where are you?"

"I'm here, like I always said I would be."

Nicola stepped out from behind a tree and tears stung his eyes, his vision swimming. The sun seemed to be shining directly on her, combining with his tears to create a shimmering nimbus around her. Her face was shadowed but he could clearly see her eyes, glimmering with life and vitality.

"Oh, baby..." he said, before his voice cracked and he swallowed back a sob.

She put her finger to his lips and he knew it was there, even though he couldn't feel it. "Ssh, keep quiet, don't wake them."

He wiped the tears from his cheek. "Who?"

"The Coughers," she said.

"What's going?" he whispered.

"I want you to see that I'm okay, that I'm safe, that you can move on."

"How can you expect me to do that?"

"Mike, you must. The more you dwell on things, the more you'll

141

be drawn back here and I don't want that for you."

"What do you mean? Where am I?"

"Think back, Mike. The wood, the track, the ruins in the trees."

He tried but his mind felt sluggish and unresponsive. Finally, memories began to emerge, of walking with Nicola, cutting through to Compass Wood from...

"Coffers Wood? That's where I am, isn't it? And that place further down is The Mill?"

"Yes."

A sound rang out, like someone hacking their lungs up, echoing around them. Nicola looked towards the source of the noise and seemed frightened.

"What is it?"

"Them," said Nicola, quietly. "Can you not feel it? The ghosts are around us all the time."

"I don't understand."

"Quickly," she said, suddenly standing on his right, startling him. More hacking sounds carried to them. "Get up, you have to move."

"But I don't want to leave you, Nicola."

"Then don't come here again, you must promise me."

"I promise."

When he woke up, long before the alarm which was set to go off at seven, he checked to see if Nicola was lying beside him. Then he checked his palms. To his dismay, they were perfectly fine.

He sat up, silent tears running down his cheeks. Another dream. But at least now he knew where he'd been seeing her.

6

A dirty brown Cavalier, its exhaust rumbling and harsh dance music blaring through opened windows, came down the road and Michael watched until it disappeared around the corner, the teenaged driver completely oblivious to him, chatting on a mobile phone.

As the noise subsided, Michael turned to look down Mill Lane. This led to the folly, where he'd played as a kid.

Four large bungalows, set back from the lane on sizeable plots of land, looked out over the fields towards Haverton. Beyond them were allotments, two fields the size of football pitches, each featuring a motley array of sheds and dowel tripods for training runner beans.

The lane rose after the allotments. At the crest of this rise was an old farmhouse that Michael remembered being terrified of as a kid - it was out of the way, had a lot of outbuildings that looked cracked and decayed and a huge Alsatian in the yard.

After this, the tarmac stopped and the lane was just hard-packed earth, with occasional slabs and patches of hardcore and a grass strip grew out of the median, like a scruffy Mohican. After the lane turned a corner, Coffers Wood spread out to the left, a "Keep Out" sign from British Steel posted at a gap in the wooden fence.

The gap was smaller than he remembered, clogged now by adventurous branches from the hedge. He stood as close as he could and peered in, the canopy of branches dappling the leaf-strewn ground and saw the mound. For the briefest of moments, he felt a sharp chill in his chest and then it was gone. Of course the mound was there, he'd seen it as a kid.

The lane wound on, growing ever more narrow, until it reached the heart of the folly, the remains of Mill House. Or The Mill, as it was known.

He didn't know what it had been - he and his friends came to the conclusion that it might have been a mill - just that it was in ruins when he first discovered it and, talking to his parents, was in ruins for as long as they knew too.

During long, hot summer holidays, Michael and his friends had come here to play war, to cut through to Haverton (through the folly, down the huge field where, if you weren't careful, you'd get chased by the farmer and across the brook on a drainage pipe) or simply to explore. All of those things got less interesting as he hit his teens and he probably hadn't visited the folly for the best part of twenty years.

The lane ended at a small turning area, with fields ahead and to the right, heading down towards the brook. The Mill was to the left, surrounded by trees, occupying perhaps half an acre, two stone gateposts guarding the way, cracked with age now and almost hidden behind years of growth from the hedge.

143

Michael stood between them and looked around in the gathering dusk. He was alone down here, protected from the noise of the main road by the fields and trees, the brook too calm to make a sound that would carry up to him. High in the trees, crows cawed and took flight.

He'd expected to feel something when he stood here, that would help to explain what his dreams meant but he didn't and the realisation choked a small laugh out of him. The sound took something in the hedge to his left by surprise and it darted away noisily.

What was he expecting to find? It was a ruin, a playground, what answers could it possibly contain for his dreams? It was just a place and, sometimes, things are exactly what they appear to be, however desperately you might want their existence to signify something. Looking at it now, as red streaks began to form in the sky above the trees, the more he thought that The Mill just was - it didn't signify or prove anything, it just existed.

He could see that there were still rough paths through the undergrowth, cut down and maintained by generations of Gaffney and Haverton kids playing there, all of which led to the centre and he stepped onto the one in front of him.

It was more overgrown that he remembered and he wondered, for a moment, if kids actually came down here to play anymore. Certainly, someone had, their existence obvious by the bleached fast food cartons, cigarette packets and drink cans that littered the undergrowth bordering the path.

It didn't take long to reach the centre of the site and it was like he'd never been away. The ruined foundations of The Mill dominated the space, the brickwork cut off at ground level. The cellars were still there, three large rectangular rooms with stone steps leading down into them, the dark blue brick covered by fading whitewash. A small, shallow ditch ran around the building and, as he had when he was a kid, he thought it looked like a moat. Off to the right, accessible through bracken that snatched at clothes, was a well.

He still didn't feel anything, apart from a warm flash of nostalgia that the place hadn't changed since he was a kid.

"What is it about this place, Nicola?"

Everything was still, even the crows. Michael walked to the edge of the foundations and stepped onto the low ledge, formed from the top of the old wall. It was three bricks thick here, most of them still as solid as the day they were laid.

He followed the line of the wall, turning left at the first branch, towards Haverton. As he looked over the hedge-line and between the trees towards the brook, he heard a cough. Surprised, he turned around, holding his arms out for balance.

He scanned left and right, squinting into the dusky gloom of the tree line, but couldn't see anyone at all. A faint pulse of unease tugged at him and he knew that it was simply because he was down here, well away from other people and it was getting dark but, really, there was nothing to be worried about. After all, the cougher was either someone coming down the lane the way he had, perhaps walking their dog, or else someone coming up from the brook, maybe taking a shortcut from Haverton to Gaffney.

He turned his attention back to the wall and looked down into the depths of the foundations, a drop of perhaps ten feett. The floor was covered by water and he could see himself, peering back. Beyond that, under the surface, there were several piles of dark bricks, obviously from where the building had been brought down. Across from him, along the other wall of this cellar room, a small tree was growing out from a large crack in the white-washed brick.

Looking down made him feel a bit giddy and unbalanced and he looked up, trying to orient himself. There was a rustling from behind him, as if someone was rushing through the undergrowth towards him and he turned sharply, pebbles of brick and mortar peppering the water. Again, he couldn't see anything except that the bracken on the Haverton side of the foundations was thick, with thorns that were large enough to be seen clearly in the fading light. Nothing could have been rushing through that, it would have been torn to pieces - he must have been mistaken.

Slightly spooked now, he stood still, listening intently. There was the faintest hum of road noise, a few birds calling and a steady drip from somewhere behind him, all things he would expect to hear. Then the rushing noise came again, this time distinctly from his right, from the thick bracken. He glanced over, knowing he wouldn't see anything and the noise stopped as he did so.

From behind and to his left, he heard another cough, followed by more. He turned and caught sight of someone moving quickly behind the first line of trees, their white gown almost luminous in the gloom.

"Who's there?" he shouted, pissed off that someone was obviously trying to scare him. The person didn't slow down or respond and he kept watch on them, meaning to see where they stopped running. He didn't know yet what he was going to do with them, but at least he'd know where they were.

The person was running between the trees, darting in and out of sight and suddenly Michael realised two things. One was that the gown was too white, almost glowing against the murkiness of the wood and the other was that the runner was moving as if unhindered by the thick undergrowth.

"Hello?" he called. The person didn't slow or acknowledge him, but disappeared behind another tree. Michael watched, waiting for them to reappear and that faint pulse of unease he'd felt before stepped up a gear. He was either being spooked by someone - kids, perhaps, annoyed that their drinking session was being interrupted - or he was going slightly mad, neither of which was something he wanted to prolong any longer than he had to.

Another chorus of coughing broke out behind him and he turned around slowly, trying to maintain his balance. He felt warm now, hot almost and he could accept that he might feel prickly heat with his unease, but it was more than that. It almost felt as though the heat was building and concentrated, like he was standing too close to a bonfire.

Then it was gone, along with the coughing.

Something reflected in the water and caught his eye. He looked down and saw himself and the head of a person who appeared to be standing to his right. It was there and then suddenly gone. The shock of seeing it seemed to fill his head with pins and needles and he fought for a moment to catch his breath. Instinctively, he looked around but he was alone on the wall.

This was too much. "Who's there?" he called, looking along the tree line, hoping to catch a glimpse of the person in white again. "Who is it?"

Bracken snapped behind him and, before he had a chance to turn, he felt hands pressing into the small of his back, pushing him forward. Caught off guard, he felt himself go and windmilled his arms desperately, trying to keep his balance. The hands let go and he knelt down quickly, making himself as small a target as possible. He looked around but he was still alone.

"What do you want?" he called.

Someone coughed, as if in response, a hacking sound from deep within the tree line and it was taken up by more, building into a chorus that seemed to surround him.

Then there was another sound, a word that he could almost but not quite hear, that sounded very much like "Mike". It was gone almost as soon as he heard it but that was it, the final straw. Whatever was happening here, it was intense and potentially dangerous now and he just wanted out of it. Steadily, he got to his feet and walked off the wall as quickly as he could, the coughs fading away as he did so. By the time he reached the hard-packed earth at the edge of the path, the coughing was almost gone, but the feeling of unease was still nagging at him. Without turning back, Michael kept going. The path was darker than before, much darker, the trees and hedges that bordered it cutting out a lot of the light. He could barely see the ground and it made the brisk flight of the person in the gown all the more astounding.

The lane, when he finally reached it, was the most welcome sight he'd seen in weeks and, as he stood on the rough gravel surface, he realised that the coughing had stopped altogether now and that he could hear crows in the trees above him.

7

"Hello Drew, it's Michael."

"Hello, how're you?"

"I'm fine, but I need to ask you a question." Michael took a deep breath, suddenly unsure of himself. He'd rehearsed the question all day, until it now seemed like a random collection of words, but he had to ask. "At the last meeting, you said something that's been nagging at me ever since."

"I'm sorry about that, I'd never want to plague your mind with anything."

"I know, it's just that I didn't understand what you meant when you said that if I had dark thoughts, I should ignore them."

"Oh really? You should always ignore dark thoughts, because they often lead to dark deeds and I don't want you to do anything silly."

"Like suicide?"

"Absolutely," said Drew quickly, "that's always a danger. We all have our low moments, but we have to push through them."

"You said something else, about dark dreams. What did that mean?" The line went quiet, until Michael could only hear a faint pulse. "Drew?"

"I'm here."

"Is anything wrong?"

"No, not at all, I'm just thinking."

"About the answer?"

Drew laughed, a humourless chuckle. "We all dream, Michael and some of them push us in certain directions. All I was trying to say was that you shouldn't always follow what you dream."

"But what if the dream feels real?"

"That's just the way it goes, some are vivid, some aren't. I take it you've dreamt of..." There was a slight pause, as Drew tried to recall her name. "...of Nicola?"

"Yes."

"And she seems okay?"

"Yes."

"Excuse my insensitivity but does she look like you remember her, from the end?"

"No, she looks like she did before, when everything was good."

"And have you dreamed of a place?"

Michael felt his pulse quicken. "Yes, I have."

"And where was that?"

"The Mill," said Michael, quietly. There was absolute silence from the other end. "At the bottom of the folly."

"I know where it is," said Drew tersely. "How long have you been having these dreams?"

"Pretty much since Nicola died, but I only recognised it last night."

"Were you told?"

"Yes."

"Okay Michael, I think we need to talk. Why don't we meet up somewhere?"

"Did you have anywhere in mind?"

"At the library. How would you be fixed for Saturday afternoon?"

8

Weekends were the worst, Michael had found. At work, if you discounted the ghoulish attention he sometimes received, he was following a routine that had existed before but Saturday and Sunday were different. He and Nicola had made a point of treating weekends as theirs and for the bulk of the time it was just them - sitting in the garden, watching TV or lying in bed on Sunday and squabbling over who got which supplement.

After she'd gone, he'd been invited to friends houses and gone willingly, but soon found he didn't want to be there. Conversational topics quickly got strained and he'd lost count of the times somebody had started telling an anecdote, only to realise that Nicola played a part in it before tailing off, embarrassed. Or, worse, talked about how awful something in their life was that made them hate their situation, then looked to Michael for reassurance, as though being told off by your boss compared to losing your wife.

Now, to fill his weekends, he'd taken to walking, spending time at the library or renting films. He tried to avoid crowds because seeing people together, being happy, made him feel sick with nostalgia.

Michael turned into Newland Street just after ten o'clock, which meant he was almost clear of the town centre - just pass the bus-bays, negotiate the crossings at the traffic lights and that was it, back into residential streets.

149

He passed some shops and then "The Society Of Friends" coffee house. He glanced in as he walked by and saw Saskia, sitting on her own by the window. She was looking out into the street and they seemed to recognise each other at the same time.

She waved and he raised his hand – should he go in and say hello or keep walking? She got up and pointed to the door, which he took to mean she wanted to talk, but did he want to do that – after all, the only thing they had in common was death.

That made him feel guilty, so he slowed to match her pace as she threaded her way between tables.

She pulled open the door and said "Hi" with the overt breeziness of someone trying to cover up their lack of confidence. "This is going to sound really stupid," she gabbled and then paused, patting her chest. "Sorry," she said and let out a small giggle, "I'll understand if you can't, but would you like to have a drink with me? You know, if you're not doing anything, it'd be nice to have a friend to sit with."

Weirdly, the desperation in her voice made him want to agree. "Alright," he said.

He followed Saskia to the counter, where she picked up a spare cup and then they wound their way back to her table. She poured him a cup from the stainless steel teapot and slid it to him.

"Thank you."

"You're welcome. So what're you doing in town?"

There was no point in not telling the truth. "Trying to fill my day," he said and watched as she met his eyes briefly, then looked at her cup. "I try to make sure I keep busy at weekends, so that I don't stop and think too much."

She nodded. "I know how that feels."

"Of course," Michael said, "sorry. Did you want to talk about something else, like the weather?"

She smiled and he thought for a moment that she was actually going to laugh. "No, but definitely something else. Tell me about you."

"Me?" He shrugged. "There's not much to tell really."

"Everyone has a life story, Michael."

"But I can't tell mine without mentioning Nicola and then I'll get upset and it'll turn into us talking about loss."

"Of course," she said, sipping her tea. "What about a funny story then? Well, not really funny, but different."

"Go on."

"A few years back, long before John was sick, I smoked. He hated it, so I used to do it on the sly, eating whole packets of Polos and thinking he'd never notice." She laughed. "Stupid, eh? I used to smoke whenever I had to go off somewhere on my own and, if there wasn't an opportunity, I'd make one. One Saturday, I went underwear shopping and John hated standing around changing rooms, so I went on my own. I parked in the multi-storey, lit my first fag of the day and it was glorious."

She smiled, wistfully and looked out of the window.

"I leaned on the wall and the view was wonderful - the sky was clear as a bell, the sun was high and bright and I could see right across Gaffney. I was aware of people around me, coming back to their cars and going home and others coming in, you know and then I became aware of someone walking along and I just knew they were coming to me." She looked at Michael. "The person stopped behind me and coughed, so I turned around and it was one of the centre security guards. He smiled and held his hands out, as if he was trying to placate me. 'Are you okay, love?' he said and I didn't know what he was talking about."

"He thought you were going to jump?"

She nodded. "Apparently, there'd been a rash of people throwing themselves off the upper floors so if they saw anyone on CCTV loitering for longer than a minute or so, they'd send someone up to check it out."

"What did you say to him?"

Saskia laughed, lightly. "I told him the truth, that I was having a sneaky fag before I went clothes shopping. He seemed to understand, but he stayed talking to me until I'd finished and then he walked down to the shopping level with me."

"Like he didn't trust you."

She shrugged. "For all he knew, as soon as he'd turned his back on me, I was going to jump. If I was him, I wouldn't have trusted me either."

151

"That'd be awful, wouldn't it? Knowing that you'd managed to talk someone around and then they kill themselves anyway."

She nodded. "But do you want to know the most ironic thing? Suicide was the furthest thing from my mind that day - I was happy with my life. Why would I want to end something that actually made me wake up with a smile?" She lifted her cup to her chin. "That day I wouldn't and now I find I can't."

Her casually spoken words hit Michael like a slap. "What?" She didn't look at him. Instead, she watched her fingers play with the handle of her cup. "I've tried to commit suicide." She took a deep breath, let it out slowly. "I'm not proud, that I've attempted it or that I've failed, but that's part of me now, of who I am."

"I didn't realise."

"Why would you?"

"My God, I…" What could he say to her? "When was this?"

"Several times. On the way home from the hospital, just after the funeral, two or three times since then."

"Jesus, Saskia, have you spoken to anyone about this?"

She shook her head and looked at him, her eyes red. "Have you tried?"

That gave him pause - he hadn't. He was devastated by the loss of Nicola, felt that part of his life had been brutally ripped away and missed her like he wouldn't have believed possible, so why hadn't he attempted suicide? Did this make his feelings of grief any less? "No," he said finally, perhaps more to himself than to Saskia. "And if I had, I probably wouldn't have told anyone."

"Why?"

"I don't know. Perhaps because then it'd be a cry for help and that's not what it was all about."

Saskia clicked her fingers and pointed at him. "Thank you. I tried because it was what I wanted to do, not for sympathy - if anything, I could have done with less sympathy from people."

"So what happened?"

"Don't ask," she said quietly and he watched tears fill her eyes.

"I don't know why I haven't tried," he said, after a while, "because being without her hurts so much. Probably the only time it crossed my mind was at the crematorium, as I watched her coffin go behind that curtain, but I didn't do anything."

Saskia pressed her fingers under her eyes. "Do you think I'm weak?"

"Why?"

"Because I tried?"

Without thinking, he reached out and laid his hand over hers but as soon as they touched, he knew he'd made a mistake. They both withdrew their hands quickly and he looked down sheepishly. "Sorry," he said, "I shouldn't have done that."

Saskia looked out of the window and Michael noticed more tears, gathering and glistening on her lower eyelids. The silence that descended on the table seemed heavy and sad, as if breaking it would involve too much effort but leaving it would suffocate them.

"Failing made me feel worse," she said finally, facing him. "He was everything to me and now I don't know what to do." She pressed her fingers under her eyes again. "I miss him, Michael, in more ways than I thought it was possible to miss somebody. You know what I mean, how it feels to be in the house on your own, looking at your past. And the loneliness? My God, the loneliness is the worst thing, that's what pushes me to the limit."

He didn't know what to say, even though he knew what it felt like, the crushing weight of suddenly being alone, however many family and friends you might have around you.

"Everybody suddenly has an opinion on how you feel, based on what they felt when their dog died or something happened to one of their friends, but they never get what I miss the most."

"Which is?"

"Him. The feel and touch of him, his smell, laying next to him in bed and feeling his hands on me. I miss holding him and hugging him and kissing him and making love with him. Is that wrong?"

"Of course not, you're bound to miss all that."

"Do you?"

He supposed he did, but with Nicola in the hospice it had been such a long time since they'd made love that it wasn't foremost of what he missed. "Sort of," he said and explained himself.

"I'm sorry, I didn't realise."

153

"That's okay."

"This is getting heavy, shall we change the subject?" Saskia said and held her cup up.

He chinked his cup to hers and smiled. "Absolutely."

"When we were at Group, Drew said to you about dark dreams and you asked me if I'd ever seen a place and I said no."

"I remember."

"Well I lied. I said no because I didn't want to get into a big discussion in case Drew caught up and things kicked off. But I have."

"Did you dream about The Mill?"

She looked at him, as if half of her had expected him to say it and the other half was completely taken by surprise. "Yes, how did you know?"

He told her his dreams.

"Bloody hell," she said. "My dreams started after John died and I don't remember the mound, but I've seen him in the wood and heard the coughing and seen the worried look on his face."

"Have you ever been tempted to go and see what's down there?"

"No," she said, firmly, "I'd be too scared."

Michael looked at her, wanting her to clarify what she meant but she didn't. Instead, she looked out of the window, holding her cup close to her face with both hands, as if her arms were a barricade to keep something away.

They drained the pot of tea in silence.

"I have to go," said Michael and he stood up.

"It's been good to see you," she said and smiled. "Do you have my number? You know, just in case you need to speak to someone who's going through the same thing?"

Whatever had scared her now seemed to have passed and she was gabbling as she had before, self-conscious and shy.

She took a pen from her handbag and scribbled her number on a napkin. He took it and the pen and wrote his number on another napkin. "Thanks," he said, "I appreciate the chat and the tea."

"You're welcome."

* * *

154

9

Later that afternoon, Drew met Michael in the vestibule of Gaffney library, holding a slim hardback. He shook Michael's hand and led him to the reading room at the back of the library.

Half of the tables were empty, but Drew still made for one at the far end of the room, under a shelf that held two dozen telephone directories. He sat facing the main door and gestured to the seat opposite.

Once Michael had sat down, Drew said, "When did you go?"

"Last night."

"Why?"

"Because I wanted to. I haven't been there since I was a kid and I couldn't work out what the connection was with Nicola, or why I should suddenly start dreaming about it."

"And what happened?"

Not wanting to lead the conversation, Michael said, "Nothing."

Drew rubbed his forehead gently with both hands. "Michael, I'd like to think that we're friends and, even if you don't, you obviously trust me." He knitted his fingers tightly. "If you want me to tell you something, you have to be so kind as to return the favour."

"I don't understand."

"I think you do. Something happened, didn't it, at The Mill?"

Michael bit his lip, trying to think of how to get across what he'd experienced without sounding like an hallucinating fool. "I don't know, I genuinely can't explain what I saw or heard or felt."

The two men stared at one another for a few moments.

"Listen Michael," Drew said, "I've not come here to make fun of you, okay?" He worried his lower lip, pulling at it with his fingers. "I've never told anybody this, but it might help. When Simon died, I didn't know what to do with myself. Everything around me reminded me of him, so I took to walking, out of Gaffney and into the countryside, head down and focusing on the road, just trying to get my feelings out and cry when there was nobody around to ask me how I felt. Well, one day I decided to go to Haverton and cut down through the folly."

Drew leaned back in his chair. "I hadn't been there for years, since I was a kid probably and I was amazed that it was exactly how I remembered it and then I saw The Mill itself. Something was nagging at me, goodness knows what because the place was in ruins when I was a kid and I wasn't scared of it, as such, but I didn't want to go through there. So I decided to cut through the field behind The Mill and then along to the main road. My days of climbing over drainage pipes are long gone, I'm afraid."

Both men smiled at one another.

"As I was walking past the entrance, I heard a cough. I assumed it was someone coming up from the brook and kept going, keeping an eye out for them. I'm quite jumpy, so I wanted to be ready for them, otherwise I'd have scared us both, leaping around like an idiot. But nobody came out and then I heard Simon."

"Really?"

Drew smiled, as if he'd run through this story in his mind a hundred times, knowing that people would smirk and think he was losing his marbles. "As real as I'm sitting in front of you. 'D babe', he said, 'come and see me, I'm lonely'. Nobody would know that he called me D babe, that was just between me and him."

"So what did you do?"

"What do you think, Michael? I'd been to my husband's funeral the week before, I saw him at the funeral home before that, I knew he'd gone. There was no way he could have been in The Mill, calling me. I refused to believe it and kept walking. Sometimes, now, I wish I'd gone in, just to see what might have happened, but I walked into the field and kept going until I couldn't hear him any more." Drew rubbed his eyes. "I believed in ghosts until Simon passed away and then I stopped. After all, if he could haunt me, surely he'd have done it at home and told me how he was and that I'd be okay without him, that he would wait for me to join him. But having said that, I do believe in other things that can draw you into a situation you don't want to be in."

"Such as?"

"There's something weird in The Mill, Michael and I don't understand what it is. Most people I've spoken to, who grew up in Gaffney, played there as kids and never had any problems with the place, unless they got ambushed by Haverton kids. But when someone's bereaved - and this doesn't happen with everyone - and they're looking for something, however unconsciously, that's the place they always seem drawn to."

"Fucking hell."

"So you saw something?"

"Sort of." Michael told Drew what had happened and, when he was done, they looked at one another without speaking. "So," Michael said finally, "what do you think it is?"

Drew tapped his fingers against the book on the table in front of him. "I don't know. Most people are too embarrassed to admit they've seen or heard anything and, after a while, they write it off in their own minds as some kind of hallucination. If they can, of course."

"What does that mean?"

"Okay Michael, let's get this straight. The other night I said to you that I wanted you to be careful and to not follow your dreams. When you rang me, I said to you about not doing anything silly and you mentioned suicide."

"I remember."

"I didn't mean that I thought you were contemplating suicide, it's just that The Mill has a bit of a history for it."

"Really?"

"Yes, but any location that's far from the madding crowd can be a suicide blackspot. If somebody wants to end it all and it's not a cry for help, they need to be away from do-gooders who'll try and save them. The thing is, The Mill's had more than its fair share over the years and, if you cross reference enough local history books, it seems to come in cycles."

Michael looked at Drew's earnest expression and shook his head - things were piling up quicker than he could get to grips with them.

"Maybe I'm just a silly man who's read too much and put two and two together and got forty-five. After I heard Simon, I decided to find out what the hell The Mill was, because I'd called it that since I was a kid and never knew why. And neither did my Mum, when I asked her. But we've had a few characters in this town over the years, some of whom have wanted to immortalise their lives and their weird little ways and they've kept a history for us."

157

Drew opened the book and lifted it up, to show Michael a photograph plate on the right-hand page. Black and white, it showed a large, three-storey mansion with trees behind it and a large drive sweeping past the front. An ornate fountain was at the bottom of some steps leading from the front door. Three people were standing in front of the fountain, a man and two women, none of them close enough to be able to discern their features clearly.

"This picture was taken in 1869," said Drew. "The man is Richard Manley-Vale, who was a very prominent local businessman. The woman next to him is his wife, Anna and the other woman is his sister, Elizabeth."

Drew put the book on the table and read aloud, keeping his voice low. "'The Mill, once owned by the Manley-Vale family, is situated at the bottom of the Folly in Gaffney. Surrounded by trees, it was once a very grand residence though only the foundations and cellars remain today. In the late 19th century, the last of the Manley-Vale line - Elizabeth, a spinster - decided to give her 'wonderful home' back to the community and it was converted into a hospice for the palliative care of TB sufferers. Unfortunately, some good folk of Gaffney believed in vampirism and never took kindly to the hospice or its residents and the building was eventually burned down, killing many sufferers. Since then, the area has fallen into disarray and no other buildings have been constructed there.'"

"I never knew that."

"Neither did I. It's not exactly hidden, since it's in this book, but it doesn't tend to get spoken of very often and it's certainly not part of any oral history of Gaffney, so far as I can tell."

"But what does this have to do with your husband, or what I saw?"

"I don't know, Michael, but I do know that a lot of people who've lost loved ones and been drawn to The Mill have experienced things they couldn't explain. Sadly, a few have taken their lives there." He closed the book gently. "I sound like a mad man, don't I?"

Before, Michael would have agreed immediately but things weren't quite so black and white now. He'd experienced things - dreaming about Nicola and seeing her in the rain, everything about

The Mill – that his rational mind couldn't explain. Perhaps that was it, the very fact that he couldn't explain what was happening in his life allowed him to accept things that couldn't be explained themselves.

"Maybe, maybe not," he said finally.

Drew smiled. "My point is, something terrible happened at The Mill, a lot of people lost their lives and I find it odd that it seems to have a draw on the recently bereaved. But if you're not there, you can't do anything silly there, can you?"

"Do you still dream about it?"

"Yes, I do. Just be careful, Michael. Your mind is not your best ally at the moment."

"Maybe not. But thank you, for telling me all this."

"Sometimes, the best we can do is pass on what we know," said Drew. "Plus, I like you, I want to see you at more meetings and see you getting stronger each time."

They chatted idly for a while, until Drew looked at his watch and declared that he had to be going. They shook hands at the library doors and Michael watched him walk away, towards the Corn Market car park.

10

Once Drew was out of sight, Michael walked down the slight hill to Market Street. His phone rang.

"Hello?"

"Michael, is that you?" He didn't recognise the voice, which sounded thick and distant.

"Yes, who's this?"

"It's Saskia. I need to talk to you, in person."

"Okay, when?"

"Now'd be brilliant. Can you come to mine?"

"I don't know where you live."

"Armada Street, number seven, on the estate by the hospital."

"I could be there in half an hour, I'm in town at the moment."

"That's fine," she said, "goodbye".

The line went dead before Michael could respond.

* * *

As soon as Michael saw Saskia, when she opened the door, he got a bad feeling about having turned up. Her eyes were red, slightly glazed and it felt as if she were looking through him, rather than at him - that's why she'd sounded so distant on the phone, she wasn't quite on the planet anymore.

"Are you okay?"

She smiled, lazily. "Yes, come in."

She stepped back, holding tightly to the door and he passed her. Once he was in the hall, she closed the door gently and deliberately, as if pretending not to be intoxicated.

"Did you want to come through to the kitchen? I was just getting a late lunch and I can make you a sandwich, if you want."

"That'd be nice," he said.

She led him down the hall to her large, well-appointed kitchen. She walked over to a worktop, her bare feet slapping on the tiled floor and stood in front of a chopping board, her back to him. He looked at her, dressed in expensive jeans and a plain khaki T-shirt and felt sorry for her - drunk before the evening, making a snack for someone she barely knew but desperately wanted to speak to.

"We're having cold chicken," she said.

"Lovely," he said and leaned against a worktop, folding his arms. "So, do you live alone?"

She nodded. "Afraid so. We'd always planned to have kids but I kept putting it off because we both had good jobs and enjoyed our foreign holidays. I thought we could start when I hit my mid-thirties, perhaps have a couple and enjoy being homebodies for a while."

"That's nice." She turned her head slightly, then went back to making the sandwich. "I'm sorry," he said quickly, "that was insensitive."

"No, it's not that, it's just... You're right, it was a nice idea, a good plan, until John went and ruined it."

He didn't want to talk about death again, so he changed the subject. "You said you wanted to talk?"

The knife blade clanged heavily, twice, against the glass chopping

160

board. "I did." She reached into a cupboard level with her head and took out two plates.

"About anything in particular?" he prompted.

"Not really." She turned and handed him a plate with a thick sandwich on it, some of the chicken falling away from the bread, then leaned on the worktop, holding her plate against her belly, her T-shirt pulled tight over her breasts. He looked away, ill at ease.

"I just thought that, as we've both been widowed, it'd be nice to see you and have a chat and some food."

He felt awful, her words seeming to hang in the air, taunting him. He'd automatically thought it was a bad idea, turning up, because she was drunk and then, to top it off, he'd stared at her breasts. What kind of pervert was he?

She smiled at him. "You're not very impressed that I've had a little drinky, are you?"

"Saskia, it's none of my business."

"During the week, I'm as straight as a die and at the weekend, I have a drink. I mean, there's only me - who cares if I couldn't drive a car now or if I fall asleep watching TV? No-one does." She looked out of the window, tapping her fingers against her lips. "I saw how you looked at me when I opened the door and, to tell you the truth, I'd probably have felt the same way except that now, I know exactly why I'm drinking."

"It's okay, really."

"Did you want a drink?"

"No, but thank you."

She took a half-empty bottle of white wine out of a cupboard and filled a glass that was on the worktop. "Cheers," she said and took a gulp. "So, what were you doing when I rang, it sounded noisy."

"I was in town." Although he wasn't sure it was a good idea, he said, "I saw Drew and we talked about The Mill. He says there's something there - he's dreamt about the place and heard his partner calling his name from there."

Saskia put her wineglass down, her mouth dropping open slightly. "No."

"I've been there too."

"What?"

Michael told her what had happened to him and the bare bones of his conversation with Drew.

"Do you believe what you saw was real?" she asked.

"Yes."

"Did you feel better, about everything, afterwards?"

"No, it scared the shit out of me. Talking with Nicola in the dream was nice, but she wasn't in The Mill."

"What do you suppose it is?"

He shrugged. "I don't know."

"What if it's the place? I've read stuff like this, what if the pain and suffering of those poor people was imprinted onto The Mill?" Animated now, she didn't wait for an answer. "If something's lingering there, maybe that's why we're dreaming of our loved ones. Perhaps we somehow tap into a primal state, where these things can see us and communicate with us?"

"Saskia, if that was the case, surely everyone would know about it?"

"What if they do?" she asked, excitement almost tangible in her voice, "but they're too scared to say?"

"What do you mean?"

Her eyes were bright, as if the conversation was sobering her up rapidly. "If someone told you there was a place where you could access spirits from generations ago, you'd think they were a nutter. But if you're bereaved, talking to others who've suffered a loss, it's different - we won't dismiss it out of hand because we want to believe it. Who wouldn't want to contact their loved one?"

He suddenly realised that he'd said too much, had got her hopes up. "Saskia, what I saw and felt wasn't Nicola. It scared me, I won't be going back there and I don't think you should go, either."

"Why not?" she asked, setting her shoulders like a petulant child.

"Because something's wrong with the place - I felt uncomfortable and Drew won't go anywhere near it." He looked at her, imploring her with his eyes. "Promise me?"

She lifted her wine glass and drained the contents. "Okay," she said, putting the glass firmly on the worktop.

"Good. When we next meet up, we can ask Drew more

questions, alright?"

"Fine," she said, dragging the word out like it was painful to say.

"You sound like it's not."

She looked at him, dipping her head slightly. "You could say that."

"See, I can read you like a book."

She laughed, longer and harder than the comment deserved, as if she needed to release tension. He didn't believe for an instant that she'd paid much attention to his warning and wished he'd kept his mouth shut.

She poured herself another glass full of wine. "So what else shall we talk about?"

He took a bite of his sandwich. "What are your plans for the rest of the weekend?"

She walked across the kitchen to stand next to him and put her plate on the worktop. She rubbed her hand on her T-shirt and he looked away quickly, but not before he saw her breast move freely under the thin material. Why was he looking at her like this?

"No plans. Like I said to you before, there's not a lot in my life now. I go to work, come home and eat, watch TV and have a drink, then I go to bed and it all starts again the next day."

"I'm sorry, I…"

"Why do you keep apologising? It's not your fault that I'm lonely. I'm not proud of it but it's nothing to be ashamed of either, it's just the way things are. I mean, aren't you lonely?"

"Sometimes."

She touched his arm and he jumped slightly. Her fingers were cool and smooth. "You miss her, don't you?"

"Yes," he said, "very much."

"We both miss our lovers."

"Yes," he said, getting more uncomfortable all the time. He knew it was the drink talking but, even so, he knew that he was going to have to leave.

"That's why it's so important to have good friends, who understand what we're going through."

She rested against him, her head on his chest, still stroking his arm. He tried to tell himself it was just a hug but he knew it wasn't

163

and couldn't bring himself to hold her.

"We're in the same place, Michael, we need the same thing."

He looked into her eyes. "But Saskia…"

"Kiss me, Michael."

"I can't."

"Kiss me, please."

"No, Saskia," he said, as gently as he could. "If I do, we'll both regret it as soon as it happens."

"I won't, I promise." She sounded agitated now. "Why won't you kiss me?"

He held her arms as gently as he could whilst letting her know that he was serious and moved her back slightly. "Don't do this. I'll go and we'll forget all about it, okay?"

He let go of her and she stood where he'd put her, her arms by her sides, her head down. "Don't you find me attractive?"

"Yes, you're very attractive, but it'd be wrong."

"How do you know?"

"I don't, but I'm pretty sure. Look, I'll speak to you soon."

He sidestepped around her and walked quickly along the hallway.

"Don't go," Saskia called as he unlatched the door, "please…"

"There's no problem," he called back, "don't worry."

"Please Michael," she said, tears evident in her voice, "don't go."

He closed his eyes, not wanting to leave her upset but fearing that if he stayed, things would get a lot worse.

He closed the door behind him and walked away, convinced that he could still hear her crying.

11

Michael walked out of the estate. A large lorry was wheezing its way up Hospital Hill, trailing a line of traffic, so he stood at the kerb, waiting for a gap so that he could cross.

He tilted his head back and rocked it from side to side, his neck creaking slightly and then looked across the road. Nicola was standing in the shade of a tree, looking at him.

Startled, he stepped off the kerb but a blaring horn forced him back. He waved away the drivers angry hand signals and looked at

164

his wife.

She smiled at him and nodded.

He smiled back, as a shuttle bus went by. He caught glimpses of Nicola through the dirty, tinted windows but when the bus had gone past, she wasn't there any more.

But he knew he'd seen her, that he hadn't just thought it.

Or had he?

Like he'd thought that Saskia was coming onto him. What if that wasn't the case, that she just wanted someone to give her comfort? He couldn't do it, because it would feel like a betrayal of Nicola but also, it would be a betrayal of Saskia too - that had been the wine talking back there and, if he'd done as she wanted, how would that have made either of them feel? How could he sit next to her again and pretend like nothing had happened.

With that thought, a weight seemed to hit him. If he'd been embarrassed by this, how must she be feeling now, having pleaded with him as he rushed to escape? What must be going through her mind? Would she now lock herself away, not wanting to go to the group because of him, spending her days working and going home to an empty house, staring at the same four walls every night before succumbing to some kind of stir crazy madness as the loneliness of her situation dug ever deeper into her mind.

He turned around, rubbing his face. He had to go back and tell her everything was okay, that he'd over-reacted and shouldn't have left like he did.

Michael rapped the knocker, hard, then peered through the lounge window. The room was empty.

"Shit."

Michael knocked with his knuckles, as hard as he could but there was still no response. Maybe she'd seen him walking up the drive, couldn't face him and so was hiding. He rapped again, then knelt down and pushed the letterbox open slightly.

"Saskia? It's Michael. I need to speak to you, about before."

Gravel crunched behind him and he whirled around, expecting to see Saskia but it was a man in his late fifties, with a shock of white hair and a ruddy face.

"Can I help you?"

"I'm looking for Saskia."

"I can see that."

"I was just here."

"I saw you."

"I need to speak to her. Do you know if she's gone out?"

"She left, a few minutes after you did. She looked very upset and I was saying to my wife that maybe we ought to ask her if everything was alright, after all that's happened?"

"Which way did she go?"

"Do I strike you as being the kind of neighbour who stands at the window and watches to see where people go."

"No," said Michael, "of course not. It's just important that I speak to Saskia."

"She looked very upset."

"I think she was."

"Did you do that to her?"

"No," Michael lied, not wanting to get into that discussion, "but I want to try and help make things better."

"Because, you know, if you did upset her…"

"I have to go," said Michael and he strode down the driveway. It wasn't until he reached the pavement that he guessed where he was going to go. Saskia was sad, lonely, upset - there was only one place she would go. He just had to hope he got to The Mill before she did.

By the time he reached the mouth of Mill Lane, the daylight had faded enough that the farmhouse at the crest of the hill was shrouded in a haze of twilight.

It was getting cooler now, the air becoming crisp and he leaned on a wall to get his breath back from jogging, his throat and lungs burning. He hadn't seen Saskia on the way here and pushed on, ignoring the stitch in his side, trying to keep up the same pace on the uneven surface after the farmhouse.

The sound of coughing drifted to him through the trees of Coffers Wood. It was some distance away but seemed to be getting closer. He tried to shut the sound out and keep moving.

"Michael." He knew a voice wasn't really calling his name, that it was just the breeze catching the trees and rustling the dying, brittle leaves on them, but it still chilled him. "Michael, don't go…"

Twigs snapped, out of his line of sight and it sounded as if someone was coming for him behind the hedge. He pushed himself harder, running now, keeping his eyes on the uneven and treacherous path.

He slowed at the bend. The field behind the fence had been stripped bare of whatever it had once nurtured, the earth dark. Lights from the road beyond were visible in snatches, showing through where the ruts in the field were deep enough.

Saskia was still nowhere in sight. He pushed himself harder as the path sloped down. His foot caught the edge of a rut, turning his ankle and he fell over, winding himself. Laying on his back, gasping for breath, his ankle singing with pain, he stared at the tops of the trees that lined the lane and the faint wisps of clouds in the gathering darkness of the sky.

"Fuck," he hissed, his breath coming in short, sharp bursts. Gingerly, he investigated his ankle with his fingertips and, whilst it hurt, it wasn't so painful that he would pass out. He rolled over and got up slowly, holding onto a tree trunk for support.

As his breathing settled he could hear more coughing, carried on the wind whispers and looked up the lane, expecting to see people walking towards him. But no-one was there, he appeared to be all alone.

"Saskia?" he yelled, "are you here?"

There was no response. Was she down here or had he made a massive error of judgement? He didn't know but couldn't turn back now. He tested his leg carefully and it didn't buckle, so he hobbled on as quickly as he could. The lane, bordered by high hedges, was dark and visibility was low. The Mill itself seemed to glow, through the haze of dusk, an almost flickering light that picked at the trees, sending shafts of light out into the darkness around it.

"Saskia!"

The only response was from behind him, sounds of feet on gravel and of legs pushing through crops that weren't there. There was more coughing too, some of it deep and sharp, some of it higher-pitched. He knew it was all in his head, that it couldn't be what he thought it was, but he didn't dare turn around, didn't want to see what was coming, just in case he was wrong.

The gateposts appeared out of the murk and he cut across towards them, hoping he didn't stumble into another pot-hole, his ankle still throbbing. As he left the gravel, it suddenly seemed to get darker – too dark, almost pitch - and then he was in the grounds of The Mill and it was light. There was no discernible source for it, but there seemed to be a glow in the air, as bright as a child's nightlight. To his left, looking back towards Coffers Wood and Gaffney, all was dark. To the right, the lights of Haverton twinkled in the night.

"Saskia," he called, ploughing along the rough path, ignoring the pain in his lungs and ankle. "I know you're here, talk to me!"

As if in response, there was an explosion of white and orange light from the centre of The Mill. Almost blinded, he stopped and rubbed his eyes, white stars dancing across his eyelids. When he opened his eyes again, he could see more - as if the intensity of the night-light had been turned up.

The sounds of people coming towards him, down the lane and across the fields, were getting louder so he pushed on, towards the centre of The Mill.

Something crashed through the bush to his left, breathing heavily and he instinctively jerked to his right, twisting his ankle again and falling against a blackened tree stump. As he clamoured for purchase on the splintered bark, he heard more ragged breath from behind him. To his right, to his left, in front - he seemed to be surrounded by the sound.

He dragged himself forward and rolled into the shallow ditch, the chill from the ribbon of water in the base of it making him gasp. He propped himself up to peer over the edge and was so shocked it took him a moment or two to realise what he was looking at.

There were at least a hundred translucent people in front of him, milling around the foundations, heads down. All of them were wearing formless white gowns, their legs and feet bare.

Through the knot of legs, Michael could see Saskia. She stood out vividly, her red jacket bright against the almost glowing whiteness of the people around her and the dark brick of the foundations.

She was on her belly, her head over the ledge, her feet making a

168

V-shape, her toes together.

"Saskia?" The milling crowd either didn't see him or chose to ignore him. "Saskia?"

She rolled to her right slightly and when he saw her face, he almost didn't recognise her. He'd never known her before John died, had never seen what she looked like when the death of a loved one wasn't draped over her like a distorting cloak, but knew she must have looked like she did now. Her eyes were bright, her cheeks had blossoms of colour, her lips seemed redder and fuller and she was smiling.

"Michael," she said, her voice faint as if she was a lot further away from him than she looked. "It's so beautiful, I wish I'd known about this before."

"About what?"

"Michael, it's wonderful. John is here, my Dad is here, they're all around, can't you see them?"

He glanced around, searching for some familiar faces, but there was nobody in the shambling mass that he recognised.

"It's so good to see him," Saskia said, grinning brightly, "he wants me to join him."

Michael felt something cold surge through his chest. "No, Saskia, stay there."

She frowned briefly, then it was gone. "Why?" she asked, cheerfully.

He didn't know for sure what he meant, just that this was all wrong and he crawled out of the ditch. Some of the shamblers looked down at him now and he could see their faces clearly, their skin tight, eyes dull and lips drawn. He could hear more laboured breathing and coughing now, but nothing else, not even the hum of traffic.

Saskia leaned back over the ledge. "Yes," he heard her say, "of course I will."

The cold feeling in his chest worked its way up, catching his breath in his throat. His hands sank into soft grass and soil, the feet of the shambling mass appearing to tread on him, though he couldn't feel them.

Saskia knelt up, her back to him and slowly got to her feet. She held out her arms, as if ready for an embrace and he saw her eyelids flicker and close.

Deep down, he knew what she was going to do and realised he wouldn't reach her in time. "Saskia, please don't," he called.

She paid him no heed and stepped forward, her left foot seeming to hang in space just beyond the bricks. Her arms reached out and around, as if she thought that someone was standing in front of her and then she leaned forward.

She dropped out of sight quickly and he heard a heavy splash. As quickly as he could, he made his way to the edge of the foundations and laid flat, half on the bricks, half on the grass, looking down.

Saskia was lying on her side, her head twisted awkwardly, her left arm obviously broken and folded beneath her. She was still smiling, even as blood swirled in the shallow water around her head.

He closed his eyes, tears burning them.

"Michael? What's wrong?"

He knew Nicola couldn't be here, knew it in the same way the shambling people couldn't be wandering around the foundations of The Mill, where so many of them had perished in the fire. He knew it with a total and complete conviction and yet he opened his eyes because he wanted to see her.

The Mill was as bright as day now and Nicola was the only person he could see. He wasn't laying on the edge of a foundation any more, but on a concrete floor. Nicola was standing two or three yards in front of him, wearing her favourite blue dress, her feet bare.

She looked wonderful. Her hair was black and glossy, shining in the light and her skin looked tanned and youthful. Her eyes were so green they almost seemed to glow and her lips were so red he just wanted to kiss her immediately.

"Michael, thank goodness."

"Nicola," he said, "I don't understand."

She raised her arms. "Hold me, please."

"I've missed you," he said.

Tears ran down her cheeks, glistening against her skin. "I've missed you so much it's been painful."

He stood up, favouring his ankle.

170

"Give me a cuddle," she said and took a step towards him.

He reached out, wanting to touch her and know she was here, to feel her body against him again. His hand touched her skin and he felt the warmth and then it was through, but that didn't matter.

"I love you, Michael," she said.

Michael reached out to embrace her, felt a brief burst of warmth and then nothing.

"I love you too," he said and then he was falling.

W F T G

Mark West was born in Kettering, Northants in 1969 and now lives back in his hometown of Rothwell, with his wife and young son.

Writing since the age of eight, he discovered the small press in 1998 and has published upwards of 50 stories in various magazines from around the world. His first collection, *Strange Tales*, was published in 2003 by Rainfall Books who are also due to publish his short novel *Conjure* in 2008. His debut novel, *In The Rain With The Dead*, was published by Pendragon Press in 2005, for which he also designed the cover art. He spent most of 2005 and 2006 suffering through a writer's block, but this story helped to break that and he now has several projects 'on the go'. You can visit him online at www.markwest.org.uk

"The Mill is a real place in Rothwell (except that we call it the folly) and when we used to play down there as kids, it was exactly as described (now the foundations are fenced off). I've long thought it would make an ideal location for a story and it occurred to me that it should be about ghosts one night as I was coming home from college in Northampton.

The idea didn't come to much, until I was trying to sort out another project altogether, a revamp of a short story about grief and suddenly everything fell into place (the final piece being a quick look at TB on the Net, which answered a couple of questions I didn't even realise I had) - that other project fell apart then, as I picked the best elements to combine with this.

The story elements came together quite quickly (using real locations throughout helped a lot, giving me a definite sense of place), though it took a while to write and was quite painful in places. But having said that, I don't think I've ever felt better working on something, especially because it pulled me out of a block that had plagued me for the best part of 18 months (and thanks again for asking, Gary!)"

THE NARROWS
Simon Bestwick

Except for the drip of distant water and the soft crying of the children, there is only silence.

Torches pick out brickwork, nearly two hundred years old and holding firm. Hand-made bricks; nineteenth-century workmanship. Thank God for small mercies.

Ochre sludge clotted at the edges of the canal. The damp chill. The black, black water.

Jean's body presses close to mine in the small boat. We're well-wrapped. Thank God we're dressed for the winter; it's cold down here. Another small mercy. Despite that, I can feel her warmth, and something stirs in me; for the first time since I've known her, I think of her in a sexual way, what she might look like naked, and I feel sickened at myself.

Is she thinking of me the same way?

I think of Anya and force myself to concentrate on the tunnel ahead. The torches give us only a few yards visibility. I try not to think of how long they'll last.

We travel on down the canal. And the others follow.

And the only sound is the soft, occasional plash of our paddles in the water.

And the drip of water from the ceiling and the walls.

And the crying, the crying of the children.

My own is silent.

When the sirens wailed, I took charge.

I don't know why that was. I wasn't the newest member of staff, but still far from long-serving. I'd only been at the school about a year.

But I took charge nonetheless.

I knew what the Headmaster, Mr Makin, was thinking. He was in his sixties, due to retire next year. All the year spent caring for others' kids, and none of his own- unless you counted a son who lived in Australia and never called or wrote. All those years, and all he'd wanted was to spend the last few with his wife.

"Ethel…" I heard him breathe in the stricken hush of the staff room.

Jean was as stunned as the rest. She was the Deputy Head and should have said something, but for the first time I could remember, she was at a loss. No-one could think of what to say or do. No-one but me.

I'd never been in serious danger before. Nearly had a car accident three years ago, avoided a collision by a hair – hardly in the same league. But they say a crisis shows you who you really are. I'd always assumed I'd fall short, feared I'd be weak or frightened.

But, come the moment, I wasn't. Even when Makin said his wife's name and sent Anya's face fluttering round my head like a moth round a light, I made it go away. She worked in the city centre; with a terrible coldness I realised there was nothing I could do for her.

I wish I'd at least called her on her mobile, said I loved her, said goodbye – but, no, I can't see that happening, can you? Switchboards have to be manned, after all. I wonder if anyone kept on mechanically doing their duty as the last few minutes ticked by.

Four minutes. That was all we had.

That endless moment broke and I was on my feet.

"The kids," I said. "Jean?"

She blinked at me. Outside, the playground had fallen silent.

"Get in the playground," I said. "Any kids live in the next couple of streets, get home. Otherwise, get them down the basement."

174

"Basement?" She blinked again. It was a filthy place, not even used for storage anymore.

"Best chance we've got." I clapped my hands. "Come on! Everyone! Go! Go!"

Where did it come from, the sudden authority? I ask myself again and again, and have no clue. And then I stop asking, because I mustn't. The ball is rolling now, and I have to stay like this. Responsibility. It's like a millstone round your neck.

The staff ran out of the room. Except old Makin. He just sat there, blinking, old eyes full of tears.

I knew what I had to do. I reached across and touched his arm. "George?"

He stared at me.

"Go home, George. Be with your wife."

"I…" He wanted to, of course, but duty pulled him the other way. I absolved him.

"We'll be fine, sir," I said. "Just go. You deserve to…" I stopped.

He nodded once, rose. "Thank you, Paul," was all he said. His head was down and he couldn't look at me, but as he left the room, he began to run, surprisingly fast for a man his age.

A moment later, I was running too.

The tunnel, and the tunnel, and the tunnel. Endless, the brick arch, low above our heads, passing by. Coming out of darkness, yard by yard, coming towards us, passing overhead and back into the dark again.

The same, and the same, and the same. Again, and again, and again.

"Paul?" Jean's voice is a whisper. Her hand on my arm. "Where are we going?"

"I don't know," I say, and then remember I have to. I have to know something. "Not yet." I think. "There'll be a gallery soon, or a landing stage. Or something."

"What then?"

How should I know? I want to scream. But of course I can't. "We'll have to see, Jean. Might be fish here." I wouldn't bet on it, though. Rats in the tunnels? Did you get them down old coal mines? You get them everywhere, surely?

Worry about food later, I think to myself. Once you're underground and safe somewhere.

Safe? Where is safe?

I stop thinking that way. It may all be pointless, just delaying the inevitable, but what am I supposed to do? Just stop and wait to die, when the poison seeps down here into the mine and the canal? No. I can't. As much for me as anyone else. If I stop, you see, I'll think of Anya. And I mustn't. I mustn't do that.

Anya was... well, Anya was my girlfriend, of course. You must have worked that out for yourselves. Except that doesn't cover it. *Girlfriend* always sounds so casual, so teenage. And it wasn't like that.

We weren't married or engaged. Hadn't even talked about it. Weren't even living together, although we *had* talked about that. Just weren't sure where we'd live. Her poky flat, my poky flat, or somewhere new.

I first saw her in a bar in the city centre, near where she worked – I went over to her, to talk to her, of course, but I never thought I stood a chance. She was blonde, with blue eyes, a classic beauty. But she liked me. More than 'liked' as it turned out.

You see loads like that from the old Eastern Bloc countries. God knows why. I once joked that if Polish women looked like her, it was no wonder they kept getting invaded. She whacked me round the head with a pillow as I recall. But she was laughing when she did it.

She wasn't a dumb blonde. She was Polish, a student. A *mature* student, I should add. At twenty-eight, two years older than me. And me a teacher. She already had a degree, taken back in Poland. English Lit. She could hold her own in any discussion about poetry. Which was good. We had lots to talk about. Keats and John Donne, Wilfred Owen (her favourite) and R.S. Thomas (mine). She was taking a Business Studies degree at Manchester Uni.

We'd been together about a year. Around the same time, give or take, as I got the teaching post at the school. A good little school, a small suburb with small classes, a plum job. I had that and Anya. I was so lucky. So bloody lucky.

I ought to have known it couldn't last.

She would've been working. She was in her final year, had two or three days free each week, so she'd taken an office job to pay the bills. Right in the city centre. Practically at Ground Zero, I'm guessing. She wouldn't have stood a chance.

I tell myself it must have been quick.

The caretaker, Mr Rutter, forced the basement door open, then stumbled away. Never saw him again. Well, I did, but I wouldn't have recognised him if not for his shoes. Old brown brogues, they were. He never wore anything else. All that was left intact of him.

He stumbled away. I have no idea where he thought he was going. I had other things to worry about.

We herded the kids down the stairs and into the basement, slammed doors shut behind us.

"Lie down," I shouted over the scared babble, then shouted it again, louder. "Lie down. Everybody. Shut your eyes. Put your hands over your ears and open your mouths." As far as I remembered, that was how you prepared yourself for the blast. I'd seen it in an old war movie, somewhere.

"Paul-" Jean's face was scared. She was about ten years older than me, competent and attractive, but didn't look much older than the kids, now. I wondered what I looked like.

"Yeah."

"What are we going to do?" she asked.

"Lie down," I told her, clambering to the floor myself. "And if we-"

That was when the bomb hit.

Brilliant light blazed, outlining the door at the top of the stairs. I looked away fast. Someone screamed – they hadn't, not in time.

A heat equal to that of the sun was consuming – had consumed – the centre of Manchester. The CIS tower, the Arndale Centre, the Lowry Hotel – all gone.

And Anya. Among all the rest, Anya too.

Then there was a distant rumbling. The sound was coming. The sound and the blast.

"Hands over your ears! Mouths open! Shut your eyes!"

And then, as I followed my own advice, the blast wave struck the school.

I've almost forgotten I'm in a tunnel. It's like watching a visual effect, a bit like one of those fractals you get on a computer, or the light effects a computer screen can create if you play a CD on it.

Got on a computer. The light effects a screen *created*. If you *played* a CD. It's all past tense now. I have to get used to the idea. All past tense.

Someone once asked Einstein, what would be the weapons of the Third World War? He said he didn't know. But that the weapons of the Fourth World War would be stones and clubs.

If anyone's left in a hundred years, and they read an account of all this – will they even understand what I'm talking about? So many reference points I took for granted, and they'll mean nothing to whoever – whatever? – survives, landmarks and signposts of a world long gone.

Christ, in a hundred years, will they still even *read*?

We used to bandy that one round the staff room, but then we were worried about literacy declining because the kids'd rather play on their Playstations and cruise porn sites on the internet. Reading? Who needs it if you can get rich and famous making a dick of yourself on a reality TV show?

Old Byerscough, the History master – he said it was capitalism's final and cleverest game to keep the working class in its place. Time was, you couldn't get an education if you were poor. Now? Now, they convince you education's for nancy-boys. Books? Being clever? Bollocks to that. Just get pissed or E'd up and have fun. And you think that's the best way, when you're just being kept happy and docile and stupid.

Past tense again. Byerscough too. He was close to retirement as well, and lived nearby, just like Makin, but he never thought about leaving. His wife had died a few years before. He died at the school. Not in the blast but after, when –

178

"Paul! Paul, wake up!"

Anya was shaking me. I must've slept through the alarm. But she'd be the one running late, wouldn't she? She had to get up before me. Neither of us could afford a place in the village where the school was, but I lived closer to it than to the city.

"Paul!" Desperation, terror. I smelt smoke. Not the alarm. A fire. The house was burning.

"Paul!" Not Anya's voice. Who was she? The bomb'd set the house on fire.

The Bomb. And I remember where I was, and Anya-

"Paul!"

"Alright!" I sat up. My brain seemed to slosh around in my skull, water in a bowl. Fingers gripped my shoulders. Jean.

I could see light through the ceiling. The sky glowed. Sunset already? No, a fire.

Fire.

The school was gone. And the ceiling with it. Well, mostly. Some had blown away. The rest had fallen into the basement. And was burning. I was lucky; I'd been under the bit that'd blown away.

The air was full of screams. Kids and staff, trapped and burning.

And the sky –

I knew if I looked, I'd see the mushroom cloud, over the city, full of ashes and dust. Some of those ashes would be Anya's. And in a few minutes, she'd rain down on me.

And she'd be bringing the bomb with her.

"Everybody out!" I shouted. Things cracked and crackled all around me. And screamed.

We got up the stairs. Byerscough stopped at the top, then turned back, starting back down.

"Alf!" I shouted. "What're you-"

He turned wild eyes on me. "There's kids still down there, man!"

And he ran back down, even though the smoke was billowing and choking.

He stumbled back up, a few seconds later, smoke-grimed, red-eyed, coughing and choking, one of the girls in his arms. He set her down, ran back into the smoke. He never came back out.

Jean knelt by the little girl. When she looked up, she was crying.

179

She shook her head.

"What do we do?" she said. "Oh God, what do we do now?"

Three of the staff were still alive: me, Jean and Frank Emerson, the Physics teacher. About a dozen kids. They were all looking at me.

"I've got an idea," I said.

The tunnel changes at last. A fork. The water laps around a big central column. The canal, going off in two directions. "Which way now?" Jean whispers.

Have to choose. Which way now? Have to pick. But what leads where? Where does each go? Which is better? Safer? Is there meaning to either word now?

"That way," I say, pointing right.

So we veer to the right. It only occurs to me later that veering to the right was what got us into this mess in the first place.

Minutes pass. I haven't looked at my watch in – not since before the bomb fell. Does it have any meaning anymore, anyway?

Then one of the kids screams.

"What is it?" I shout, trying to keep panic out of my own voice.

It's one of the boys, one of the younger ones. "A monster," he shouts. "A monster in the water."

I flick the torch-beam over the black surface. "There's nothing there."

"There *was*, Mr Forrester, sir. There *was*."

What did it look like? I want to ask. But stop myself in time. "It's alright," I tell him. "It's OK. Being down here, it – it plays tricks on your mind. Don't worry about it." *Don't worry about it*, that has to rank as the most fatuous remark of the day.

The kids are mumbling amongst themselves. From the boy who cried out, I make out disjointed words: *grinning, claws, teeth.*

A chill up my back, and it's not just being down here. No. The boy's hallucinating. Who can blame him? I'm surprised I'm not. Will I sleep later? And will I dream? God, please not.

"Let's keep going," I say.

We stumbled through the remains of the school. Passed what was left of Mr Rutter on the way. "Don't look," I told the kids. Bile

180

crept into my throat. The smell of roast, charred pork.

To get where we were going, we had to pass the Physics lab. It was, for God knows what reason, the only part of the building left more or less intact. Frank Emerson let out of a shout. "Wait up!" he yelled, and dashed into the lab.

"Frank!" I yelled. "We haven't time-"

"Trust me." He forced the store room door open and came out again seconds later, clutching what looked like a metal box with a microphone attached.

"What?"

He clicked the 'microphone' on and there was a soft crackling, ticking sound. "Geiger counter," he said.

I was about to ask where that'd come from – not exactly standard-issue in schools these days – but it didn't matter. Never look a gift horse in the mouth and so on. "You're a genius," I said. "Come on."

Worsley village – now it's a posh, desirable residence sort of place (*was, then*, past tense once more, Mr Forrester) but in the Industrial Revolution it'd've been anything but. The Bridgewater and Liverpool/Manchester canals all met here, and the whole area was a big coalfield, bringing up about 10,000 tons of coal a day.

Why do I mention this?

Because of the Delph, where we were heading.

There was next to nothing left above ground. The houses were gone, and where most of them had been there was only fire. There was nowhere to hide from the dust that would soon be falling.

It might already be too late, of course. I'd been to the Imperial War Museum up at Salford Quays the year before; one of the exhibits had been an atom bomb. Deactivated, I presumed. Beside it had been a diagram, a sequence of concentric circles marking out distances from the blast, and a table showing what would happen within them.

Nothing would be left for a mile or so around the blast site. Anya was dust, again. But where Worsley was:

All those not killed by the blast would be dead of radiation poisoning within hours.

181

Where we dead already? How long would be a fatal exposure? I didn't know, but I couldn't just stop, couldn't just quit. Easy to do so; easy to stop and spend the last of my time railing at the sky and the mad, sick bastards who'd done this to us. The politicians on both sides...

I'd grown up in the shadow of the Cold War; when it'd ended, I'd been in my teens, but I knew enough by then to have felt some of the dread that my parents – who would also be dead now – must've spent most of their adulthood under. And a weight had lifted. One less worry. Or so I'd thought.

Now...

Beside the Delph was a shed, belonging to the local boating club. We smashed the doors down. Inside, boats. Dinghies and open-topped canoes. And paddles. We took what we needed.

And torches, too. We were lucky. There were half a dozen, and a box or two of batteries. We took them as well, and then scrabbled over the fences, lifting boats and children, and headed down into the Delph.

'Delph' simply means a delved place. Delved; dug. An old sandstone quarry, half-filled with orangey-coloured water. The canals round Worsley are full of it – iron oxides from all the heavy industry.

If you go into the Delph, you'll find a hole, a tunnel entrance. Gated up. We forced the lock – me, Jean and Frank Emerson, chest-deep in that water. And then we climbed into the boats and paddled through, into the dark.

You see, the Delph is an entrance, to one of the biggest engineering feats of the Industrial Revolution.

I said the whole area had been a big coalfield. The coal had to be transported. And what was the main means of transport in those days?

Canals.

Entered, via the Delph, are forty-six miles of underground canal. Extending down on four levels, deep and deep and deep. To the galleries of the mines.

That was where we were headed. Deep underground, the one safe place I could think of.

If you're so clever, tell me where else we could have gone.

I knew the Delph had been closed off because of carbon monoxide seeping up from the old mines. I could only hope it'd dispersed by now. But even if it hadn't, it beat radiation sickness. Carbon monoxide, you got groggy, disorientated, queasy, yes, but in the end you just drifted off. That had to be better than the alternative.

And so we paddled, and soon the light died and we used one of the torches to destroy a tiny portion of the dark ahead, so we could see where the hell we were going.

I tried looking at my watch a moment ago. Blank. Of course. It was a digital. EMP: electromagnetic pulse from the blast. Wiped it out. Thank God the Geiger counter still works. I wonder if anyone here has an analogue watch. Only chance of keeping track. Mobile phones might have clocks but they'll have likely gone the same way as the digital watches.

There's no way of gauging the time. The same unending tunnel, after the brief variation of the fork, in unending repetition. It just goes on. Perhaps it'll be like this forever. Perhaps we're all already dead. Perhaps we died in the school, or on the way to the Delph, or at some point on this journey and this is all the last hallucinatory moment of dying, stretching on out forever...

No good thinking that way. I force myself to keep paddling. My hands are numb. The damp chill of the air, a nip at first, but like a swarm of soldier ants eating through to the bone bite by tiny bite.

The air is stale and foul. An olfactory memory skitters past; the summer just gone, walking in a meadow, the smell of fresh-cut grass, flowers breathing perfume into air, soft, clean, clear air.

Treasure that memory, Paul. You aren't likely to have another like it.

Cold. The air stinks. My teeth have begun to chatter. What it must be like for the children, back in the smaller boats, I don't like to think. Is Frank Emerson alright back there? I ought to shout to him but I can't seem to. My jaw won't let me, refuses to let me waste the energy.

"Paul?" It's Jean. She's been crying. So have I, silently. I can feel the burn of the dried salt on my cheeks. Anya.

I'm wandering, vague, keep greying out. Radiation sickness? Or carbon monoxide? Or just going cold and tired? Be ironic that, if it's hypothermia and exhaustion that finishes the job. Maybe a kind of bleak triumph there, a bitter laugh at the death that thought it'd have us.

"Paul?" Jean again. Her voice is cracked. She's been thinking about her husband, must've been with all this time on our hands, just paddling – well, the endless tunnel can sort of hypnotise you. Better if it does, in a way. If not, your mind begins to wander. I'd've been thinking about Anya so, so much if not for that lucky effect. But Jean-

I met her husband once. A small, quiet man, balding and moustached. Bespectacled. Smoked a pipe. Scottish, like her. Glaswegian, or was he from Edinburgh? Sipped a Britvic orange in the pub at the staff do last Christmas while Jean got tipsy on Dubonnet. Did he work? From home, I think she said. What was he? An accountant, I think. They lived in the village. His – their – house was.

Can't remember. Burned to ashes anyway. Doubt he'd've had a chance. But at least, with Anya, I can be sure she's dead. Horrible, how easy you can accept that, the fact that the person you love the most in the world is gone. Oh, my heart's been ripped out of my chest. Well, there it is. There you go. Never mind.

Except I *do* mind, but what to do? It's keep going or stop and die. Some instinct or drive, something in me, won't just let me lie down and quit. It's not the responsibility for the kids that keeps me going. That's getting it backwards. *That's* why I seized control when the sirens went. It was my excuse for living. Anya would have approved.

"Just because I'm dead, Paul, doesn't mean you can give up."

No ma'am. I know that, darling.

"Keep going. We'll be together again one day."

Yeah, right. Now I *know* that's my imagination. Anya would never have said anything so trite, so twee, not even to motivate me. She'd been raised a Catholic, but lapsed long ago.

She was the most honest person I knew. *When you're dead,* she'd

184

told me bluntly, once, *you're dead, that's it. You're a match that flares in the dark. You burn a few seconds and then you go out.* A little poetic, but it was the small hours of one morning and we'd been smashed on bisongrass vodka and a couple of joints. In vodka veritas. *You have seconds in the dark. Out of the dark and back into it. You have to use it while you can. Don't waste it.*

It would be nice to think of my survival as my tribute to Anya, that I'm doing it for her, but-

"Paul?"

God *damnit.* I turn to Jean. "What?" My voice is gravel.

Her teeth are chattering too. Hard to tell in the gloomy back-spill of light from the torch, but I think her lips are bluing from the cold.

"We can't keep going much longer," she whispers. "Look at us. We're nearly all in. The kids must be finished. I don't know how the keep going."

"Yeah. I know."

"We're gonna have to stop soon."

"I know." But where? That's the big question, isn't it?

I'm about to confess I have nothing left, no ideas, when I become aware of something. A current in the sluggish water, pulling the boat sideways.

"What-"

I flash the torch. There's a sound too, a new one – I've missed it from being so lulled by the repetitive journey. It's water, rushing. I flick the torch-beam ahead. It skates along the wall on the left, and then plunges through into darkness.

"What's th-?"

Something's punched a hole in the tunnel wall, or it's caved in. What could do that? I don't know. But water's draining through the hole, pouring through.

We draw level, and I use an oar to brace us, stop us sliding through till I know.

I shine the torch through the hole.

Water slides down in a low black gleaming slope, into a deep pool – no, not a pool, a small *lake*, on the floor of a great big fucking cavern.

I let out a shout. There are yells down the tunnel; the kids, startled.

"Paul," says Jean.

"Sorry." I shine the beam around. A big chamber. A natural cavern. A high ceiling. Stalactites. Stalagmites. And around the pool, a shore of crumbled stone. Dry land. A place to rest.

"Is it safe?" asks Jean.

I laugh. "God knows," I tell her. "What's safe?" I turn back to the others. "Through here," I call.

We pull the boats onto the blessed dry land and stumble on up, legs weak and shaky. A couple of the younger kids, deathly tired, have to be carried ashore.

We sit and take stock. Frank Emerson stares at the clinker on the ground and grubs through it, picks up a lump of something black and brittle. A grin spreads across his cadaverous face; not a pleasant sight.

"What?" I ask.

He grins wider. "Coal!"

Of course. We grub together a heap of it. Thank God for my lighter. Anya used to nag me about my smoking, but thank God for it now.

(What'll we do, I wonder, when its fuel is all gone?)

The fire smoulders into life and we switch off the torches as a little puddle of heat and light spreads and gathers round.

We're all tired. Time to sleep. No strength to consider what other dangers there might be down here. If we don't wake up, so be it. We're too tired to care now, after all we've been through.

We have no blankets. I'm shivering – of course, we all were standing in that water – God, so cold. How have I held out this long? I'm lucky to still be alive. Thank God for the coal heat.

We huddle together for the warmth as we sleep. Jean on one side of me, one of the younger boys on the other. Yesterday I'd've run a mile before being in this kind of proximity to one of the kids. Inappropriate contact. Now it's irrelevant; now it's about survival.

Anya, I think, and then, thank God, I drift off to sleep before I can think anymore.

I dream of fire. A room of fire. In the middle of it, a table. Anya sips coffee there, putting another cup in front of me.

"Thanks," I say.

"It's alright."

"No, I mean it. 'Specially with you being dead and all."

She snorts and flaps a hand, the way she always used to when she thought I was being silly. She keeps the left side of her face turned to me. The right side is eyeless and black, charcoal, the skull beneath half-bared. Grins at me whenever she turns without thinking. "Are you alright, Paul?"

"I think so. Relatively speaking."

"Relatively speaking."

"Well, you're dead."

"Don't go on about it."

"And the world's ended."

"Don't be so dramatic. The world's still there. It's just the people that are gone."

"Of course. I forgot."

"Don't worry about it. You've a lot on your plate right now. Just be careful."

"Of what?"

"Of everything, Paul." Her hair catches fire, her clothes. I don't. I remain unscathed, just watching as the flames crawl over her and the rest of her face blackens and her one blue eye melts and trickles down her charcoal cheek like a tear. "Of everything."

I wake up. Jean's gone. Sound nearby.

I rise, looking round. Jean squats nearby, gathering up more coal. The fire's almost dead, smouldering. How can I see down here? The darkness should be total. Then I see dull green patches of luminescence smeared on the rock. "What's that?"

"Fungus of some kind, I should think." She isn't shocked by my sudden whisper. She's almost glacially calm. "Are you alright?"

My joints are a little creaky and I've a banging headache, but otherwise I feel fine. "Just hungry. And thirsty."

"You think that water's safe to drink?"

187

"We may have to chance it. We could try boiling it."

"Aye." She heaps coal on the embers of the fire, watches it start to smoulder. "Alan probably looks like that now."

"Alan?" I realise she means her husband.

"Aye. He has to be, doesn't he? I mean, no way he could've survived."

I don't know if that's true as yet – he might've got into the cellar, if she had one. I don't know if he did, and it doesn't matter. Things like that she doesn't need or want to hear. "No," I tell her, "no way."

"Anya worked in the city centre, didn't she?"

"Yes. She wouldn't have had a chance either."

"No." She sits beside me, huddles close, takes my hand. Is it just warmth she wants, companionship? I can't see myself having anything else to give, but I seem to – I feel my body stirring in her presence. It never has before today. But we never so narrowly escaped death, losing so much in the process, before.

It might be good for us, or it might not. I can't tell and I won't risk it. Not so soon. I squeeze her hand, and when she puts the other on my knee I gently but firmly remove it, but don't let it go.

Her sigh is a warm breath in my ear. "OK," she says. "For now."

We settle back down to sleep once more.

This time I don't dream.

The next – day? – God knows. There is neither time nor light down here, save the light we make. But I have to call it something. The next day, we explore the cavern.

Big, roomy. Plenty of coal, big chunks of it in the walls. We can hack bits loose with rocks. We won't freeze. We might starve or die of thirst, but we won't freeze.

Thank God, in one of the boats, someone had stored a kettle. I don't know what for. One more piece of luck, like the torches and the Geiger counter and the whole ceiling of the basement not falling in on us. Blind chance, saving us all.

Well, the fifteen of us, anyway.

Me, Jean and Frank Emerson are the only adults. The rest: nine boys, six girls. Most of the kids are the older ones, between fourteen and sixteen years of age. Two ten year old boys, one nine year old girl. The older kids- stronger, more grown-up, more independent. They were the ones who fought their way out of the basement. The younger ones – scared, huddled, either frozen where they were or running around in hopeless panic – never had a chance. All the little ones... I think of Alf Byerscough going back down there, never coming back. There was a brave man. A hero.

And dead. Better a live coward... or is it? Look where it's got me: a hole in the ground. But still alive.

Frank heats water in the kettle, lets the steam collect in the upturned hull of a boat, angled so it trickles down and collects in a corner. There's a tin cup too. A small water ration for everybody.

Food is a more pressing concern, at least until one of the younger boys yells and points at the water – the same one thought he saw a man in the canal yesterday. But he's seen something this time, something big and white and floundering. A fish, a big one. I whack the water hard with an oar – it flops to the surface, stunned.

"Bream," pronounces Frank, who used to go fishing. It's white and eyeless. "They tend to go for muddy water."

Muddy isn't the word for this water, but I'm grateful nonetheless. It's a big fish, but between fifteen people it doesn't go far. We need more.

"There might be rats," says one of the boys. Jeff Tomlinson. Sporty, practical, goes camping a lot, reads books on wilderness survival. Should've known he'd make it. "We could eat them."

"If we can catch them," says Frank.

"Maybe the rats'll be blind too," says Jeff.

"Have hearing like a bat."

I wonder if there'll be any of those down here too.

"Mr Forrester." It's one of the girls. Jane Routledge. She's at the end of the cavern, pointing.

"Look at this, sir." She's a scarily calm girl. A kind of brittle shock, a shell around her.

At the end of the cavern, the water branches off down channels, streams disappearing into holes in the walls. Small narrow caves, winding. Looking round I see others in the walls. Some are

189

draining off the water. Others are dry, dusty. Off into the mine. Or maybe not. Was this cavern part of the mine? I doubt it somehow.

I venture a few feet into the nearest cave. Not far. Something about it makes my scalp prickle. I touch the walls. They feel – *ribbed*. These are not natural. These have been dug.

I say nothing about it, but something about the caves draws the kids.

By what I guess to be the end of the day, they're going into them, but not far, never out of sight of the main cavern, on my instructions. Last thing we need is any of them getting lost.

Also, by the end of the day, the caves have been given a name.

The children call them the Narrows.

"Like a big worm's been through them," Jean whispers. "Isn't it?"

I give her hand a squeeze. "Don't."

We're at the far end of the cavern. It's late, as we reckon time now. The children and Frank are asleep around the dying fire. Jean and I... we're warm enough and restless enough to pull away. I shine a torch down one of the narrows. It glances off the ribbed, irregular stone. I can see about ten yards down it, before it bends right and is lost to view.

"They're weird, aren't they," she whispers.

"Yeah." We move to the neighbouring entrance. "The kids seem to like them, though. Gives 'em something to occupy themselves with."

"Aye, well. Just don't let them go playing in it. Bloody easy to get lost or stuck, place like this."

"Mm." I shine the torch again, then frown. "Hang on."

"What?"

"Look." I cross back to the first cave. "See that?"

"Bends right. Aye. So?"

"Look." I step to the right and shine the torch down its neighbour. "See?"

The neighbouring tunnel extends in a straight line for longer than the first – fifteen, twenty yards, easily – before veering off and up.

190

Its walls are smooth and unbroken, right the way through.

"That can't be," says Jean.

"I know."

We cross back to the first one and look again. "Must be a dead end," Jean says.

"Mm. Hang on." I venture down the tunnel, shining the light.

"Paul!" she hisses.

"It's okay. I'll be right back. Just..."

I trail off; I've reached the bend in the first narrow. No dead end; the torch picks out another long low tunnel, stretching away from me.

I can't see a break in its walls either. But there must be. Some trick of light and shadow the composition of the walls lends itself to somehow. Must be. An optical illusion that makes the entrance invisible.

"Paul?"

"There's a tunnel," I say. "It must... Jean?"

"Aye?"

"Go to that next narrow," I say. "Just hang about there."

"But –"

"Just try it."

Muttering, she does. I start down the cave, stooped, flashing the torch from side to side. This narrow and the second are about five yards apart, if that. A yard; that's about a pace for me. I count my steps: one, two, three, four... "Jean?"

"Paul?" Her voice is faint.

"Jean?" I shout a little. "Can you hear me?"

"Where are you?"

I shine the torch around. The walls are unbroken. I flash the beam ahead. "Can you see that?"

"See what?"

"The torch light. Is it coming through into your narrow?"

"No, it bloody isn't, Paul, and it's bloody dark out here. Will you come back now, please?"

"Okay." I feel a beading film of sweat on my forehead. The narrow looks straight and level but it must go under or over the neighbouring one. It's the only explanation.

I backtrack to the bend in the narrow. Shine the torch around-
This isn't right.

I left a long straight tunnel, with the main cavern at the end to my left, but where the main cavern and Jean ought to be there's just a flat wall of black and yellow stone, with tunnels branching left and right. And to my right, where there was a dead end, the narrow now extends on for as far as I can see and there are very visible openings in it – two on the left and one on the right – where other narrows branch off.

Panic squirms low down in my belly. I turn back towards the T-junction. "Jean?" I shout, and I can't quite keep my voice level.

"Paul?"

It's coming from behind me, down the mysteriously extended narrow. "Jean!"

"What?" She sounds pissed off. "Where are you?"

Good question. "Jean, just keep shouting me, alright? I'm sort of – lost here."

"Lost? How the hell are you-"

"Jean, just do it!" I yell. First time I've really lost it since we got down here. Since the bomb, in fact.

"Okay. Okay. Can you hear me?"

"Yes, just about. Keep talking."

"Talking? More like shouting."

"Just keep it up."

I head towards her voice. My hand is shaking on the torch.

"What should I say?"

"Anything. Sing if you want."

"Sing? I canna sing for toffee."

"It doesn't have to be tuneful."

She breaks into a halting rendition of *Scotland The Brave*. I can see what she meant. At least it's not *You Canna Shove Yer Granny Aff The Bus*. Small mercies again.

It rings in the narrow. I pass the first of the entrances on my left. When I reach the second, I realise her singing's coming from there.

There's no guarantee that sound's a reliable indicator of location, as everything else I'd normally rely on has gone screwy, but what else can I do. I start down this new narrow. It slopes steeply upward, but I follow it.

The singing gets louder. Water splashes around my ankles. Something white and blind wriggles past on its way down. I keep on climbing. The water flowing down this narrow is fast and cold and quite deep. Why didn't any of it spill out into the other, longer one I've left behind?

The singing stops. "Jean?" I shout.

"Alright, alright." I hear her coughing. Then she starts again, the *Mingulay Boat Song* this time.

"Heel ya ho, boys, let her go, boys, sailing homewards to Mingulay..."

Where is Mingulay anyway? The Hebrides? Orkneys? Shetlands? I'm pretty sure it's an island of some kind anyway.

The singing's good and loud, at least. The narrow steepens till it's almost vertical. I clamp the torch between my teeth and use my hands to climb.

At last, I reach the top. Been climbing too long. Flat floor, water gushing across it, and I can hear Jean's voice, loud and clear, close-to. I look up; the narrow has a mouth and water glistens beyond it. It opens out. I hear voices, too.

Someone shouts as the beam of my torch flashes from the narrow-mouth and I stumble out, almost falling headlong into the lake. Across the water on the bank, Jean and Frank and the others spin from the mouth of the narrow I entered and stare at me dumbfounded.

"No-one goes in there," I say later, huddled round a fresh fire some way from the circle of children, sharing its warmth with Jean and Frank. "No-one."

Frank looks at me doubtfully. "Paul, I know you've had a shock, but-"

"No buts," I say. "I didn't imagine what happened in there."

"Are you sure?" he asks gently.

I glare at him. "Frank –"

"Paul, all I'm saying is we've all been through a hell of a lot. You especially. You've been responsible for all of us. It'd be unbelievable if you didn't feel the strain somehow. And you have to keep everything so bottled up and reined in, it's not surprising if-"

193

"Are you a psychoanalyst now?" I know I'm overreacting, taking it out on Frank, but I can't stop myself. Luckily he seems to understand that too.

"No, Paul, I'm not. All I'm trying to say is this: stress, lack of sleep, grief, trauma, all those things, they can cause you too hallucinate. As can simply being underground, in the dark, in tunnels. I've been caving once or twice. You'd be surprised what... look. All I mean is this. What you saw down there is physically impossible. Right?"

"I know that." I rub my face. "But I saw it."

"I'm not questioning that." I look up. "All I'm questioning is that it was *objectively real*. Be honest. What's the most likely explanation? Either the tunnels really did shift and change around like you say, or you experienced a hallucination brought on by your emotional state and the conditions down here. And I don't doubt the narrows themselves could be disorientating too, once you got out of sight of the main cavern. You obviously lost your bearings and were lucky to find your way out again. But out of those two explanations, which makes more sense? Which is more probable? That's all I'm saying."

I bow my head. I have to admit he's right on that one. But that's what *really* frightens me. Because if you can't trust your own senses, the evidence of your own eyes, what *can* you trust?

In the cold light of day... I've had the occasional weird experience in my time, and most could be put down to hallucinations, like Frank says about this, or something more mundane. But it helps when you can get away from the place where you saw the weird thing or heard the weird sounds and go somewhere normal, four-square, the land of Starbucks and McDonalds, busy city streets and cars, brand names and day-jobs. *The cold light of day.*

Except that it might still be cold back up there – but light? I think of all the predictions I heard and read: the nuclear winter, the great clouds of smoke and ash blotting out the sun and plunging the world into a new Ice Age. And even if we could get back up there, even forgetting that the radiation would kill us in hours, the world of Starbucks and McDonalds, busy city streets and brand names – it's all gone. The day job, the worries about bills and rent and mortgages, shopping at Morrisons or the local market – *it's all gone*. There *is* no normal any more. The world is what's around us now, wherever we're clinging on to life a bit longer. The world is this cave. And reality... *what's* reality? Frank's right. We can't trust what we hear or see – with everything we've been through, it'd be a miracle if we didn't see or hear things that weren't there. And it isn't safe to be here. Nowhere is, anymore.

Panic wells up; I fight it down. I know that if I give into it once, that'll be it. Nothing will ever make sense anymore and I'll either curl up catatonic or run screaming into the water till I drown to escape the knowledge, or not believe a real danger till it kills me or run to my death from an imaginary one.

So I push it down and instead I let myself realise the magnitude of our loss. Not just Anya, but Poland is gone. Not just the school, the village, Manchester and Salford, but Britain itself in any meaningful sense. America, too? Or – what if the bombs only fell on Manchester? If there weren't any others? It's impossible to say. And impossible to believe.

It's all gone. Names fly past, already robbed of meaning: Adidas, Reebok, Microsoft, BBC, ITV, Sky TV, Sony – all the brand names, all the twenty-first Century totems. They mean nothing now. Will mean nothing to anybody till whatever archaeologists of the future there might be dig them up and mount them in museums, try to decipher what they meant to us.

I can't get a handle on it. Only think of Anya, imagine her there in front of me. And there she is, sat beside me, whole and unharmed, unmarked. Not burnt up like in my dream, but the Anya I kissed goodbye the morning before the bomb fell. There are now four of us round the fire: me, Jean, Frank and Anya. Jean holds my left hand, Anya my right. She looks at Jean's hand on mine, then up at me, raises an eyebrow. I pull my hand free of Jean's, embarrassed, caught out, almost caught cheating.

"Paul?"

I blink, and Anya's gone. But I can still feel the warmth of her hand where it held mine. Jean. Jean drove her away. I turn to shout at her, then stop myself. She was never there. Never here. It wasn't real, however real it was.

195

"Paul, are you okay?"

"Yes." I nod, but I'm not. God, how could I be? Come that close to raving and shouting over *something that wasn't there*. I'm crazy. Or going crazy. But what's crazy? What's not? What's mad and what isn't? How much more food will we find down here? And if there isn't enough to eat – how long before we start eyeing each other like that? Before we're killing each other, smashing each other's heads in with lumps of rock, roasting pieces of each other in our coal fires?

I try not to think about it, but I can't stop. What criteria will we use, to choose who lives or dies? The smaller children are of least use. Will we eat them first? But there's less meat on a nine-year-old kid than on a grown man or woman. Will it be the biggest of us, to go the furthest, last the longest, before we have to do it again? Me? Frank? Jean? Or are we of more value? In what way? We've as little idea as anyone else of what to do next. Hell, Jeff Tomlinson probably has more idea. And we're adults, we're authority, the powers that be, as far as the kids are concerned, who killed Mum and Dad and their friends and brought them down here to this. How long will the shreds and tatters of our authority as teachers last? How long before they realise there are more of them than there are of us and like any who hold power, we only do so because they allow it? I see myself, my torso and an arm, all that's left, lying by the fire, flies crawling across my glazed eyes, the gnawed bones of the rest of me in the embers of the fire. Kids' famished faces, eager and greedy and animal, smeared with my blood and grease.

When are you insane? When you think about it? When you imagine it? Plan it? Or when you do it? Or is it insanity, will it be when it comes, or will be only necessity, need, do or die? Will the mad ones be the ones who won't do it, clinging to an outmoded way, as mad in this time as worshipping the Sun God would be to the people we were last week?

Oh God.

Oh. God.

I can smell the roast pork stink that came off Mr Rutter's corpse, and saliva fills my mouth.

I'm crying. Softly. Again.

"Paul, it's alright." Jean's arms are around me. "It's alright. We've all been through so much. It's alright."

I nod, squeeze her hand. I look at Frank. "Get some sleep," he says. "You'll be okay."

We both know that's a lie. For all of us. "Frank," I say.

"Yes?"

"I still think – the kids mustn't go into the narrows again. Whatever it was in there. If it happened to me…"

"Then it could happen to anyone else." He nods. "Yes. I thought of that too. I just wanted to make sure."

That I knew it wasn't real. I nod. But, of course, I don't know. None of us can, anymore.

Taking Frank's advice, I get some sleep. It's deep and dark and blessedly silent. I wake once, and in the dim emberlight of the waning fire, someone tall is standing over me.

"Wh –?"

"Sh." Anya kneels by my head. Warm light glows on her face. She strokes my forehead, my matted hair. "Sh. It's alright, Paul."

"Anya."

"Sh." She bends and kisses me: my forehead, my eyes, my cheeks, my nose, my mouth. The last, long and deep.

At last, she squeezes down next me and huddles close, kisses me again. "It's alright, Paul. Sleep now."

Polish women, I think, *are so beautiful.*

And I sleep again.

In what passes for the morning, when some vague consensus of reality is established by enough of us all being awake at once, I have no idea if I was dreaming or not.

When we were journeying, searching, at least we had some momentum, a purpose, a goal, a quest. Now – now all we have is an increasingly desultory routine, with too little in it to fill the aching gaps of time in these days that aren't days and nights that aren't nights.

We hunt the lake for fish, catch two more blind bream. We consider the greenish fungus on the cave walls, and can't be sure if we dare eat it or not. Soon we'll have no choice.

Jeff T sees a rat skitter across the cavern floor and chases it, but it bolts into one of the narrows and is gone. "No," I shout as he makes to follow.

"But sir-"

"*No*, Jeff. It's dangerous in there."

He looks at me with a smirk playing round his lips, a smirk that says *coward*, *weakling*, but more, worse, *nutter.* And he was one of the good kids, respectful, obedient, yes sir no sir. Now it's a direct challenge, open insolence, and I have nothing to back me up, I daren't meet it. It could be the blow that shatters all discipline, all balance.

I look away. Jeff wanders off. He mutters something. There is muffled laughter in response. I look up, fists clenching. Jeff and a couple others smirk back at me. Jean takes my arm and draws me aside.

We catch two more bream in the lake. Have to take one of the boats out on it to find the second; only one's dumb enough to come close to shore. How many does the lake hold? And what will we do when they're all gone?

We cook and eat the fish. Hunger rumbles in us. Fish are low-calorie. We're getting weak, tire quicker. At least it makes for an early night.

I sleep-

And am shaken awake. A boy, crying. "Sir! Sir!"

"Wh —" I sit up. Everyone's awake. "What? What?"

"It's Jeff, sir, Jeff and Mike."

Mike? Mike Rawlins, one of the smirkers. This was the other one — James? No. Jason. Jason Stanton. *Not so cocky now*, I think. His face is grimy and cut and he's soaking wet. Tears have cut clean streaks down through the black coal dust on his face and his eyes are red.

"What about them? What happened?" I look around. No sign of the boys in question. Torches are lit, flashed around the cavern. "Where are they?" I demand.

For answer, Jason Stanton points a trembling hand towards the back of the cavern, and the black mouths of the narrows.

Jeff said I was crazy, apparently. A nutter, fruitcake, a screwball, a patient. And other things too. A stupid cunt, for one.

Kids, eh?

He reckoned we could catch rats for food. Not a bad plan. Good source of protein. Reckoned we could get lucky in the narrows. Asked for volunteers. Jason and Mike stepped up straight off the bat.

Jeff, of course, was the man with a plan. He had a ball of string; tied one end around a rocky outcropping near the mouth of the narrow they used. They took a torch and two of the 'spears' we'd made lashing sharpened rocks to the hafts of oars. And they went a-hunting. Stupid, stupid kids.

But I can't deny a sneaking, ugly relief; the first challenger to my authority, to ours, that of the adults, is gone. The most capable. The one who sneered. Major challenge removed and an object lesson in daddy knows best. Adults are always right, because we say so. It's a lie and I've always known that, but right now I've never been so grateful for it.

The three of them went in, paying out the string as they went. They'd go a distance, wait. Listen. Switch off the torch at times. Listen. No sound. Any rats there were silent.

So they moved on. And paid out a little more string as they went.

Time passed. And in the end they started to get bored. And tired. And fed-up. And low on confidence.

(See, Jeff? It's not so easy, is it, being in charge? Wait till you have the responsibility. Easy to criticise, from the sidelines. When it isn't you.

And yes, I realise, thinking that even to myself, how like the politicians I always most despised I sound. *Wait till you see what I've seen, then you'd know I'm right.* Oh God. All the things happening to me that I can't bear. Is this the price of survival? How much of myself will I give up to stay alive, of what I was?)

So they retraced their steps, following the string, and then they found-

The string was lying in the middle of a narrow, the tied end frayed and unravelled.

Shouted recriminations, near-panic, quelled by Jeff's fists – Jason has the split lip to prove it. Jeff taking charge. They headed back up the narrow. The string couldn't have trailed far. They can follow their tracks in the dust of the narrow's floor. Retrace their steps to the cavern. If they stay calm.

They follow the marks in the dust.

To a fork they don't remember.

And the dust of each branching narrow's floor is disturbed (*by what?*) and it's impossible to tell which is which, which they might have come down.

Panic in the air again; Jeff quells it. They go right. More narrows branching off. *Which way?*

At last they hear the trickle of water. We go towards that, Jeff tells them. It'll be runoff from the cavern. See? We'll be okay. Forrester found his way out like that, didn't he?

(Not quite, Jeff. But it was worth a try.)

They keep going and they find the water, alright. But it's not the cavern. Oh, it's *a* cavern, yes. But not the one they were looking for. A small chamber, almost wall to wall water, running down from a narrow high up in the cavern wall.

Mike yelping, shouting that he saw something in the water. Big, white, moving. Not a fish. Jeff slaps him into silence, the crack of flesh on flesh ringing in the wet, trickling dark. He saw nothing. Imagining things, seeing things that aren't there. Like that puff Forrester did.

They climb the wall to the narrow the water's coming through, none of them admitting what they know; the torch's beam is starting to dim.

They follow the stream that trickles down the narrow's floor, praying for the cavern that's hearth and home in their mind's eye now.

And it opens out into another cavern. The floor awash to ankle or maybe even knee height with fresh water. They don't check the depth in this cavern. There are houses there.

("What?" "Houses?" "What're you–" "Sh. Go on, Jason.")

Not like houses you'd see up top, Jason says. Crude ones. Can't even call them huts. Just stacks of rocks, heaped up drystone, covered over with big heavy flat pieces, slabs. No windows, but a hole that might be a door. Jason reckons he counted about a dozen of them.

And the cave is not silent. Things are moving around. Inside the houses. Slithering and shifting, slumping and flopping around. And there are other noises too. Not noises a fish or even a very big fucking rat could make.

The boys start to go back the way they came, and then – more sounds, the same as from the houses, coming up the narrow, towards them. The dying torch shines: shadows flick across the wall.

They have to go round the edge of the water, past the houses, towards the only other narrow they can see. The noise from the houses grows louder; none of them look back at the sound of splashing in the water.

The torch goes out a few yards into the narrow.

Jason breaks and runs. He's screaming, but he thinks they aren't the only ones he hears.

He runs on – in the dark, cannoning into walls, scrabbling on, feeling ahead with his hands, terrified of what his fingers might touch.

But somehow- by pure, blind, lucky chance, it can only be – he finds himself crashing headlong into our own little lake. Screaming, splashing, blundering, and then sees the dim distant glow of the fire, catches its gleam off the upturned hulls of boats, flounders and staggers to the shore and shakes me awake, all believing in Mr Forrester now, wanting answers, wanting someone to make it alright.

"This is why I warned everyone not to go into the narrows," I say. "As soon as you get out of sight of this cavern – they can start playing tricks with your head. It's very easy to get lost in there. We don't know where they all go."

Jason cries like a baby, and no-one blames him. Jean holds him tight, rocking him. All the kids' eyes are wide.

"Sir –" it's one of the little ones. "Sir – what about the monsters?"

201

"There aren't any," I say.

"There are," sobs Jason.

"No," I say. "Jason, listen. That place – the narrows – they play tricks on you, remember? They-" I look up, catch Frank's eye. He nods.

Frank Emerson – one thing about him, he can explain anything. Always had the highest pass rates in the school; he could make anything crystal clear and easy to understand. I've never been so grateful for that as now

Hallucinations, Frank explains. It happened to Mr Forrester too, though not as badly because he didn't go as far in, wasn't so badly lost. Jeff and Mike are still in there somewhere, but there's nothing we can do. We can't go in there or we could end up lost as well. The best we can do is call them, shout down the narrows, hope they hear and find us that way.

The kids are wide-eyed. We're just leaving Jeff and Mike in there. Teachers don't do that, abandon their charges. But it's different now. The rules have changed. I used to despise people who said that too.

And so we try. In relays, groups of us, all through that night that is not a night, screaming ourselves hoarse.

But from the narrows, there isn't a sound.

Waking in the 'morning', the mood's sullen and still, scared. We know they're dead. If they're lucky. My big fear was that we'd hear them but not be able to call them home. We'd have to listen to them dying slowly. At least it looks like they're doing that out of earshot.

Unless the things in the houses that don't exist got them.

Otherwise – we try not to think of them, still hopelessly lost, starving, dying by inches in there, wandering around.

As we are. Will be. Jeff and Mike are just us in fast forward.

Jason has slept the night in Jean's comforting, maternal embrace. She releases him, comes over, leans against me.

I feel her weariness, her need, and I know I will sleep with her tonight.

We catch a bream. It's all we eat today. We've all lost weight;

I've tightened my belt as far as I can, but my trousers still keep threatening to slip down.

We go to sleep still hungry.

No-one goes near the narrows today.

Jean and I wait till the others are asleep. Then she crawls to me, takes my hand, draws me to my feet, and we head off to as quiet a part of the cavern as we can. There's not much in the way of privacy here – we have a corner for purposes of nature, but even that's not very private. And we'd hardly go there. Inside one of the narrows might be private, but we'd fuck in the middle of a circle of the kids before we did that.

We kiss and fumble with each other's clothes. In the dark, I fondle the pale blurs of her breasts, make her wet and open with my fingers. She moans into my neck, muffling her cries in my flesh, rubbing my cock. She moans with Anya's Polish accent.

We fuck on the gritty floor, taking turns on top. In flickers of chancy firelight, I see Anya looking down as she rides me.

I wonder if Jean sees Alan.

Our fragile, glass-brittle equilibrium, such as it is, shatters for good and all the next day.

At first it looks lucky. A dead bream bobs in the shallows when we wake, wafts to shore. An easy breakfast.

It's only later that Frank takes my arm.

"Paul, we've got a problem."

"What's that?"

For answer, he picks up the Geiger counter and walks towards the shore. I look round. Jean and the remaining ten children are further down, towards the top end of the cavern. We're up near the narrows; everyone else is, understandably, giving them the widest possible berth.

Frank switches the microphone on. A moment later, the Geiger counter begins to crackle and tick. Before he switches it off, it's almost to a screech.

"It's bad, isn't it?" I ask. Foolishly.

"You know it is." Frank nods towards the breach in the tunnel wall, the one we came through. "The radiation's seeping down here."

I sag. This doesn't end. It just doesn't end. "Oh shit."

"Yeah. Yeah."

"What can we do?"

"Get away from it," Frank says, simply. "Go deeper in. It's the only way."

I turn and look unwillingly at the narrows.

"Look – Paul. I know it's freaky in there. But if we just keep going-"

"Are you mad?"

"No. Look – most of the disorientation was about trying to find your way back. We won't be. We can survive: we know there's water in the narrows."

Water and what else, Frank? Low, crude houses? White things that flop and grunt and hiss in the water?

"We don't know where any of them go anyway," he says. "So we can't get lost as such. It's as good a chance as any of finding somewhere safer."

"What about…" I point back towards the breach in the wall. "We could head on down the canal."

"And go where?"

I shrug. "We don't know what else could be there. Might be something better than this place. And whatever you say about *that*" – I point at the narrows – "I don't want to go back in there. I know" – he opens his mouth – "it's not about what I want. But it's bad in there, Frank. You talk about it but you don't know what it's like."

"I've got an inkling," he said. "I heard what Jason said, like everyone else."

"That stuff, about the houses…"

He spreads his hands. "Let's not go there, mate."

"But that's the point. We'll have to."

"Alright. Maybe the houses were real. Maybe some people got trapped down here back in the day one time and had to rough it, or they were used for storage. Or something. Doesn't mean they've got something out of a midnight movie living in them."

204

I find myself wishing he hadn't put it into words. "I don't like the idea of putting the kids in there."

"I know." He chews his lip.

"If we tried the canal," I say, "at least we'd know where the hell we were."

"Yeah. Yeah."

In the end, a compromise is reached. Frank and two of the older boys – volunteers, one of whom is Jason Stanton, unsurprisingly up for anything that poses an alternative to the narrows – will head down the canal in one of the boats. I can see why Frank's reluctant; we spent hours – even days, it felt like – leading down the canal before we found the cavern, and that was sheer luck. By the time we give up and turn back, the radiation might've seeped so far down we can't get to the narrows at all.

But that's no loss to me; Frank doesn't understand. He can't. He hasn't been in there.

They row the boat off. Jean and stay with the rest of the children and the Geiger counter. Frank told me what to look for. When the radiation gets too high, keep moving away from the water's edge, and if you have to, head into the narrows.

I'll die first, I think.

The plash of oars recedes. Long silence falls. Jean sits beside me. We haven't spoken since we fucked last night. Don't know what to say to each other. I try to pretend it didn't happen. I saw Anya while I fucked her. I'll call it a dream. In this blurred twilight place that comes easy.

"Do you think they'll find anything?" she asks at last. Perhaps she's made the same decision as me.

"I hope so." But I doubt it. It's almost as if Frank *wants* to go into the narrows. Maybe he does, because he never has; he wants to experience it for himself.

That's crazy, I tell myself. But we'd all be crazy *not* to be crazy, in one way or another, down here. I know my own madness pretty damn well by now. But Frank's? He seems so together, so calm and controlled. But that could only make him the craziest one of all, just waiting to-

Then the screaming starts.

205

Jason. I know that voice. Howling, pleas and promises and threats. "No! No! Please! I'll – no! You fucker, I'll kill y-"

And Frank screams too, and the other boy. Terror or rage, I can't tell.

The water thrashing and churning. Who's fighting who, or what? At last, silence falls.

Much later, a broken oar drifts over the lip of the breach and bobs slowly across the lake to the shore. I pick it up. Its blade is smudged red, and cracked.

After a time, I remember to switch on the Geiger counter.

The screech is piercing. I turn it off. But they're all looking at me now. All but the youngest kids understand what it means.

Jean looks to me for a lead. No help, no decision there. Once again, it's all down to me.

"Alright," I say. "Now. Whatever happens, you stay close to me. Hang on to the person in front of you. Do *not* stop unless everyone else does. Understand?"

"Yes, Mr Forrester."

I meet Jean's eyes. She's pale, close to welling up.

Torches, batteries. No food. There isn't any. We've brought what coal we can, stuffed in our pockets, tied up in an old jacket.

I flick the torch into the mouth of one of the narrows, and then another. Where do you start? Which do you pick? It's all *terra incognita.*

In the end, I pick the longest narrow in sight. It extends a good fifty yards without a bend. This one.

"Alright," I say. "Let's go."

We start down it, torches shining ahead. A small hand is hooked into the back of my belt. It's the same all the way down the line.

I'll die first. That's what I thought. But – what was it pushed me on? The same refusal to die that drove me down here? Or was that what it was, after all? Was it something else? Did something call me down here, lead me into this? A secret love of the dark, a curiosity about the places like this? If so, the narrows are the logical conclusion. Was it really a struggle to avoid going back in or a struggle against what kept me out?

Everything's coming apart; even my own motivations. I can't be sure what I want anymore, who I am, what makes me tick.

Or maybe it was simpler. Maybe I could've faced dying, but the kids – the kids and Jean – I know enough about radiation sickness, read and seen enough to know it's a bad death, maybe the worst. Could I have even put myself through it? In the end I couldn't put the children through it. Couldn't watch them die like that because of me.

Or... I just don't know anymore. It feels as if everything's been pushing us – me – towards the narrows. The radiation, whatever happened to Frank. Sooner or later, I had to give way.

What *did* happen to Frank and the others? Something in the water? Something like what Jason heard in the narrows? Or did Frank decide it was a non-starter? Was the tunnel blocked further down? Was he going to turn back and the fight was between him and Jason?

We'll never know. No-one was going to chance trying it again. Maybe we should have.

Too late now.

"Paul?"

"What?" I snap out of the reverie. Snap being the operative word. I look back. Jean, scared face above a line of others like hers.

"I – sorry – Paul. If we go any further we'll be out of sight of the cavern."

She's right. We're about at the first bend. When we round that, the real narrows begin.

"Okay," I say. "Let's stop. Everybody sit down. No-one goes anywhere. Not even to pee."

We sit. I can just see the rocks and the glimmer of the lake. Now we're so close to leaving it behind for good, I feel a pang of loss. Like it's home we're leaving.

This is the furthest we can go and hope to turn back. But of course we can't. The radiation...

After a while, I switch on the Geiger counter. It ticks and it crackles, but it's not too loud. Not yet. I switch it off again.

One of the girls, one of the older ones – Laura, Laura Rodgers – is crying quietly. I can find nothing to say to her.

Time passes. I switch on the counter again. It screeches in the narrow like a wounded bat. I switch it off. My eyes meet Jean's.

I force myself to stand. "Alright, everybody," I say. "Let's go."

The tunnel is endless.

Yard after yard. It stretches on forever.

A torch gives out. Dead batteries fall to the floor. New ones are pushed into place.

They will not last forever.

We keep walking.

Laura Rodgers keeps crying.

Finally we reach a fork. Left or right? I pick the left. We've gone right enough times now, and look where it's got us.

We've stopped twice. The first time, I waited till the Geiger counter screamed at me to move. The second time, I didn't even switch it on.

I just keep walking, leading the children on. Like a Pied Piper, going into the magic mountain. Hushabye. No trees sprouting candy canes here. My stomach growls. I don't think about it. Something scurries, small, somewhere. I can't see it. A rat. *Food.* No. Don't go looking. You'll get lost and you'll never find your way back. Back to what?

I keep walking. And walking. And walking.

Laura Rodgers keeps on crying. It gets harsh, worse. I should tell her to stop, but I can't seem to. All I can do is put one foot in front of the other.

Her breath starts hitching. It's building. To a scream.

Stop her. Calm her down.

But even as I think it, she shrieks.

Yelps, cries of alarm, a struggle, blows.

"No! No!" She screeches, and breaks out of the line and blunders back down the narrow. She's not a big girl, only about fifteen and hardly tall for her age, but she knocks Jean aside like a puppet when she tries to hold Laura back. She runs off, still screaming.

"Laura!" I shout. "*Laura!*"

But she's gone. Running back down the narrow towards the cavern. Except of course it won't be there. Still screaming, all the way.

The shrieks and sobs die, echoing into silence. And Laura's gone. We wait for a last screech, the sound of her meeting some final doom, but it doesn't come. She just recedes. Disappears. Is gone. Swallowed up.

The kids are crying. The three little ones, back at the far end with Jean, are almost in hysterics. She holds them tight.

"Everybody stay still!" I shout. I flash the torch, do a quick head count. Everybody here. Except one. Laura Rodgers. The first of us to go.

Me. Jean. And nine kids now.

"Everyone grab on to the person in front of you," I say hoarsely. And we move on.

We stop again for a rest. I switch on the Geiger counter, remembering this time. A faint crackling murmur. Safe. For now.

We're all tired. And hopeless.

But this has to end somewhere. Doesn't it? There has to be a place where the narrows end.

Yeah. Maybe a blank wall.

An hour – ? – later, I switch the counter back on. It's louder. Much louder. Too loud.

"Come on," I say, and stand.

We walk, and walk, and walk.

New narrows everywhere now. Gaping in the walls, beckoning us down them, like sellers in a bazaar. *Come this way. No, this way. No, that. That. The other.*

"Shut up!"

"What? Paul?"

God I've spoken aloud. Cracking up. "Nothing," I say. "Sorry."

We keep going. "Rest stop," I gasp. We sit. I do a head count and –

"Jean?"

"What?"

"Someone's missing."

One of the boys. Danny Harper. "Where's Danny?" I say. "Where did he go?"

No-one seems to know.

"Who was behind him?"

A hand goes up. Lisa Fowler. "Where did he go?"

"I don't know, sir. I didn't see. I was just holding on to him. Whoever was in front of me."

"Did you let go? Even for a moment?"

"I... I don't know, sir." But her eyes are downcast.

I glare at Jean. "Didn't you see anything?"

"We're all tired, Paul," she snaps. "Can barely focus on whoever's in front of us. Don't start-"

"For Christ's sake! We've lost another one!"

The shout fades to silence. Pale faces stare at me, angry and frightened.

I can say nothing to them. He must have slipped down one of the narrows. Saw something, or thought he did. Heard something, or thought he did. And now he's gone.

Let's go.

Further on up, the narrow begins to twist and turn. Like we're riding a snake that's realised we're there and is trying to shake us off.

It bends cruelly, sharply, pinching almost too narrow to climb through at all.

And for one boy, it is.

Toby Thwaites. His panicked scream explodes like a bomb. *"Mr Forrester!"*

I stumble to a halt. Turn back.

"I'm stuck! I'm stuck!"

Toby, halfway down the line, is wedged solid. Stuck behind him, Jean and the three little ones. Leaving me with the two girls, Lisa Fowler and Jane Routledge.

Jean and I stare at each other, past Toby's shoulder.

We try everything we can to move him, but it's no go.

"Don't leave me," sobs Toby. He's fifteen years old. "Don't leave me."

210

"We won't, Toby," I promise him. "We won't."

But we all know it's a lie.

So we wait, and eventually he falls asleep.

"What do we do?" whispers Jean.

"Have to try and go around," I say dully. "Meet up again. We can't stay."

No. We have to keep going. Have to try and find a way out. Even through we know now we never will.

Jean reaches through and clasps my hand.

"Good luck," I say. We know we'll never see each other again.

And we don't.

I watch Jean and the kids go back down the narrow, back the way they came, into the dark, and gone.

"Come on," I say to the girls.

The narrow straightens out again soon enough after that. It's done what it set out to do. We all hope we'll be out of earshot before Toby wakes up and starts screaming at us to come back.

We aren't.

Further down, the voices start.

First one is Laura Rodgers. "Mr Forrester? Mr Forrester?" Crying, desperately. "Please. *Please.*"

We keep walking.

"Help! Help! Hello? *Hello?*" I know that voice. It's Jeff Tomlinson.

"Can anyone hear us?" A stripped, hysterical scream: I think it's Mike Rawlins.

"Paul? Paul? Are you there?" It's Jean. I shout her name. She shouts mine. But she only gets further away.

Until she's gone.

The last set of batteries for the last of the torches. I'm stumbling, shuffling. So are Jane and Lisa. We press close, link hands; I lead them on. My left hand holds Lisa's right; her left holds Jane's.

"Listen." It's Jane. Her voice is a croak. "Can you hear it?"

"Hear what?" asks Lisa.

"Water. Listen."

Yes. It's there. Trickling. I realise how swollen my mouth and tongue are. How dry.

"Keep going," I manage.

The trickling seems to get louder and louder.

"Keep g-"

There's suddenly less weight on my left hand. I turn. Lisa stares back at me, then looks round to stare down an empty narrow. A few yards behind us, the sound of water echoes from a hole in the wall.

We go to it. A narrow, extending for maybe five yards, then branching off into three new ones.

"Jane? Jane!"

But there's no reply.

Walking on. So tired. Sounds of things moving in the darkness beyond. Big things. Heavy things. A hissing sound, close by. Lisa gasps, clutches my arm. A grunt from behind us. We walk faster.

Water, trickling.

At last, too tired to keep on. We need a place to stop, but the endless narrows – there's nowhere.

But at last, the narrow opens out. Only briefly, two new ones beyond, but it's a small chamber.

We lie down. I curl up; Lisa huddles against my back.

I sleep. No dreams. I wake once; I hear Lisa, crying. "Mum?" she calls. Her voice cracks with terror and relief. "Mum? Mum, is that you? Where are you?"

I should wake up and stop her. But I'm so, so tired. I go back to sleep.

I wake up alone.

I've been walking a long time now.

The beam of the torch is faint and flickery. I don't have the Geiger counter anymore. I don't know when or where I left it behind.

Voices. All around me. Calling my name. Pleading. Praying. Damning me.

212

Jean.
Lisa
Jane
Danny
Laura
Toby, poor Toby,
The little ones
Jean.

The torch goes out.

I shake and rattle and bang it, but it's good and dead this time. At last, I let it fall.

The darkness is total.

I walk into it, hands in front of me.

Dreading what they might touch.

Can barely walk now. So tired. So hungry. So thirsty. Oh. God.

Plod. Plod. Stumble. Shuffle.

Hit a wall. Ow. Feel at it. Push myself clear. Arms out to either side, then in front. To the sides again. And out front. And so on. And on.

Something stings my eyes. What..?

Light. It's light. It's been so long since I saw it.

Where is it?

Up ahead. I can see it now. There's a bend in the narrow. I stumble towards it. An exit, at last?

I round the corner. And stop.

Anya steps out; she is in silhouette and her outline looks thinner than I remember, but it's her. "Hi, Paul."

A noise comes out of my throat. I want to believe this, but-

"Paul?" She takes a step forward; a slow, dragging step. I stumble backwards. "Darling?"

I back-pedal faster. Then, with a horrible crack, my ankle goes as a lump of rock gives underfoot. I fall down, crying out.

"Sh. Baby. Sh." She's holding out her arms. "It's alright." I cover my face as her dragging footsteps approach. "It's alright."

I pray for death to reach me before her.

213

But it doesn't.

W̶ F T G

Simon Bestwick lives in Lancashire, works in a call-centre to pay the bills and scribbles down/types up his dreams and nightmares for fun and beer money. In his early thirties, he is told he looks older but sounds a lot younger. (In which case the call-centre's probably the best place.) Over fifty of his short stories have been published or are forthcoming in various magazines and anthologies – most recently in Ellen Datlow's *Inferno*, David Sutton's *Houses On The Borderland*, Barbara and Christopher Roden's *Acquainted With The Night* and *At Ease With The Dead*, Pendragon Press's *Triquorum*, and *All Hallows*. He does not have a tall, blonde, Polish girlfriend; any applicants for the post can contact him via his blog at www.geocities.com/sbestwick2002[1].

"The Narrows: *The story came out of a combination of three elements. First was the title, which was in my notebooks for several years in search of a story that could do it justice. Second was the underground canal system used in the story; it exists, although inaccessible to the public and dangerous due to seepage of carbon monoxide gas. For artistic reasons, I've taken liberties with the real-life town of Worsley, particularly the Delph, to make access to the system possible. The third and final element was the desire to write a totally black and pitiless story, one where reality itself warped into the ultimate nightmare. Hopefully I've succeeded. Nuclear war was a very real fear of mine as a child, and sadly hasn't gone away; it made the perfect starting point for* The Narrows."

---

[1] For the benefit of the literal-minded or dim, that was a joke (unless, of course, any attractive young Polish ladies *do* wish to apply, in which case, feel free.)

FOOLS RUSH IN
An Afterword

Let's call this one the Accidental Anthology. I didn't mean to edit; it wasn't my fault. Personally, I blame the parents, or the government. The devil made me do it.

But let me be serious for just a moment... It all started early in 2007, when I was chatting to Mark West on an internet forum. I'd only just got to know Mark – but not yet met him; he was still merely a cyber-acquaintance – and genuinely liked the guy, so when he told me about the bout of writer's block he was experiencing I empathised completely. I'd just gone through a three month block of my own, you see, and the only thing that got me writing again was a deadline for a story I'd been working on. The thing is, a sense of commitment and a no-nonsense work ethic pulled me through, forced me to sit down in front of the blank laptop screen and write until I barged through the blockage using a combination of brute force and plain idiocy.

Eureka!

What if, thought I, like the fool I undoubtedly am, Mark had a similar deadline imposed upon him? How about an anthology? Better still, how about an anthology of novelettes? (I've never been one to make small leaps. Only big ones. Stupid and reckless ones that often end in a broken limb)

Flushed with a sense of my own brilliance, I told Mark that I was compiling such an anthology and that I'd like to include an original story of his. At that point, I wasn't doing any such thing; of course I wasn't. I was far too busy to be editing anything other than my

215

shopping list – and even that was tricky. I kept forgetting that we'd run out of eggs.

The next day was when the Fear struck. I'd committed: I was going to have to pull something out of the hat and edit a book. Not a bit of a book, or half a book, or even three-quarters of a book, but an *entire* book. With words and stuff in it. I stared at my computer screen in search of inspiration, but the soft porn and football sites were offering up none. Slowly and quietly, I began to shit my pants.

At about the same time I'd been corresponding with Simon Bestwick, another writer whose work I've long admired, and who actually inspired me to start writing seriously back in the mid 1990s, when I first discovered the wonderful world of independent publishing via magazines with titles like *The Third Alternative*, *Peeping Tom* and *Nasty Piece of Work*.

Eureka #2!

Wouldn't it be great if I asked a clutch (or should that be a murder? What exactly is the correct collective noun for a group of horror authors?) of my favourite small press writers, all with their roots firmly embedded in that same period, to contribute stories to my mythical book? I could even give it a snazzy retro title like *We Fade to Grey* (Okay, I know it's the wrong era, but I'm sure you get the point).

I snapped out emails to British horror writers *extraordinaire*, Bestwick, Young and Finch, not at all confident that I could convince them. Twenty-four hours later each one had replied and agreed to write something. Within six weeks I had the finished tales saved on my hard drive, and was absolutely thrilled – and just a little bit stunned – by the sheer quality of what they'd delivered.

My brief to these authors had been simple: scare me, move me, stir my emotions. I think the stories here deliver on all these levels, and they do so in an impressive variety of ways.

Simon Bestwick has written possibly the best (and without a doubt the scariest) story I read in 2007. Stuart Young's tale shows us what the shoddy BBC TV series *Torchwood* could and *should* be like. Paul Finch recalls those gritty, creepy low budget British horror films from the 1970s, probably starring Oliver Reed in maniac-mode and shot on location in the lovely English countryside. Mark West, the man without whom none of this madness would have been possible, has produced the subtlest thing he's ever written — a beautiful, haunting, heartbreaking ghost story.

Mark Morris — God bless him and all who sail in him — put the icing on the cake with an insightful introduction. Don't ask me why he said yes to my request when I emailed him. Mark's possibly the busiest man in genre fiction, but somehow I managed to coerce him into reading the unedited manuscript. It must have been the beer. Or those photographs I have of him dancing with a bikini-clad sheep named Polly. Photographic evidence of a similar nature certainly had something to do with Pendragon Press agreeing to publish the book.

I hope *We Fade to Grey* will prove successful, both financially and critically, mainly for the authors involved, and of course for the publisher. But also because, damn fool that I am, I want to do another one. Yeah. Imagine it. Volume 2, and 3, and 4…now wouldn't that be grand?

Gary McMahon
Somewhere in West Yorkshire
Lunchtime
2008

… and if you liked this anthology, then perhaps you may also like to read this…

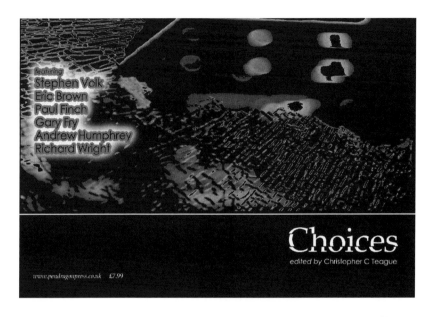

featuring
Stephen Volk
Eric Brown
Paul Finch
Gary Fry
Andrew Humphrey
Richard Wright

Choices
edited by Christopher C Teague

www.pendragonpress.co.uk   £7.99

Featuring the *British Fantasy Award*-winning novella
"Kid" by Paul Finch

Coming Soon from
www.pendragonpress.net

Kingston to Cable
by
Gary Greenwood

Broken Symmetries
by
Steve Redwood

The Winter Hunt and Other Tales
by
Steve Lockley & Paul Lewis

Silversands
by
Gareth L Powell

Fade-Out
by
Gavin Salisbury

The Places Between
by
Terry Grimwood

Check out the website for further details, and sign up to
our (in)frequent e-newsletter to be kept abreast of all
future developments from Pendragon towers.